GEMINOS

A JOSH BRANNON SCI-FI ACTION THRILLER

Nigel Billington

GEMINOS by Nigel Billington, 1st Edition.

ISBN - 978-0-6397-5248-8 (e-book)

ISBN - 978-0-6397-5249-5 (paperback)

ISBN - 978-0-6397-5250-1 (hardcover)

Cover Artwork

Cover design: Nigel Billington. Cover photographs: pixabay.com

Why do you not

know what you

already know?

CHAPTER 1

JOSH WAS UP EARLY, sitting quietly looking out through the windscreen. It was 6am and still dark outside. He felt more comfortable in the dark, protected by the shadows. The street lights shone dim light down the near empty street. The postman passed by on his early rounds, not paying attention to the solitary man sitting in his car.

A voice came through in Josh's radio earpiece; "All call-signs, Zero, radio check over." It was the hourly check call from the operations room at office headquarters.

Putting his hand in his jacket pocket, Josh prepared to acknowledge the check call in sequence, along with the other operatives on the ground. A string of acknowledgements was radioed in turn, "Alpha okay. Bravo okay." Josh pushed on his radio's pressel switch in his pocket and spoke into his hidden microphone, "Charlie okay." Other call-signs likewise radioed through that everything was fine, and the net went dead silent again.

"Operation Sting Bolt" was in full swing—a joint operation with the London Metropolitan Police. Josh was waiting patiently for the order to go. The raid was planned for 7am, so in the meantime he had to sit tight, keeping observations on the target address further down the street.

Waiting was something he disliked, but with an operation of this much importance, everything and everyone had to be ready. He was just one piece of a larger game that involved over fifty personnel—armed police, undercover operatives, and technical teams. This was an operation that could bring down one of the biggest terrorist cells the country had ever seen.

Josh knew his orders, he was "eyes and ears" only and backup if needed. The police were to take the credit for this one. It was their operation despite the significant work the "office" had contributed. Josh had also played a part in the Op; a minor part corroborating low-level intelligence. He didn't care though, about getting any credit, just wanted these guys taken out.

Half an hour ticked by and Josh was beginning to prepare himself, mentally and physically. He brushed his hand over the outside of his jacket and felt the hidden armoury underneath—SIG Sauer P226 pistol and HK MP7 submachine gun. The magazine of the MP7 pushed into his body making it a little uncomfortable, but it wouldn't be long now until the operation would be sprung into action.

Fifteen, ten, five minutes to seven. "All call-signs this is Zero, radio check over." The control room came back on the net for a final check to make sure everyone was ready. As before, Josh acknowledged the check call in sequence with the other call-signs on the ground. He was feeling calm and eagerly waiting for the order to go.

He kept checking his synchronised watch for the last five minutes; finally, it changed to 07:00hrs. The firm voice from Control came up on the net again. "All call-signs this is Zero, stand by, stand by. Operation Sting Bolt is a go. I repeat operation Sting Bolt is a go. Charlie acknowledge over."

Josh pushed his radio's pressel switch, "Charlie roger, out."

Suddenly, two strings of heavily armed police, ten in each string, appeared from both ends of the street out of the vestiges of the night. Dressed in blue overalls and wearing Kevlar helmets, balaclavas, goggles and carrying automatic rifles, they shuffled quickly along the pathway. The multiple tapping sounds of light boot steps on the path made little noise as they stealthily made their way. With both strings of armed officers working as cohesive units, they moved fast, converging at the front door of the target address Josh had been watching from afar. He knew the plan inside out, as well as the contingency plans if things went wrong. Every eventuality had been covered; every possible outcome had been meticulously examined with one goal in mind—capture or kill.

CRASH! A sudden loud noise broke the early morning silence.

A handheld battering ram had been used by the point men of the police entry team, to smash through the locked front door. The point men immediately stepped aside, giving way for the rest of the team to rush in through the open doorway. They began shouting, "POLICE!", as they stormed inside the building out of sight to Josh. His orders were to observe only at this point, but he was itching to get involved. Less than thirty seconds in since the initial building breach, a hail of loud shots sounded out from the address, echoing loudly in the quiet of the morning. Josh pulled his weapon out from under his jacket in preparation for the order to go in.

Control spoke on the radio; "All call-signs this is Zero; phase one complete, phase two initiated. Bravo and Charlie remain on the plot. All other call-signs return to HQ. Bravo and Charlie acknowledge over."

"Bravo, roger that."

Josh spoke into the mic of his radio to acknowledge the order; "Charlie, roger, out." He pushed his weapon back under his jacket, with the feeling of disappointment the operation had gone according to plan—well almost. He knew there were casualties, most likely fatal. He wanted in on the action but not this time—once again.

The operation had been planned over three months; the part Josh had been involved in anyway. More than likely, it had been going on for much longer—during the undercover and intelligence gathering stage. It seemed now that Josh was only getting to see the tail-end of operations, and was purposely kept out of the really meaty stuff. He seemed to be in someone's bad books, and was being kept on a very short leash. And he suspected he knew why, and by whom.

Sitting in his car, he continued watching the early morning activity from a distance. More police were entering the building along with SOCO—the crime scene team. The paramedics were still on standby though, a sign that none of the terrorists had survived; all part of the risk of getting involved in terrorism. Josh also knew the risks of his own job—being a government operative—and the only person to blame for any dire outcome, was ultimately him.

"Charlie, Bravo over." Josh's radio piped up again. It was Malik Asif, the other remaining member of the team who had been instructed to stay behind with Josh. He was situated at the rear of the property, on the adjacent street.

"Send over," answered Josh, speaking into his mic.

"Channel two, over." Malik wanted a less formal chat on the net, and requested a change of radio channel, so that only they would be heard.

"Channel two, out." And Josh reached for his radio, turning the knob to channel two. "Go ahead Malik."

"Josh, my side's secure, nothing much happening. Got the police swarming the place, so just seems like routine stuff now. How's it your side mate?"

"Yeah, same here. Lots of uniforms in and out," replied Josh.

"Okay, I'm coming round to your location," said Malik.

"Roger that. I'm changing to one." And Josh switched his radio back to channel one.

Just as he had changed channels, he heard a single shot, originating from the rear of the target address, from Malik's side. Josh knew there was a problem, as Malik had not radioed out but was silent. Josh started his car, pushed it into gear and screeched off.

"Zero, Charlie, shot heard, wait out." Josh immediately radioed control with an initial contact report that a shot had been fired.

Staying in low gear, for speed, he came to the end of the row of houses. He pulled out of the junction without stopping, narrowly missing a car, and drove into the street at the rear of the target address. Speeding up the road, Josh could see several armed police pointing their weapons from defensive firing positions. He slammed on his breaks, stopping in the middle of the road, and jumped out. He pulled out his submachine gun and took up a firing position next to his car, using it as cover.

"What happened?" Josh shouted to a nearby officer.

"Single shot fired, man down, no eyes on the shooter!" shouted the officer.

Josh suspected one of the terrorists had remained hidden and had taken an opportunity to escape. And without looking, he knew Malik was the "man down". Without thought for his own safety, he sprinted past the armed officers to Malik's car. The door was open and Malik was lying on the floor, blood seeping through his upper garments. Josh quickly unzipped Malik's jacket and removed his weapon, placing it beside him on the ground. He ripped open the rest of his upper clothing, revealing a small bullet hole centre of his chest. Blood was flowing out and Malik was looking pale from the blood loss. He wasn't responding, and Josh could see he was on his way out. Josh put the palm of his hand over the hole and pushed down hard to stem the blood flow.

"MEDIC! MEDIC!" Josh shouted, knowing the paramedics were already on the scene.

The medics though, were prevented from attending, due to the uncertainty that the shooter was still watching, and perhaps wanted a further target. Without waiting, Josh pulled Malik up off the ground, flopped him over his right shoulder and stood up. He ran with the dead weight on his back, into the rear of the target address, through to the other side where he knew the medics were waiting. He carefully lowered Malik down onto the road.

"He's got a gunshot wound to the chest!" he shouted to a paramedic, who immediately took over.

Josh ran back through the house to the other side, to assist with locating the shooter. The armed police had already fanned out over the open wasteland at the rear, to extend their perimeter, but they were simply securing the area—nothing more. Call-sign "Hotel One"—a police helicopter on standby for the operation—had been called in immediately and was hovering overhead, searching for the suspect, but so far nothing was being reported.

Josh pressed the transmit button on his radio, to give a "situation report" to the control room. "Zero, Charlie, sit rep, over."

"Zero, send."

"Bravo is down, single bullet wound to the chest. He's with a Papa unit right now. No sign of the shooter or firing point. Hotel One is on site. Over!"

"Roger Charlie. Remain at location until further notice. We have direct comms with Hotel One and have re-assigned all call-signs to assist in the search. Zero, out."

Josh walked back to move his car from obstructing the road; parking it near the terrorists' house. He looked over to Malik's vehicle; the crime scene team were busy putting up a white screen around it. Police were beginning to respond to the neighbours emerging from their homes, who were hoping to get an eye-full. Still dressed in pyjamas and night gowns, officers instructed them to keep inside, but curiosity had them peering out through the windows. This wasn't an everyday occurrence in this quiet middle-class neighbourhood.

The police and forensic teams had begun settling down into the routine of the preservation and evidence gathering stage—forensics busy documenting, photographing, and bagging evidence, while police kept the spectators and newly arrived news reporters away. This was how it was: months of planning and preparation culminating into a brief dramatic scene that would only last minutes.

Josh opened the boot of his SQRV—Surveillance and Quick Reaction Vehicle—and pushed back the cover that hid his weaponry. He made his MP7 submachine gun safe—removing the magazine from the weapon and round from the chamber—and placed it inside the car. He pulled the cover back over and closed the boot. His job was done, but he had to follow orders and stay on site.

He took the opportunity to look around, to get more facts. He hadn't been involved in Operation Sting Bolt as closely as he wanted, so wasn't privy to everything. He began thinking about Malik and why he was slow to respond, which was most unlike him. Josh was beginning to hypothesise what had happened.

"We were on the radio...we stopped talking...shot fired. I raced around. His car door was open...he's on the ground...bullet wound centre of chest." Josh was imagining the situation in his head, picturing the possible scene Malik had faced. "He was facing the shooter...his weapon still concealed—not drawn. Why didn't he challenge? Where was Armed Response?" he thought.

Josh approached an armed police officer standing guard near the back door of the house. "Was a good Op, hey?" said Josh casually, as though just wanting to make small talk.

"Yeah, looks like we hit the jackpot today. Beers all round tonight," replied the officer from behind his balaclava.

"Yeah, good stuff, beers all round for sure." Josh was building a rapport with the unknown officer. "It was my colleague, got hit over there." Josh nodded in the direction of Malik's screen-covered car. "Did you see what happened?"

"Nah, I was inside. There was another team out here." The officer then walked off to stop a nosey neighbour who had appeared from her home to get a closer look.

Josh continued, approaching and asking the other officers if they had seen anything of Malik getting shot. They all said the same story, that they were inside and another team was securing the rear of the house. But Josh couldn't find anyone from the so-called "other team" to clarify what had happened. It was as if they never existed.

He spotted a suited man walk out from the terrorists' house through the back door, with a police sergeant from the Counter Terrorism Specialist Firearms Unit. Clearly, the "suit" was of some higher rank and importance involved in the operation. They appeared to be walking around making assessments of the situation. Josh approached them, taking the opportunity to ask some questions.

"Excuse me sir." Josh knew he would get further by granting them some importance. Both men looked at him.

"Yes?" replied the "suit".

"I'm looking for the team tasked to secure the rear of the address during the breach. Just trying to get some intel on the shooter that took out my colleague. These guys said they were inside." Josh indicated the officers he had already questioned. "But I can't find any of the unit that was covering the rear. Any ideas sir?"

"What's your name and unit?" questioned the "suit".

"Brannon, office support."

"Ah, spies! We have a real-life spy here Sergeant Crofts," said the man, looking at the heavily armed officer standing next to him. "Brannon, we have multiple police units here drawn from all areas, some have been stood down and are being debriefed as we speak. We will find the terrorist responsible for your colleague."

"I appreciate that sir. Sorry, I don't know your name?"

"Sir Godfrey," and without saying anything further, he walked off with the sergeant.

Pulling out his mobile phone, Josh speed-dialled a number and put it to his ear. The call was answered almost immediately.

"Flash speaking."

"Flash, Brannon. I need a favour."

"Brannon, I'm in the middle of integrating a four-phase...."

Josh interrupted before Flash could bore him any further with his tech-talk; "I need to find out who a "Sir Godfrey" is and his connection to Sting Bolt. Call me when you have something."

"Well that's easy. He's a politician, and his connection would be that he is an advisor on the operation. He was there from the start. I'm surprised you don't know that," answered Flash.

"Thanks Flash. Been a bit kept in the dark lately," and Josh hung up.

He walked unchallenged into the house—having free access and some authority; afforded to him by the secret government organisation he works for. It was an ordinary terraced house in a middle-class suburb, mostly made up of families of various races and religions: White, Indian, Pakistani, Muslims, Sikhs, Christians. All were living in harmony, trying to survive and live the best way they could. The downstairs had a pokey living room and kitchen, with a steep stairway going up to the bedrooms. Looking at the scene inside, all of the action had obviously taken place upstairs—catching the terrorists by surprise, which was the plan.

Josh climbed the stairs, bumping past a crime scene officer on his way down with an armful of packed evidence bags. At the top was a flurry of activity for such a small area. There were at least four people in white coveralls from the forensics team busy marking out, photographing, and bagging items. They were all too busy to pay any attention to an outsider—Josh, except to keep him from contaminating their crime scene. He remained outside the room they were busy processing.

Standing in the doorway, Josh was craning his neck to get a better look at a dead body. From his angle, all he could see was a bare hairy muscular leg hanging over the edge of a bed. It looked like the surprised man had attempted to get out of bed during the raid, but was stopped short with a bullet or two. Strangely though, the leg was that of a white man and not a tanned Muslim, as expected. Intrigued, Josh stretched a little further. He was suddenly given an eyeful of the dead body, as the forensics team moved out of the way to focus on the window area.

WHOOSH!

Josh began experiencing a feeling he hadn't felt for some months; a familiar feeling he now knew the meaning of. The strange mind-absorbing sensation of déjà vu—the indication of a "Time-fold"—seemed to be warning him of something. He knew the sign. And as always, the reaction distracted his attention.

"Why is this happening again? I thought it was over," he thought, as his mind briefly recalled the incident in the bunker four months earlier. "Who is this person?"

His head cleared, allowing him to fully inspect the corpse lying on the bed. Seeing the pale face of the man produced a further reaction of disbelief. The deathly looking face appeared very different than when he was last seen alive. Not just different from the fact that something was missing from the body—a life-force or something—but the age. He was almost unrecognisable. The last time Josh saw this person alive was when they were both in their teens. It was his old school friend that had died at the young age of fourteen. It was the same friend that appeared before him as a "ghost" where he used to live; the same friend that first started the sequence of déjà vu and Time-fold events.

Maybe beyond four months ago, Josh would have been completely stunned and at odds with what he was seeing, but not anymore. He knew that what he was looking at was in fact a facsimile, or wrap-over, as Professor Montague had explained to him back in the bunker. Simply put, it was his old friend, but not of this lifetime, and not of this dimension.

Somewhat still surprised, Josh instinctively knew this operation was intimately connected to his past, to the string of events that led him to Sofia, the underground bunker, professors Montague and Balantyne, and to View Corp. He had no doubt in his mind that events were starting up again, that his past was coming back around.

CHAPTER 2

KNOWING THE IDENTITY OF the corpse and the connection to the actual organisation he appeared to be a part of, Josh knew Operation Sting Bolt was a smoke-screen for something more. The supposed terrorist cell that occupied the dwelling was reported to be linked to a Muslim terror organisation, but Josh now knew that was a lie. He knew the operation was to get to View Corp, and although he didn't want to admit his concern for her, he knew Sofia was in serious danger.

A forensic officer was pushing past him with an armful of evidence bags. "I thought this was supposed to be a Muslim set-up?" inquired Josh. He wanted to get an initial assessment from the officer. "This guy's not Muslim."

"It takes all sorts, I guess. They're known for radicalising and recruiting westerners. Probably a convert," replied the officer, who continued on down the stairway.

Josh wasn't satisfied with the glib response. He should have been surprised by the officer's answer, but knew if they were told these guys were Muslim terrorists then that's what they would believe—without question. He found it frustrating; people not looking and questioning the things that don't add up. Rather than trying to make sense of illogical situations they would accept any degree of lie. Perhaps the possibility of discovering any kind of truth would be too much to face. Better to take the easy option and sit in front of the TV and be told what to believe. Better to believe a lie and live a "comfortable" life. But to Josh, "comfort" came at a price—loss of integrity, a price not worth paying. It was better to live an uncomfortable life than one filled with lies and dishonour.

Standing in the doorway, Josh began analysing the room. There were bullet holes in the wall around the inside of the doorway he was standing in. He assumed they were caused by his old friend Liam—the facsimile, as the police entry team burst through.

He began imagining the scenario in his head. The sudden crash of the downstairs front door being smashed in: a noise that would almost certainly have jolted the occupants awake. The shouting of warnings and heavy thumping of police footsteps up the stairway. The bedroom door being forced open. Liam firing his weapon. And the police retaliating with fatal shots. On the surface, the picture was making sense in his head as he matched it to the crime scene. He also knew there had to be at least a second occupant: Malik's killer. This is where his mental construct, cross-checked against the actual scene, became questionable.

"Can I help you Brannon?"

Josh turned. Sir Godfrey and Sergeant Crofts were standing at the top of the stairway looking at him.

"Catching a look at the terrorist sir. Always good to know one's enemy," Josh replied, stepping out of the doorway. "Strange that he's Caucasian sir, don't you think?"

"There's nothing strange about it Brannon. They convert and recruit anyone to forward their cause, even Caucasians. There's no more for you to do here. Let's let SOCO get on with it shall we?" and Sir Godfrey stepped through into the room followed by Sergeant Crofts; both ignoring crime scene protocol.

It was obvious they wanted him out of the way. Josh walked down the stairs, somewhat niggled by Sir Godfrey's and the crime scene officer's response to his question. In essence, they were saying the same thing. Although the answers were not verbatim, they followed the same line, the same story. And Josh readily picked up on Sir Godfrey's vibe, something he was communicating without actually saying. There was a dark streak in him that he covered up with his refined and educated persona—a veil that would only fool a fool. Josh sensed there was more to him than met the eye, something malevolent. Whether this had any bearing to Operation Sting Bolt or not was unknown, perhaps it was just his dark side; a dark side evil people try to hide.

At the bottom of the stairs, reimagining the scene in his head from earlier, Josh began looking for illogical aspects to the operation—things that didn't make sense. He started looking for places Malik's killer could have hidden. The house was too small. Even if it were possible to have someone secreted in one of the cramped-sized cupboards, the place would have been too difficult to get out from; it was swarming with armed officers. It just didn't add up. He needed to locate the officers that had covered the rear of the house during the initial breach, to question them for answers. He then began wondering who the second person could be, even contemplating it could be Sofia. "But why were they here?" he thought.

Josh walked over to the crime scene investigation van parked directly opposite the front door of the target address. The officer he spoke with upstairs was standing by the van. He was busy passing the bags of evidence to another officer in the back, who was systematically recording and storing them in a lockable cage.

"What weapon did the terrorist use?" Josh directed his question to the officer inside the van.

"There's no weapon yet; nothing processed anyway. You'll need to ask inside." The officer was too busy for questions and carried on with his job, documenting evidence.

"Thanks." Josh could sense something was off. A weapon should have been the first exhibit to get processed. They would have wanted the ballistic report as soon as possible—to compare against other incidents for possible matches. And while analysing the upstairs room, before Sir Godfrey's interruption, he recalled seeing no weapon. There was a possibility it had fallen to the floor, maybe even kicked under the bed by the officers during the sudden firefight. But officers were trained to secure weapons so they couldn't be further used against them. He couldn't see the room completely to be sure. So, there was still a chance for it to be found, but he suspected otherwise. He knew the weapon would have been the first on the list to be found. And why were the crime scene investigators not asking the same questions?

"Brannon, still bothering my staff I see." Sir Godfrey and Sergeant Crofts had once again appeared from behind.

"Just asking about the weapon the terrorist used upstairs sir. Apparently there's no weapon." Josh watched Sir Godfrey's reaction.

"They're still collecting evidence so the pistol will be processed in due course."

"You saw a pistol then sir?" said Josh sharply.

"I'm sure something will be found." Sir Godfrey backtracked on his statement. "I think you're best needed back at your HQ Brannon, looking for the second terrorist who killed your colleague. The more time you give them the harder they are to find." And with that, Sir Godfrey walked off. But this time Sergeant Crofts spoke up. "Stay on your side Brannon, and keep off the fence," he warned. "We know what we're doing." And Crofts turned and followed his boss.

The warning wasn't subtle and Sir Godfrey's lie shone through like a beacon; to Josh anyway. He could easily see through a person's social veneer and read between the lines well enough. It wasn't hard, you just had to look.

Josh watched them both walking up the road; Sir Godfrey making a call on his phone. Maybe it was time to do a disappearing act back to the office after all, and start some digging around. He was in the fortunate position to know roughly what was going on, and needed to find Sofia for more answers.

BEEP-BEEP, BEEP-BEEP! BEEP-BEEP, BEEP-BEEP!

Josh's phone began ringing. "Brannon," he answered.

It was Harris. "Brannon, you're not needed there anymore. Return to HQ for debriefing," and Harris ended the call without waiting for confirmation of his order.

Harris was still the thorn in Josh's backside that he couldn't seem to pull out. He had been keeping Josh on a very short leash ever since his return from the bunker four months earlier—the time when he broke free from the effects of the Time-fold. It appeared that that wasn't part of some plan that Harris seemed to be a part of, and ever since, Josh has been regarded with immense suspicion from his superior. And strangely, no mention of the incident or the case he was put on at the time has ever been made, just as though it never happened.

"Hmm," muttered Josh. He looked over at Sir Godfrey. "Seems like I am treading on someone's toes," he thought.

Sir Godfrey and Crofts were standing looking back at him. It didn't take much to know who had put pressure on Harris to remove him from the scene. The best thing about treading on people's toes is that you get to find out who's who and what side of the game they're on. Josh decided it was time to get going, regardless of Sir Godfrey's intervention and Harris's order. He needed to dig elsewhere to find out more about his old friend and why he was beginning to experience the Time-fold phenomenon again. He would only get his answers from people he knew: View Corp.

Under the suspicious eyes of Godfrey and Crofts, Josh headed for his service vehicle. He walked through the target house to the other side where he had left his car. Sitting inside, he watched briefly the officers still scouring the area for clues to the unknown shooter. He gave a disappointing look at their efforts and started the engine. Slowly, he drove up the road passing Malik's covered vehicle. He looked down at the ground, spotting traces of Malik's semi-dried blood as he continued on past to the cordon at the end of the road. A police officer lifted the tape, allowing Josh to drive under.

It was fifteen minutes past ten and Josh was heading back to the office. He was interested to know what his debriefing would be with Harris—another bollocking for sure. Through some kind of luck Josh was still in a job, maybe by the skin of his teeth, but he was still employed. The case he was put on four months ago, the case that led him back to the bunker and View Corp, was suddenly dropped. Since that time, he had only been put on low-class assignments without any explanation, until now. Operation Sting Bolt was the first real assignment he had been involved in, and now he was beginning to wonder why. He wasn't stupid. It was no coincidence that he suddenly came upon his old friend Liam, and the start-up of his déjà vu experiences. This was planned, but why?

A twenty-minute journey back to HQ, Josh was routinely checked in through security. He drove through and parked up in the vehicle compound. He disliked being at HQ, preferring to be out in the field. He liked getting into the thick of things; the danger kept him alive. He had been feeling stultified the past four months and had considered quitting, but knew Harris would enjoy that moment, so decided to wait it out. Until now, nothing was giving him much reason to stay: now he had one.

"Alright Josh, same shit?" said Mohammed, standing in the gym doorway along the corridor.

"Same shit Mo."

"Wanna come and fight it out mate?" Mohammed enjoyed his martial arts sessions with Josh, as he kept him on his toes. He liked the fact that Josh didn't always use conventional martial arts moves, but mixed it up with his own strategic tricks, causing Mo to think differently.

"No, not now mate. I need to eat then get debriefed."

"Well, anytime," nodded Mo, and he entered the gym.

Josh walked to the canteen. Like a famished animal, his stomach was starting to growl impatiently and he needed to feed it. There were a few guys already eating; guys that had also been on Sting Bolt that morning. Josh grabbed a tray and began checking the menu.

"What do you want Josh?" asked Mel. "I'm afraid the cooked breakfasts are off the menu now, as it's gone ten, but I can do your usual for you if you like?"

"That'll be good. Thanks Mel."

"Go and sit down and I'll bring it over." Mel gave a flirtatious smile and went to cook his meal.

Josh turned and sat himself at the table with his colleagues. They were finishing up eating and swallowing the last of their tea.

"How's it going Josh?" asked one of his colleagues.

"Okay," replied Josh, keeping the conversation short.

"You hear about Malik?" asked his colleague. "He didn't make it." Josh's mood sank. "I hadn't heard."

"We heard what you did for him. Put yourself in danger. You did a good job mate."

"Yeah, well done mate." The others acknowledged Josh's efforts to save Malik.

"Did any of you see anything?" inquired Josh.

"Not from where we were. We were kept on stand-by; told to stay put when we heard your contact report over the net."

"Who told you to stay put?" quizzed Josh.

"Harris," they all replied; each one looking disaffected with Harris's order not to go in.

"Hey, don't forget to clean yourself up." Another of the group pointed with his cutlery knife at Josh's jacket.

Josh turned his head to look. He hadn't noticed, but Malik's blood was staining his jacket on the shoulder, where he had carried him. Josh took it off; placing it on the seat next to him.

His colleagues stood up from the table. "Catch you later Josh," and they left the canteen together.

Mel came to the table. "Here ya go Josh. And here's a nice cuppa for you." She placed his food on the table with a strong cup of tea, just how he liked it.

"Thanks Mel."

He caught her glance at the bloodstain on his shoulder. Malik's blood had not only covered the outside of his jacket, but soaked through to his top. And despite seeing it, she said nothing. She knew the rules, the rule not to ask, and walked off. It was a strange game they were in—trying to keep their own secrets secret but trying to find out other peoples.

Josh ate fast, he always did. He felt he would be missing something if he ate slowly. Life seemed too short to waste it on trivial things like food.

"Cheers Mel. I'm done." She smiled at him. He placed his empty plate on the stack of dirty dishes and left the canteen.

He walked to the debriefing room and began writing his report. It was mandated that everything and anything that had occurred had to be disclosed: no matter how insignificant it seemed. As Josh began covering the part of the incident concerning Malik, he couldn't help but mentally picture his face. The strangeness of life and death made him wonder if it was all worth it. Malik was dedicated to his job, to his country, but what now for him? Thinking about his own experiences with the Time-fold phenomenon, Josh wondered if Malik was still alive; alive in another dimension. It was a thought that comforted him.

"Ah Brannon." Harris had sneaked into the debriefing room. It seemed to be a common occurrence that morning, that the snakes were sneaking up on Josh—first Sir Godfrey and Sergeant Crofts, and now Harris.

"Sir," replied Josh.

"Just making sure you are where you should be, and writing your report. Make sure you include everything," and without waiting for an answer, Harris walked out.

He knew Harris wanted him to include his conversations with Sir Godfrey. Harris either wanted it as ammunition to use in Josh's personnel file—to get rid of him, or to spy on his own. Either way, Josh would include it. But what he knew he couldn't include, was his strange connection to the "terrorist" Liam. Not that he would be believed, but it would most certainly be added to his psych report.

It was almost noon and Josh wrapped up writing his report. The rest of the team had already finished theirs before he got back. He placed it in the basket with the others, ready to go for evaluation. Curious, he pulled out the rest of the team's reports and read through them one by one. Every one mentioned that Harris had prevented the team from reacting to Josh's initial contact report—when he radioed through after hearing a shot: the shot that killed Malik. There was no reason given, just the order to stay put. Reading further, one report mentioned a police team leaving the scene. The timing of them leaving was shortly after the shot fired.

Josh replaced the reports in the basket. He needed to feel Harris out, to get what he knew. He left the debriefing room and headed for Harris's office down the corridor. He knocked on the door and waited for permission to enter. There was no answer so he opened the door and walked in. The office was empty, Harris wasn't there. Immediately Josh's attention zeroed in on a brown file on Harris's desk. It was colour-coded red and marked "Top Secret".

"Hmm, strange he would leave it out," thought Josh, wondering further if it was an integrity test, and was being recorded. Often the company would set up these little tests to see if their own employees could be trusted: planting seemingly insignificant items, like money or leaving "valuable" documents around, to see what an employee would do with them.

He scanned the room and noticed a new object—a book standing up on its end. Josh had been in Harris's office many times, and his almost photographic memory helped to flag the book as something out of the ordinary. It was a test. Josh knew that inside the book would be a hidden camera. Most of the main areas were already covered by internal security cameras, but there were blind-spots, and certain rooms were intentionally not covered—Harris's being one of them. Josh walked out, knowing he had passed the test—passing, not because of not looking in the file, but because he was clever enough to spot the trap in the first place.

Walking along the corridor, Josh spotted Harris walking towards him, likely going to his office. "Sir, can I have a word?"

"What is it Brannon?" snapped Harris. He seemed agitated.

"About the Op this morning, and Malik," replied Josh.

"Malik?" Harris showed some confusion about the name at first, "Oh, you mean Asif." He couldn't even remember Malik's first name, only his last. His complete arrogance and disregard for his team was apparent. "Well, what is it?" he continued.

"Any news on the shooter?" asked Josh.

"No nothing. Is that it?" Harris began to walk off.

"No, that's not it. Just wondering why you stopped the team from responding to my radio call?"

Harris halted and turned, "I—I make the decisions Brannon not you. I make decisions based on intel." He balked a little, not able to handle the question put to him.

Josh knew the pencil pusher was lying through his teeth. "What intel sir?"

"That's need-to-know!" snapped Harris defensively.

"What do you know about the additional police team that evacuated the site, shortly after Malik's shooting?"

"I don't know what you're inferring, or even suggesting Brannon, but you need to toe the line. You are speaking to your superior!" barked Harris, and he started walking off again; avoiding all questions.

"By the way, I like your new book sir," remarked Josh sarcastically, referring to the spy camera test set up in his office. Harris said nothing.

Josh was angry inside. He knew Harris was up to his neck in something, something that was more than official government secrets. He knew Harris was compromised; corruption was written all over his face. Poking the snake was fun, but one day the snake will bite back. Josh knew it, but also knew Harris was under orders. For some reason the snake was holding back, maybe just out of pure cowardice, but more likely because of other plans that had yet to be laid.

CHAPTER 3

JOSH WALKED TO THE changing room to get cleaned up. His bloodstained clothes had to be removed, as he knew Malik's blood was a sign of victory for the other side—whatever side that was—and would have a negative effect on his colleagues.

He pushed his jacket into a plastic bag. Looking in a mirror, he could see the blood had seeped all the way through to his undergarments. It was good practice for operatives to have spare clothing, not just for changing disguise in the field, but for such occasions as this. He removed his sweat-top and t-shirt then leaned over the sink to wash his shoulder clean. Not bothering to dry himself, he put on his spares. He pushed the soiled tops in with his bloodied jacket, inside the bag, and put them away in his locker.

Refreshed and wearing clean clothes, Josh's next step was to get answers. He needed to find out why the Time-fold phenomenon was happening again, and the connection to his old friend Liam. He already had a suspicion of why Malik was killed, but needed proof. He also needed to find out the "Who"—the shooter. He knew that if he could identify the "Who" to Malik's death, he could extract from them who else was in the house during the raid that morning. A new puzzle was beginning to form, and he knew precisely where to start.

Josh left the changing room and stopped by the gym; needing the help of Mo to cover his back with Harris. Josh wanted to take some time off and needed a reliable alibi. He entered the gym, and watched as Mo had a half-defeated student on the floor in a joint-lock.

Straining his head, Mo looked up. "Hey Josh...changed ya mind?" he groaned, as he battled his student. He was figuring Josh had changed his mind about taking him up on his offer of a sparring session.

"Yeah, I need some 'practice'," emphasised Josh.

Mo knew what he meant—Josh was beyond needing practice, he was a master without the belt—it was a subtle code between them only a good friend would understand.

"No problem," panted Mo, and continued countering his student's efforts to escape the hold.

Josh left the gym and strode along the corridor for the vehicle compound. He walked up to his SQRV, opened it, threw his phone on the front seat, and closed the door. Instead of using the SQRV, he jumped into his own car: his own to cover any tracks of where he was planning on going. He couldn't afford to be tracked through the GPS tracker fitted to his company car, and phone. He knew what technical surveillance capabilities the company had, and he didn't trust Harris not to check.

He started the engine, pulled off, and drove past security into the street. As per standard protocol upon leaving the "office", he drove around to make sure he hadn't been tagged by a hostile surveillance team—driving down one road, making a U-turn, and driving back up. After completing standard anti-surveillance moves, watching for tails, he figured he was unfollowed, and headed for his destination.

Swerving fast through the city traffic, he headed out to familiar ground. About a forty-five-minute drive from the city, Josh turned into a dirt track out in the countryside. The familiar scene had him pulling up old memories. Instead of caution, as in previous visits, he drove as though going to meet an old friend. He pulled up in a small wooded area near some fields, his vehicle parked out of sight, just off the track. He stepped out of his car, closed and locked the door. With his right hand he felt the outer left side of his clean jacket, feeling his 9mm automatic pistol through the garment. Although intended as a friendly visit, he still needed to be prepared.

He walked a short distance up the dirt track, to the concrete building he had last seen four months prior—the hidden underground bunker where View Corp was situated. Surprisingly, the heavy steel door was ajar—unlocked and unsecure.

"Something's wrong," he thought.

He instinctively reached inside his jacket and pulled out his 9mil. Simultaneously, he pulled back on the top slide with one hand and pushed forward on the pistol grip with the other: cocking the weapon and pushing a round into the chamber. Holding his weapon up to point the way, he slowly opened the steel door. With the door further open, Josh entered the building. It was dark; no internal lights and he could barely see. He had a mini-torch in his tactical vest under his jacket, but preferred not to use it and make his presence known—just in case he wasn't welcome anymore.

He descended the concrete stairway to the bottom, using what minimal light was available that shone through from the doorway at the top of the stairs. It was getting too dark. He had no choice but to use his mini-torch, so pulled it out and switched it on. He held the light in his left hand, resting it against his 9mil—both weapon and light pointing in the same direction. He slowly scanned the area ahead of him as he walked along the corridor, but was stopped short. He was stopped by a walled mass of collapsed steel and rubble that blocked the way, as though an intense force had ripped the bunker apart from within.

"What the hell happened?" he thought.

He shone his light through the dark gaps of fallen concrete to see if he could somehow make his way through. It appeared as though the whole lower section of the bunker had been destroyed. He knew he wouldn't be able to push his body through, and he wasn't sure how stable the building was. It was too risky.

Josh backed up the way he came, heading up to the surface. At the top, he knew there was another way in. Walking cautiously between the trees and through the undergrowth, he made his way to the opposite side of the bunker complex. The main complex couldn't be seen on the surface, but strangely, Josh could picture the hidden sub-structure in his head. He was mentally picturing the layout of the corridor and rooms beneath his boots, as though he could see down through the earth.

He made his way to the external bunker doorway, the same doorway he had used before to gain access. As he neared the dirty grey concrete outbuilding, poking up from the ground, he fleetingly recalled his past experiences: first entering the bunker as a boy with his former older self, and then with his younger self—both facsimiles. And, unlike previous occasions, revisiting that specific part of the bunker had no effect on him, as though any Time-fold effect had been resolved—straightened out. There was no déjà vu, or sudden dampening of his awareness.

Knowing how to gain access, up the gradual embankment around to the opposite side from the heavy metal door, Josh crouched down to the narrow window at ground level. Oddly, he recalled the last time he climbed through—with his younger self four months ago—the window had been covered by brambles. Now though, after the passing of four months, it was still free, free from not only brambles, but any form of natural growth that should have occurred. It was wrong. He wasn't a horticulturist but he knew there should be at least some regrowth. It was something that was missing that should be there. This made him even more wary.

He lay down on the ground, and with legs first, pushed his way through the window slit to the other side. On the inside, from what he could remember, nothing seemed to have changed, except it was dirtier with thick grey concrete dust covering the floor. As with the other bunker entrance, there was no light, except natural light passing through the narrow window. Josh pulled out his mini-torch again, turning it on to shine the way.

Quietly making his way down the stairway, he remained overly cautious. The bunker's structure had been severely compromised. He had to inspect the walls and ceiling for extreme weakness and potential collapse. Reaching the bottom, he passed through the open steel door. On the opposite side, Josh was only permitted to walk several steps before being stopped again. A chaotic mix of concrete rubble and steel from the ceiling was again blocking his way. The internal explosion was powerful enough to have ripped through the whole of that bunker section.

"This can't be right," he thought.

Josh was unsure if the bunker had been occupied at the time of the explosion, but he was already forming a hypothesis. In truth, he knew what had occurred there. Although he was semi-acceptant to the idea, it was still somewhat unbelievable. He sensed he knew of two bodies that would likely be lying on the floor in the corridor. He didn't know why he was thinking what he was thinking, but the unlikeable truth seemed to be revealing itself.

Guessing aside, he was desperate to know for sure. He shone his light through the debris, looking through the spaces between the various sized concrete pieces and structural steel. He identified a pathway of small spaces he could squeeze through. He removed his jacket and tactical vest, placing them on the floor, then proceeded to push his body between the fallen concrete. Navigating through the tiny spaces was hard, hard enough to force him to have to purposely scrape his body against the mishmash of debris, or it wouldn't let him through. It was as though the jagged concrete was desperately guarding a secret it didn't want him to discover.

It was becoming tighter and his way became barred. He knew he couldn't go further and had to go back. Josh rested a little and looked around at the mess. Something caught his eye, something stood out. It was a piece of dusty white clothing. Determined to prove his idea right—what he sensed had happened—he wriggled a little further in. He reached with his hand, grabbed the cloth material and pulled. A dusty limp hand flipped up. Josh had pulled on the sleeve of a coat revealing a body. He was right. He didn't need to see the face to know who it was. He knew it was one of two people.

Josh let go of the sleeve, letting the dead hand rest in peace. His intuition had been proven, so he began to make his way back. It was impossible to turn his body, so he inched his way backwards—feet first, through the concrete mess. Gaining more scrapes along the way, he finally made it back through. He stood up, and without delay grabbed his jacket and tactical vest from the floor, then made a fast exit; back to the top of the stairway.

At the top, he placed his jacket and tac-vest on the ground, turned off his light and put it away. He quickly brushed and patted himself down, allowing the concrete dust and small fragments of debris to fall freely from his clothing. He then got kitted up—putting on his tac-vest and jacket.

Josh knew that present-time circumstances were being manipulated again, to expect more Time-fold phenomena, and so had to be ready. Nothing in his training had prepared him for this four-dimensional assault. His mind now, was becoming a much more needed weapon, as he recalled—when a boy—the moment his older self was struck by bullets upon leaving the bunker. Would that be his fate now? He was unsure.

Before leaving the bunker, he checked his 9mil over. There was nothing worse than getting caught up in a firefight, and having your weapon jam due to dust and grit in the firing mechanism. Thorough preparation and good execution were key elements in any battle scenario. His weapon was serviceable and Josh was now prepared to fight it out.

Looking through the narrow window, Josh scanned the immediate area outside, searching for unexpected and unwanted guests. He couldn't see far, for the undergrowth restricted his visionary arcs left and right, as well as limit how far he could see in front. He couldn't delay any longer, and had to take his chances and leave. In nearly one smooth action, he pulled himself up, squeezed through the window and pointed his weapon—readying for a contact. He dashed fast, away from the bunker, zig-zagging left and right to make himself a harder target to kill. He raced toward a dense area of bushes to give him cover from view. He was safe.

Outside in the fresh air, crouched down low, Josh took a deep breath to saturate his lungs. He coughed hard, expelling concrete dust particles breathed in from inside the bunker. He looked through the undergrowth from his hiding position, further checking the area; still no sign of hostiles. He was satisfied he was safe and so housed his 9mil inside his jacket. He stood up and began making his way back to the car.

Heading down the track his car came into view. As usual, before approaching it he stopped, crouched down and checked around for dangers: devices, hostile surveillance teams, and possible enemy ambush positions.

"All clear," he thought, then stood up.

Walking up to it, he pulled out his keys and remotely unlocked the door. He stepped inside, closed the door and wound down the window. Sitting quietly, he began taking stock of the new situation he had found himself in. Thankfully, he had a better understanding of what was going on than before. But still, he had to think differently, and as cliché as it sounds, he had to think outside the box, because the box was no longer three-dimensional, but had a hidden fourth. And as far as he could make out, due to the absence of any déjà vu, the destroyed bunker was real and not a Time-fold. That concerned him.

Josh was catching on fast. He knew this was intimately connected to him; the fact of seeing the facsimile of his friend Liam earlier that morning. He needed more answers, but his primary sources of information had been killed. Killed by whom was still unknown, but he couldn't help but consider a remarkable possibility. He was disappointed and frustrated he couldn't get the answers from the only two that seemed to know most about it—professors Montague and Balantyne: both now lying dead in the bunker.

"Sofia!" Josh's thoughts suddenly jumped to Sofia. She was in danger and he needed to find her fast.

CRACK!

Josh immediately pulled his weapon, pushed hard on the car door with his shoulder—swinging it fully open—and jumped out. He pointed his 9mil over the roof of the car in the general direction of the sound—the crack of a breaking stick underfoot. Sharply focussed, with all senses aligned and scanning for movement, Josh caught sight and zeroed-in on a figure lurking nearby.

"Armed security services! Stop or I fire!" yelled Josh, with a clear warning he intended to use deadly force.

The figure suddenly froze, partly hidden behind a tree.

"Step out with your hands up!"

The figure complied, stepping out away from the tree into full view.

WHOOSH!

A Time-fold effect struck Josh, temporarily distracting him from the source. It lasted but a few seconds then wore off. His focus quickly returned, allowing him to see who was standing before him.

"I don't believe it," he thought, as he slowly lowered his weapon.

A boy had stepped out, looking completely stunned. Holding his hands part way up in the air, as a sign of submission, he was staring hard at Josh with a look of total disbelief.

"But—but I saw you get killed," said the boy. "You were killed. I saw it, in there," and he pointed in the direction of the bunker.

Josh knew exactly what the boy was talking about. Somehow the event of four months ago was being continued—the boy's timeline had been crudely spliced together with his own. He could only guess as to why, that whoever or whatever was behind it, had not achieved their goal: to destroy View Corp. It meant View Corp was still a major threat, in spite of the deaths of Montague and Balantyne.

The boy was standing, waiting for some kind of explanation. He was frozen, dumb-looking, with his mouth open. And this time Josh had no idea of how to respond, as he had no idea how this was now playing out. He had not personally lived this moment before, or had he?

"We need to go," said Josh firmly. "Get in the car!"

Josh put his weapon away, as he quickly paced around the opposite side of the car towards the boy. He took hold of the boy and marched him along, literally pushing him into the car's passenger seat. The boy said nothing. Josh closed the door, walked to the driver's side and got in. The boy looked across at Josh, looking at his torso area, inspecting it thoroughly.

"What is it? asked Josh.

"You were bleeding. Bullet holes...you had bullet holes. You died. I had to run away." The boy recounted the traumatic spots of what had happened in the bunker.

Josh also remembered that exact moment for him—when he was the boy. Recalling those shadow memories made him realise once again, nothing is at it seems—even momentarily doubting his own existence.

"There are things we both need to understand, things that need answering. We both need to work together on this one. Okay? Okay Josh?" said Josh softly to the boy.

The boy slowly looked up. "Sure, sure," he nodded hesitantly. His face was full of confusion and uncertainty as he slowly clipped in his seat belt.

CHAPTER 4

JOSH STARTED THE CAR engine; driving and making a U-turn back down the dirt track. He joined the main road and sped off. He had to get back to HQ before his absence was known to Harris, if not already. But first he had to deal with the boy who was sitting quietly, still shocked at Josh's "resurrection".

"Why did you go back to the bunker?" asked Josh, breaking the silence.

"I don't know. I didn't want to but felt I had to. I don't know why." The boy became a little agitated.

"Okay. When you saw me again, up in the woods, did you experience anything?"

"I guess I was scared. I didn't expect to see you again. You were killed. I saw you...with bullet holes." The boy was again recounting that fateful experience. "How are you alive? Are you a ghost?"

Frustratingly, Josh wasn't getting any useful intelligence from the boy, but knew he had to allow him to naturally pull himself out of the shock. The more aware he was, the clearer the information would be—information that was desperately needed. Josh knew that people in shock, in lower states of awareness, rarely spoke with any accuracy, and had a poor understanding of reality. It was a fact of life.

"You remember about View Corp?"

"Yes, some kind of terrorist organisation. You were looking for them...in the bunker. You killed those two men...blew it up."

So far, everything the boy was saying was a duplication of what had happened in the past. But clearly things had changed, something in Josh's own life had been altered, and he needed to probe further.

"I don't expect you to understand, but things have changed since the last time I saw you."

"'Since the last time I saw you,' are you fucking joking?" The boy's anger was a good indication his awareness was coming up. "The last time I saw you was last night, dead in that place. How can anything have happened since? How can any of this be happening?"

"So, this all happened just last night?" questioned Josh.

"Of course, you were there! Don't you remember? Or at least I think it was you. But that doesn't make sense. If it was you then you wouldn't be here, or you would have holes in you." The boy was starting to think more clearly, questioning the circumstances. "I just don't understand."

"Okay. So, when you saw me in the woods did you experience anything strange?" Josh moved back to his earlier question.

"I felt that feeling again, the one I keep getting, like this has all happened before."

"Déjà vu," answered Josh, "The feeling you've experienced something before."

"Yeah. Déjà vu." The boy seemed more settled and began looking out of the car window at the countryside.

Evaluating the information in his head, Josh concluded that everything that had happened with the boy, was the same that had happened to him, except the part of going back to the bunker—this was new. Josh never went back to the bunker when he was the boy. He never saw his older self again. "But if we both experienced the same Time-fold in the woods, it must have happened before?" thought Josh.

"How did you get here?" he asked the boy, trying to lighten the mood.

The boy looked round. "I hitched," he said. "So, I guess you're some kind of assassin," he grinned. The boy was in a better frame of mind now.

"I never thought of it like that," replied Josh.

"Look, I know you can't say coz you're some kind of secret agent or something, or whatever, but I need to know what's going on. I need to know what's happening to me." The boy was justifiably concerned.

Josh knew the boy deserved to know, even if the truth was beyond anything he was able to comprehend. They had both come back around, and whether by nature or by external manipulation, were joined again. Their lives, coming together, were positioned at an inverted fork in the road of time, which was pointing them both in the same direction. They had to join forces. Explaining to the boy everything he knew—the fact that the bunker situation had been four months ago for him, and had turned out differently—Josh waited for a response.

The boy chuckled. "So, you're saying, I'm not real? I'm some kinda what...a ghost, in your time? This 'wrap-over' thing; 'facsimile'. I'm from another, what, world? How do you explain that I can feel these things? You're even talking to me. Doesn't that make you kinda crazy?"

"I'm not saying you aren't real. But what I am saying, is that both our realities have crossed over—your world and mine."

"So how do I know this isn't my world, my time? It could be mine. Maybe you're in my world and you're the one that's not supposed to be here?"

The boy was making valid points, giving Josh new viewpoints at which to look at the whole situation. "I don't know the answer to that," replied Josh thoughtfully. "But what I do know, is that we both need real answers."

Pushing down on the accelerator, it wasn't long before they reached London. Josh now had a new companion and wasn't sure what to do with him. He knew the boy was important somehow and needed him close by, but couldn't take him to HQ. He needed to put him somewhere, out of the way, where he wouldn't get into trouble. There was only one place he could take him.

"So, this is my new flat then?" said the boy smiling, as he entered Josh's flat. "You know, we are the same person...so what's yours is also mine...in my future maybe, but it's still mine."

Josh gave no response to the boy's cocky banter, just let him have his moment of fun. "Stay here and don't leave the flat. Do not use the phone. And don't answer the door to anyone. Okay?" instructed Josh. "And no snooping." He was beginning to feel like the boy's father. "I'm gonna be gone for the rest of the day, maybe more. Here's my mobile number," and Josh wrote his number on a pad, leaving it on the table. "Don't call unless you have to."

"Sure, no sweat," smiled the boy, while resting back in a comfy chair, his arms stretched up and hands clasped behind his head, like he owned the place.

Josh left the apartment, closing the door and making sure it was locked behind him. He knew the boy wouldn't be able to resist not snooping—he knew because he would also want to snoop. It didn't matter anyway, there was nothing in the flat from the office; operatives knew better than to take any work home with them. His filing cabinet was in his head.

He drove back to headquarters. It was late afternoon and Josh knew Harris would likely be at the pub with the other "suits", having a tot of his favourite whisky—his daily routine. It was a routine that could easily compromise him. Harris was an office spy, and although intellectually clever, wasn't street-smart. Routine got intelligence officers and field agents killed. But Josh liked Harris's routines, making him predictable. He grabbed his phone from the front seat of his SQRV where he had left it. Oddly, Harris seemed to have ignored him; no missed calls, nothing.

Entering the building, Josh went straight to see Mohammed. He poked his head through the gym doorway. "All good Mo?" he asked.

"All good Josh. Great session," replied Mo, with a secretive nod.

He gave Josh the all clear that Harris hadn't been hunting him down. Josh nodded back and the secret bond was upheld. He left the gym and headed for Technical Branch. He needed to find out which police unit had been covering the rear of the target address during Operation Sting Bolt.

In T-Branch, the lab-coated nerds were too busy to pay Josh any attention. They were busy developing and experimenting with new technologies that would put the UK at the head of the spying game. Josh looked across to Flash's corner where he was sitting with his head down, concentrating in a book. Josh walked up behind him, grabbed a chair and sat down.

"Good to see you're not wasting taxpayer's money," interjected Josh.

Flash was startled by the surprise interruption. He suddenly slapped closed a computer-electronics book he was pretending to read. Concealed inside was a comic book Josh had caught him with.

"What do you want Brannon?" Flash was a little defensive from his secret being discovered.

"I need to find out which police unit covered the rear of the building this morning during the Op."

"Why don't you ask Harris?" replied Flash.

"I need you to find out for me," insisted Josh.

Flash knew Josh didn't want his digital fingerprints all over this, otherwise he would have logged in himself to look at the files. It wasn't like he didn't have clearance, he did. He just didn't want anyone knowing he was investigating his own. He needed a hacker's light touch, one that wouldn't leave any user log files.

"Ah, okay...well it's quite simple really Josh...just need to log in," and Flash entered his username and password into his computer. "Okay...now I need to...," he began tapping on the keyboard, creating a system workaround that would lead him through one of his illegal backdoors he had previously created. "Here we go. And here's the folder." He double tapped on his computer mouse opening a folder titled "OPERATION STING BOLT". He scrolled down the page. "Looking for the... ah here it is," and Flash tapped on a computer file listing all the agencies involved in the operation.

Josh leaned in, looking closely at the various agencies and their assigned tasks during the Op. One oddity that immediately stood out, was the number of agencies involved for just one, possibly two "terrorists". It was overkill. "It says here one of the local Counter Terrorism Units was assigned. Who's the unit I/C?"

Flash clicked on a link for the officer in charge. "It says, 'Sergeant Allan Crofts.'"

Josh sat back; a moment of relief came over him: relief caused by the discovering of a truth. A piece of the puzzle had just mentally clunked into place inside his head. "The truth shall set you free Sergeant Crofts," he murmured to himself.

"Do you know him?" asked Flash.

"Not entirely, but I will," warned Josh. He then changed the subject, "I need to borrow it."

Flash looked at him and began slowly shaking his head. "I can't. You'll get me into trouble."

"Come on Flash, I'll look after it. It'll be good as new when I return it."

Feeling obliged, Flash opened a drawer. "I'm not supposed to just give out equipment like this," he complained. He reached in and took out the handheld computer device Josh had used before, and reluctantly handed it over.

"What do you call this thing anyway?" asked Josh as he took the device and put it in his jacket pocket.

"I don't know. Never thought about giving it a name. I'll call it... 'Sniffer', after a hound dog I used to have. He could sniff out anything," and Flash smiled at his newly named invention.

"Sounds good to me," agreed Josh. "I let you get back to your "book".

Flash smirked while Josh stood up and walked off, leaving the room. As soon as Josh had gone Tomblin came skulking over. He had been watching from his desk, their secret rendezvous.

"Hey Flash, how's it going?"

"What do you want?" snarled Flash. He could see through Tomblin's façade. He was sniffing around for titbits as usual.

"How's Josh?"

"Is that a spine I see Tomblin? Ah no, sorry my mistake," Flash criticized Tomblin's wormy character.

Tomblin's lips shrivelled from annoyance. He snapped back as best a worm could do, "You can call me by my first name you know. That's what friends and colleagues do."

"Yeah okay, thanks for the advice, Tomblin. I'll remember that," and Flash opened his book and continued reading his comic.

Tomblin was so transparent you could almost see he was spineless. Flash knew he was Harris's stooge and was just out to get information so he could report back. It was funny, everyone spying on each other, made Flash wonder if there was any time to do any real spying. No one trusted anyone. There were too many secrets, too many crimes within the company that were being covered up.

Sitting in the canteen, Josh stopped by to get some food while waiting for Harris to get back. Mel had knocked up some left-over lunch for him which he was happily throwing down his neck. Most people ate because it was time to do so—by the clock. Josh ate because he was hungry, regardless of customary habits. Routine was something he had managed to break free from. He realised routine was a mental state that could trap people, trap them in life—the nine-to-fivers.

Finishing his last mouthful, he was itching to get going again. He didn't want to waste time feeding his body. He needed to get back on with his investigation. That was another strange thing. Before the morning, before Operation Sting Bolt, he had been kept on a very short leash. Harris had been checking his every move, every activity he was on for the past four months. But now, it was as though Harris had let him loose. Something didn't add up. Something stank.

Josh got up from the table. "Thanks Mel."

"Anytime," replied Mel, smiling.

He left the table. Next stop was Harris's office. Josh needed to know what his next assignment was going to be. And as much as he wanted to do his own investigation, he needed to keep a low profile while doing it. Josh walked into Harris's office without knocking. He had become accustomed to pissing him off.

"Yes!" snapped Harris; he was back from his late afternoon tipple and annoyed at the sudden intrusion. He was sitting at his desk, busy looking through papers and files.

Although Josh didn't enjoy Harris's company, he always found it worthwhile paying surprise visits to his office. Not to annoy him, that was a secondary pleasure, but to see if he could pick up on anything that may be of interest to him—particularly relating to his past experiences. Harris always had case files on his desk and occasionally, unbeknown to him, Josh could pick out key words from the paperwork: words that allowed him to accurately guess their overall content. It was a knack he had.

"Just checking in sir," said Josh. "I've been at a bit of a loose end since getting back from the Op. Nothing much to do," he lied. He wanted Harris to believe he had been at the office all day; not conducting his own inquiries. "I think Mo's getting the idea I fancy him."

Harris was too much of a snob to appreciate Josh's humour. He hardly looked up but kept his nose in his paperwork. This suited Josh perfectly; taking the opportunity to stretch a little further to read the file's content without arousing suspicion.

"Check in at the usual time tomorrow Brannon. I might have a job just up your alley. Report at 08:00 hours. That's all."

"Righto sir," and Josh walked out of the office, purposely leaving the door open to cause his boss some annoyance.

For the short time he was in with Harris, he had managed to glean some key words from the case file Harris was reading, but nothing of real interest to him. What he could piece together though, was a low-key operation concerning a bio-tech company. Perhaps that was his next assignment. In the meantime, this was his opportunity to go home and get back to the boy. He had further questions to ask him, now that he would be more relaxed.

He grabbed his gear from his locker—the bag of bloodstained clothing, and headed out to his car. He dumped the bag on the back seat and got in. Just as he was about to turn the key in the ignition, a familiar face appeared, driving through from security. The car parked up and a man stepped out. It was the very man that had recruited him from out of the army. The same man Josh had followed in the past, who had met up with the CIA officer—William Byrnes, who had been shot in the street. This was one part of the puzzle that he never figured out: why the CIA wanted his personnel file. And also, who his recruiter was.

Josh watched as he walked into the building, carrying a black briefcase. He suspected he was going to visit Harris, but for what, he didn't know. Josh stepped out of his vehicle and casually walked back towards the main building. As he got closer, he casually looked across at his recruiter's black saloon and memorised the vehicle registration number. He continued to the office block doorway—as a pretence he had forgotten something—then turned about and headed back to his car, making it appear as though he had remembered.

Taking a pen and paper from inside his car door, Josh noted down the vehicle details from memory. He started up the car engine and drove off to security. He approached the boom and spiked barrier as always, but instead of driving through, he stopped. He wound down his window and glanced over to the armed security officer at the window.

"Alright Josh?" asked Tim.

Tim was an old-timer at the office, in his early fifties, and ex-military like Josh. He had been security there for the past ten years or so, and knew most of the faces that came and went. Josh made a point of getting to know him from the start. Most intelligence operatives liked to try and bond with the upper hierarchy types for intel, and all but ignore ordinary folk. But Josh knew the potential value of ordinary people in his game.

"Alright Tim. You got the night shift again?"

"Yeah, get a break from the missus," he smiled.

Josh smiled with him. "How's ya extension coming on?"

"It's okay, just finished the roof. Still a way to go though, and it certainly ain't cheap."

"It's a good job you got your army pension then."

"Yeah, that's for sure."

Josh was purposely building up the relationship before he asked for something. He knew people were more willing to give or do things once a bond was made, rather than going straight in like a bull. Sometimes though, he had to use the bulldozer method to get what he wanted, but it was always easier with co-operation.

"Hey Tim, who's that guy that just came in; black saloon?"

"You mean the hard looking bugger in the suit?" replied Tim.

"Yeah, that bugger." Josh matched Tim's attitude to help build the rapport even more.

"He's been here before. His name's Nugent, Chris Nugent. Got a special pass, one of those fancy one's that'll get you in anywhere, even Parliament."

"Has he come to see Harris?"

Tim nodded, "Yeah."

"What's his story?"

"I'm not sure. I figure he's one of those middlemen ya know, a go-between. Works somewhere between us and the political nobs up in Parliament. He's not a talker when he comes through here, so I don't bother. I wouldn't mess with him though; looks like he can handle himself. And my own personal opinion, but you didn't hear it from me, is he's a doer."

Josh knew what he meant by "doer"—someone that took deadly action when needed. "Why do you say 'he's a doer'?" Josh listened intently as Tim began revealing more.

"Just something I saw a little while back. He came through one evening. I was on night shift. I think he came to see Harris. He had some blood on his shirt, not much, must've rubbed off from his side-arm. I don't think he even knew it was there, and I'm sure not gonna say anything. Anyway, usually he doesn't have anything in his car, on the seats I mean; a real stickler for security. But that evening he had a box, you know, one of those metal lockboxes; a real old looking one. It was odd, only because his car is usually clean. Well, I don't want to speculate, but I think someone got 'done' that evening, if you know what I mean."

It suddenly dawned on Josh what had happened—where the blood had come from: on Nugent's shirt.

"When was that?" asked Josh.

"Um—I think it was maybe four months or so ago," answered Tim.

Unexpectedly, Tim gave Josh more valuable information than he thought he would get, particularly about the lockbox. Tim carried on the conversation with more small talk about his home extension, but had to let Josh go as another car was waiting to pass through. He opened the barrier and Josh continued out.

Driving home, Josh's attention was on Tim's revelations. It was easy now to put two and two together. Josh knew the lockbox Tim was referring to was the same one he had taken from the old electrical shop, around four months ago. The same time he took out "Stone Face", Stephen Hoffman—the man who had killed Sofia's father. Another mystery was suddenly solved. He never knew who had knocked him out in his parking lot at home that evening, now he did. It was his old recruiter: Chris Nugent. But why he wanted the box, and what was in it, was still a mystery.

CHAPTER 5

Arrived home, Josh pulled out his keys, unlocked and opened his flat door and stepped inside, pushing it closed behind him. He walked into the living room expecting to see the boy. The T.V. was on but muted. The flat was quiet. Josh felt something wrong and drew his 9mil pistol. He checked around the apartment but there was no sign of him: he was gone.

Feeling annoyed, Josh laid his weapon down on the living room side table and began wondering about the boy's whereabouts. He told him to stay put but he didn't follow orders. He was now a problem. There was no forced entry into the flat, so Josh considered the possibility of him leaving was of his own volition, unless he was somehow tricked out. Looking around, Josh suddenly spotted a folded piece of paper. It was taped to the back of the main door of the flat. He walked up to it and pulled it off. Unfolding it revealed a note, a short message written in black ink: "He's with me." It was signed underneath with the letter "S".

It had been a while since he last saw or had any contact with her, but knew from the elegant handwriting and obvious initial, Sofia had taken the boy. Why she took him and how she knew he was in his flat was a mystery. All he knew was that they—View Corp—were ten steps ahead of him. He had to start thinking fast as he had a lot of catch-up to do.

He put the note on a plate, and using a lighter from the kitchen, set it alight. Once the flame had died out, turning the paper ashen, he rubbed the flaky remnants to a fine dust. He washed the plate and his hands of the ash, the final particles of the note. He didn't want any evidence of Sofia or the boy lying around, just in case.

Josh was always strict with his own personal security, but in his game, there were no absolute measures any operative or intelligence officer could take. No matter what strategy one took, the enemy would always find a weakness. Both sides were continually looking for the holes of the other, while trying to plug their own—that was the game. They were all at it—all governments and their spy departments. No one was innocent, in spite of any government's wailing accusations of being victimised by the opposition's intelligence. They were also busy doing what they blamed the other side of doing. Still, it was evident his own personal security had been compromised; he needed to plug his own holes. His was a compounded problem though. He was dealing with something much more complex than conventional spycraft, which made it all the more difficult.

His next step had to bring him closer to finding the truth, and he knew who he wanted to begin with. He sat down and pulled out "Sniffer"—Flash's newly named device—placing it on the living room table next to his laptop. He opened the laptop and booted it up. He connected to a Virtual Private Network for added security that would go some way in covering his digital tracks. He picked up Sniffer and connected it to his laptop.

The company's intranet was protected with a ring of several security systems working in unison—breaking the outer level security would alert the whole system and demand a protocol reshuffle. In essence, the whole system was like a moving organism that would change to protect itself from attack. It was new and highly effective against state-sanctioned hacking from hostile countries. Flash though, unwittingly, had made Josh aware of the upgraded system through his bragging—he helped design it. So,

Josh was unsure if Sniffer was "intelligent enough" to circumvent the system without alerting it. It was time for a test.

After secure connection to the internet had been established, Josh typed in the company's intranet IP address on the device and pressed the "Enter" button. He watched as Sniffer began doing its part. Behind the scenes it was searching for low-key terminals that had not been logged off by the user. Flash had programmed it to first start with simple unnoticeable holes in systems it could easily exploit, before working its way up to a more advanced re-programming status, whereby Sniffer would create its own holes.

"So far so good," he thought. He continued watching, ready to disconnect if he suspected his hack had been detected and was being traced. "ACCESS GRANTED." Suddenly a message popped up on the small display. Sniffer had done its job admirably and Flash would surely be proud.

Josh connected to the personnel database that stored all of the various databases for all government, non-government, military, and police force personnel. He typed the name he wanted information on: C.R.O.F.T.S. A.L.L.A.N. and pressed the enter key. In next to no time the results came up—five hits. Only one of those entries was listed under "Police", making things easier.

He clicked on the entry and the personnel file displayed on the screen. The I.D. photograph on the file assisted Josh with a positive identification. He had found who he was searching for. It was a severe and somewhat younger looking image, but nonetheless it was Sergeant Crofts. Josh began silently reading his profile.

"Current status: sergeant in the Counter Terrorism Specialist Firearms Unit based at Scotland Yard. Seven years in CTU. Before that, an ordinary beat officer. Various citations and awards. Personal and history: went to college then joined the Metropolitan Police Service; seems like he's been there ever since. Married with two kids. Nothing out of the ordinary...nothing out of the ordinary," repeated Josh. "Except it's too ordinary," he thought.

Josh knew criminal types; he could spot one a mile away. Their faces, their demeanour gave them away—an unmistakable look that might as well say "lock me up" printed on their face. Criminality took its pound of flesh from those that would do its bidding. Over time, the innocence and beauty of a person would become tarnished and ugly, just a small price to pay. And even Josh had a mild criminal history; trouble with the Law in his teens. Most soldiers, even police officers, had done something they were guilty of; even if they hadn't been caught. No one was squeaky clean like sergeant Crofts, which made it even more convincing he wasn't all he seemed to be. He didn't look squeaky clean.

Picking up a pen, Josh noted down Sergeant Crofts's current address. He had all he needed so far; the rest was going to come from the man himself. He knew Crofts was bent, and not just him, Sir Godfrey as well. He couldn't go bashing down Sir Godfrey's door to extract information, he was a politician, but Crofts, he was ripe for picking.

Josh disconnected Sniffer and pushed down the lid of his laptop—putting it to sleep. Not wanting to be trackable, he picked up his own mobile phone and slipped it in his pocket. In light of everything that had happened over the past several months, he convinced Flash to secure it for him. Flash had programmed it with a rotational output and encryption signal—meaning the phone continually jumped carrier signals and couldn't be tracked, unlike his company issued phone. He grabbed his keys and pistol from the side table, and promptly left the flat to pay a visit to Crofts at his home.

The Crofts' residence was situated in a middle-class estate. All of the homes looked well-kept: nicely painted, gardens perfectly manicured with a surrounding low fence, and a car parked in every drive. It was a middle-class utopian dream. A dream for those that had given up on adventure and any possibility there could be more. Josh hated the humdrum replication of it all. Introduction of anything that would upset their set pattern of life would be looked upon disdainfully. Well, too bad, he was there to upset it all.

As he drove by Crofts's home, he looked across for signs of life inside. It was still. A lone car was parked in the driveway that according to the vehicle licensing database was registered to his wife. The second car registered to the address—to sergeant Crofts, was absent. Josh could only assume his wife was home and that sergeant Crofts hadn't returned from the station yet.

Parking further down the road, Josh had direct line of sight to the Crofts' residence. It was now going to be a waiting game; one he was prepared for. The evening was starting to draw in, allowing the semi-darkness to cover his presence. The shadow of night was again becoming a warm blanket for him; his preferred time of day. Hiding in the shadows was his modus-operandi in life. Keeping himself in the dark, away from others, was an existence he preferred.

An hour had passed by and Josh was sitting relaxed, surveilling the house, when suddenly he perked up. Lights shone bright in his rear-view mirror as a car drove towards him from the rear. He slid his body down in the seat; making himself hidden while the car passed him by. Sergeant Crofts had arrived and pulled into his drive. Street lights were bright enough to allow Josh to see Crofts get out of his car and disappear into his home.

Waiting thirty minutes to allow Crofts to settle down indoors—into his cosy evening routine with his family—Josh reached down. He reached for a tiny vehicle tracker he had stored in the car door's side compartment and switched it on. He tapped on the tracker's app on his phone, checking the signal between the app and the tracker—the signal was strong. He then slipped the device into his pocket. He looked up out of the car window and thoroughly checked the residential area was clear of people. Once satisfied he quietly left his vehicle; casually walking towards Crofts's home.

All the neighbours had their curtains closed and seemed to be settled in for the evening. It was a good sign. Josh reached the residence and immediately walked up to Crofts's car, ducked down and attached the tiny magnetic tracker to the underside. It took but a few seconds. He stood back up and casually walked off back to his own car. His trick to not getting caught was to make it appear he belonged in the area. By acting calm and casual, any inquisitive neighbour he may have mistakenly overlooked probably wouldn't think twice about what he was doing. It worked most of the time.

Sitting inside his car, Josh prepared to wait it out and see what Crofts would do. He had no idea if Crofts would be leaving the house that evening or not. Another hour passed and still no more activity. Josh was considering calling off his own surveillance when a light shone out from the house, coming through the opening of the front door. Crofts reappeared, getting into his car. He reversed out of the driveway into the road and pulled off, driving away in the opposite direction from where Josh was waiting. Josh started his engine—readying to follow—and turned on the tracking app.

Allowing Crofts to get a head start, so as not to arouse suspicion, Josh then pulled off. He was quick to catch up as the housing estate roads were quiet, so he slowed down to a safe distance. It only took a short drive before they ended up on relatively busier roads, giving Josh opportunity to blend his car in with whatever vehicles were about that evening. Crofts was heading out of London along the motorway, and Josh, staying back even further, continued on his tail.

Further along, Crofts turned off down a slip road, off the motorway and onto a minor country road. Josh sped up a little to close the distance, so as not to let him get too far ahead. It was always a big concern of being blown when tailing someone, particularly when conducting one-man surveillance—which was never recommended. He knew a task like this would usually need a minimum of two or three surveillance teams, but he had no other option. At least he had his tracker as back-up.

The country roads were dark—no street lighting at all—and little to no other traffic to hide behind. It was beginning to make Josh's car stand out like a sore thumb, with its glaring headlights. He had to back off and rely completely on the tracker. Following the tracker icon on his phone, Josh continued after Crofts who had been making turns into even more secluded roads. It wasn't much longer before the tracker icon finally stopped moving on the display. It was indicating the tracker—and Crofts's car—had stopped down a dead-end lane, in what appeared to be an isolated area of hedged fields and trees. Josh turned his headlights off and carefully drove along the lane in darkness.

BANG BANG!

Two loud shots suddenly sounded out from the right-hand side, landing two bullets in Josh's car—one in the door and one shattering the driver's side window. It was an ambush and Josh was in the kill-zone. He knew it was a light one-man ambush so immediately spun his car ninety degrees right and flicked his headlights on full, so as to flood the area with light and blind the shooter. The light shone brightly into a country hedgerow along the side of the road.

BANG BANG!

Two more shots were fired, one hitting a headlight and one into the windscreen—zipping past Josh's left ear. He threw the car door open at the same time as drawing his 9mil from inside his jacket—cocking it simultaneously. The three actions melted into one—all one smooth instinctive move developed from hard training.

BANG BANG! BANG BANG!

Josh retaliated immediately, returning fire with four shots in the direction of the gunshot sounds; an immediate action to the threat that would cause the unidentified shooter to take cover. He sprinted diagonally across the road—away from the single light beam of his car—to the same side as the shooter, and into the cover of darkness. He pushed his body through a thick hedgerow along the roadside and took up an aimed kneeling position on the other side. It was dark, with just splintered rays of light shining through the hedge from his car headlight. He knew the shooter was close by, so waited for noise and movement that would give away their location. A light noise of shifting foliage and cracking twigs under foot immediately grabbed Josh's attention. A shape, a silhouette began slowly moving twenty metres away.

BANG BANG!

Josh double-tapped, pulling the trigger of his 9mil, firing off two well-aimed shots at the dark figure. It dropped to the ground. Josh sprinted forwards, weapon at the ready for another go. Lying in the field, two shots to the body and still grasping his own pistol, Sergeant Crofts was dead.

Looking around the area, there were no signs of life nearby that would have been alerted to the skirmish. Crofts had chosen the perfect ambush site. Unfortunately for him though, he came alone. He had grossly underestimated his target, and had met more than his match going up against Josh. Had he not been so arrogant, he would have brought a team. Only then, possibly then, they could have done a better job.

Josh began checking through Crofts's clothing. He did so carefully, to minimise transference of any particles from him that could be identified through forensics: sweat, fingerprints, fibres.

Lightly feeling—with the back of his fingers, the outside fabric of Crofts's pockets, and peeling back his blood-soaked jacket, Josh was looking for anything incriminating—looking for answers. Crofts, being out of uniform and wearing civvies, was clean of any intelligence. He had come out for the sole purpose of taking Josh out, and paid the ultimate price for his failure.

Now Josh had to sanitise the scene as best he could. He went back to his car—the engine still running, and drove it to the roadside. He turned off the one light that was still working and the engine. He opened the glove compartment for a torch and shone light onto the road. The light bounced back from broken glass. There were a few glass fragments from his broken headlight scattered around, so he picked up all he could see. Luckily, the penetration of the two bullets Crofts had fired at his car windows had only caused shattering. They were still in their frames.

There was a thick black tyre mark ingrained in the road, caused by the sharp turn Josh had made while trying to extract himself from Crofts's kill-zone. That also needed to go, or at least camouflaged. He took a sock from an overnight kit bag he always kept in the boot of his car, and secured it to a piece of wire. He pushed it down into the fuel tank, soaking the sock with fuel, pulled it out and squeezed it over the tyre mark. Repeatedly soaking the sock, he adequately covered the tyre mark and set it alight—burning and melting any rubber residue. Once the fire had died out, he took handfuls of mud from the field and covered the mark—treading it in with his boot.

He then searched for sergeant Crofts's car. It was parked up further along the road—he had parked and doubled back to set his ambush. Careful to not leave fingerprints on any surface, Josh opened the car door. He poked around a little, seeing nothing of interest at first, but then spotted a plain envelope. He opened it.

Inside was a bundle of fifty-pound notes, at least a hundred. Josh put it back where he found it.

He finished up at the car, removing his vehicle tracker, and now he just needed to check one... two more things. He walked back to Crofts's body lying in the field. He knelt down beside it and pulled open the clothing to expose both bullet holes. He rolled the body over on its side to check for exit wounds. Unfortunately, both bullets had lodged inside and he needed to dig them out. He pulled out his knife and without hesitation cut a slit across each bullet hole. He pushed his muddy fingers inside, forcing them through the broken rib cage. Feeling around he felt a solid object. He pulled out the first bullet and pushed his fingers into the second hole. Slightly deeper, the second bullet had embedded itself in the heart organ. And as resistant as the body was in letting it go, the second bullet was finally extracted.

Returned to his car, Josh used the fuel-soaked sock to wipe his hands of blood, and dropped both recovered bullets inside. He gave a last check of the scene and was semi-satisfied he had removed evidence of his presence. But he was no stranger to the capabilities of forensics. His last act before leaving the scene: setting both Crofts's car and body alight.

With flames beginning to light up the night, Josh got into his car and drove away, back the way he came. He only had one headlight and so had to stay off the main roads to avoid being pulled over by police. He also needed to fix his car windows and change all of his tyres so they couldn't be matched to the crime scene. He needed his car "cleaned". He needed the assistance of Jonesy.

"Jonesy, I'm coming over. I've got an emergency I need your help with." Josh phoned Jonesy for a late-night favour.

"Mister Brannon, it's late. Come in tomorrow and I'll sort you out, no problem," replied Jonesy.

"I'll see you in an hour. Make sure you're ready," insisted Josh, then terminated the call.

It took twice as long to get where he needed to go, using the minor back roads, but he finally reached Jonesy's workshop. Josh parked up and a shutter door began opening. He got out, leaving the engine running. Jonesy, a short stout fellow in his early sixties came over. He looked at the war-torn car, giving it a quick assessment while shaking his head.

"I can see your emergency Mister Brannon. It's gonna cost a little more this time though. Prices have gone through the roof. Difficult to keep me ole wife happy ya know."

"I need it done tonight. And ALL tyres replaced. I'll wait inside."

Jonesy didn't argue. He got into the car, drove it into the workshop and closed the shutter. Josh walked into Jonesy's office and washed his hands in the sink—washing off the mix of fuel, mud, and blood. He dried them in a dirty old towel draped over the sink, then laid down on an old oil smelling couch. Josh was thoroughly tired. He easily dozed off amid the clanging and tapping noises coming from inside the workshop, as Jonesy got to work.

CHAPTER 6

JOSH WAS JOLTED AWAKE by the clanging noise of a fallen spanner striking concrete; the noise coming from the workshop. It was 7am. Jonesy had been at it through the night, fixing up the car. Josh rose from the smelly but surprisingly comfortable couch, and stepped through into the workshop. He began looking over his car, inspecting Jonesy's work.

"You've done a good job as always Jonesy," he praised.

"It's not perfect; not my usual standard Mister Brannon, but it'll see ya alright. The spray paint's still a little tacky but looks like new."

Jonesy looked tired; his eyes red from the strain of keeping himself awake all night. He had replaced the bullet-shattered windscreen and side-window, and covered the bullet hole in the door—filled and spray-painted. He had also replaced the headlight that Crofts had shot out, and all four tyres at Josh's instruction. The car looked as though nothing had happened to it; like it had never been caught up in the shoot-out.

"They need burning Jonesy." Josh gestured at the stack of four tyres that had been removed from his car—tyres that could connect his car to the scene of Crofts's death.

"Yes, will do Mister Brannon. I'll do it later; gotta spot I can do it that won't draw attention."

"I need it done now," asserted Josh. He knew that he could only trust Jonesy so far. He needed to see the job through himself;

to be sure the tyres got burned and not sold on. Jonesy was a businessman now, and anything to get a quick buck would be welcomed, even if it meant selling incriminating evidence.

"Sure—okay," Jonesy agreed. "I've got a place I can do it outside, but will make a lot of smoke."

Josh said nothing, just waited for compliance. Jonesy picked up two tyres, one in each hand, and carried them outside. He came back for the other two and Josh followed him out to a low brick wall where he stacked them against. Jonesy got himself a blow-torch and a can of fuel. He poured just enough fuel over the tyres—just to get the fire started, and with the blow-torch set the stack alight. Within a couple of minutes, the flames had engulfed all four tyres.

"You'll need to get rid of those too I think Mister Brannon," suggested Jonesy, looking at the clothes he was wearing. "I've got a new set of overalls you can use; just your size."

Jonesy disappeared into the workshop, returning a few moments later with a new set of blue overalls, still wrapped in plastic. Josh stripped down to his underwear—placing his shoulder holster and pistol beside him. He dropped his soiled clothes in a pile on the ground. Jonesy picked them up, and along with the fuel-smelling sock Josh had used earlier, threw everything on the fire. Josh dressed himself in the overalls while keeping an eye on Jonesy. He picked up his holstered pistol, stuffing it inside the waist of the overalls and zipped them up.

"You might want these Mister Brannon." Jonesy held out a small see-through plastic bag, containing the two recovered bullets that had killed Crofts. "I've cleaned em up nicely, just in case you wanna keep em. Nice what a little soak in vinegar can do."

Josh took the bag and pushed it in his pocket. "Send me the bill, the usual way," he ordered.

"Will do Mister Brannon. You off now? Keys are in the car."

Josh was satisfied everything had been taken care of and walked back into the workshop. He opened the car door and checked inside. Jonesy had not only cleaned the exterior, but interior as well—even the foot pedals. He knew Jonesy would do the best job; he was the best—an expert. He used to work for organised crime: as a "cleaner", but turned supergrass. His court testimony put some of the biggest London criminals of his time behind bars for many years—some still serving their sentence. His real name was Harry Slater, but under the National Crime Agency's Witness Protection Programme it was changed to James Jones. In return for spilling the beans on his former bosses, he was given a new life in anonymity. And now he's a garage owner, a mechanic, who had done a few fix-up jobs for Josh in the past.

The engine revved as Josh turned the key and pushed down on the accelerator. He slowly drove out of the workshop, past the thick black smoke billowing upwards from the burning tyres. He knew Jonesy would put the flames out as soon as he was gone but that didn't matter now, the tread had already melted—all evidence destroyed.

Heading back onto the main roads, Josh drove his freshly sterilised car, without concern of being stopped by police. With one hand on the steering wheel, he wound down his window and reached into his pocket for the plastic bag Jonesy had given him. He ripped the bag open and flung the two damaged bullets into a passing field, and wound the window up.

He now needed to get home fast, freshen up, and get to the office. He was sure that the disappearance of Crofts would soon be reported, either by his wife or by his own unit for being absent from work. Either way, he needed to see what would transpire and make sure he was out of the picture. He needed to stay in the shadows.

Having driven fast, weaving through the early morning traffic, Josh had arrived back at his apartment. He was busy showering to rid his body of additional traces of evidence. He placed his underwear, boots, and the overalls Jonesy had supplied him, inside a plastic bin bag. His 9mil pistol was stripped down; the parts bathing in vinegar in the kitchen: at Jonesy's advice.

Finishing up, Josh dried and dressed himself in clean clothes. He went into the kitchen and removed the weapon parts from the vinegar and wiped them dry. He thoroughly cleaned the barrel through and wiped over the parts—removing any residue carbon and lightly oiling them up. He put the parts back together, inserted the magazine and pushed the clean weapon back into its holster.

It was late and Josh needed to get going. He grabbed his car keys and the plastic bin bag and headed to his car in the parking lot. He threw the bag on the passenger seat of the car, stepped in, and drove out into the morning traffic. Checking his phone: 08:45hrs, he was late, but no missed calls.

On his way to the office, he slowed down, stopping by a homeless man rummaging through a street bin. Josh wound down the electric window. "Hey!" he called out. The man looked across with a scowl. Josh grabbed the bin bag containing the clothing—the last of the evidence, and threw it out of the window to him. "Your lucky day!" he shouted and sped off.

At the office, Harris wasn't his usual self. Josh was late but no words of displeasure left Harris's lips. Something was wrong. Josh suspected it could have something to do with the visit from his old recruiter yesterday—Chris Nugent.

"Brannon, your new assignment," said Harris, as he pushed a brown file across the table to him.

"Right sir; something to get my teeth into," replied Josh, and picked it up.

"Its routine stuff, so nothing to get into a flap about. Brannon...you're on your own on this one," he said slowly. "No need for support."

Harris was saying something without actually saying it. Josh sensed a hidden warning blending in between his words, and was sharp to pick up on it. The tacit warning instantly put him on guard, but he kept a straight face so as not to let on he was suspicious.

"No problem, sir. Reporting as per SOPs?"

"Just when you have something concrete. That's all Brannon," and Harris picked up another file on his desk and began reading.

Josh walked out from the office, taking the file to the debriefing room. He took a seat at a table and placed the file in front of him. He opened it and began to read:

OFFICIAL
IG/43 File Summary
Condition – Red

An unknown whistle-blower has contacted the Department of Trade and Industry concerning irregular practices at the bio-technology company: GeneRobotix. The whistle-blower gave no specific details; only that it involves making a trade deal with a blacklisted country.

Assignment is two-fold:

1: Make contact with the source and ascertain their bona fides.

2: Get intelligence of what is being traded, who internally at GeneRobotix is making the trades, and to whom – which country and official representative.

The rest of the file gave details of GeneRobotix's products and structure as a company—addresses in the UK and abroad, as well as the CEO, executives, and investors. There was nothing about this case that warranted Harris's hidden warning. The fact that the file's government security classification was only "OFFICIAL"—the lowest security rating of all—gave Josh doubts he was assigned anything that would be even remotely interesting. The only advantage this case seemed to offer, was the release of Harris's continual grip; one he had had on him over the past four months. If Harris was finally taking the leash off, giving him flexibility to work the case, then Josh would happily take it.

Using a computer—through the Department of Trade and Industry's databases—Josh pulled up the trade disclosure documents for GeneRobotix. He read through the documents to get a fair understanding of the company's business dealings; their products and international customers. So far, on the face of it, the company's dealings looked legitimate—nothing wrong. Josh checked his watch; it was time to get going so wrapped up what he was doing. He needed to go and meet his source—the GeneRobotix whistle-blower.

Finished with his preliminary assessment of the case, Josh had driven to the rendezvous. Meeting intelligence sources was always a risk, you never knew if you were being set-up or not. The source had specified the time and location, and Josh was reluctantly following their rules. Usually, the office would call the shots on meeting locations, so they could control the environment—dominating the area with company resources in case things went belly-up. Josh knew of intelligence officers being snatched during a meet, but that was usually on "TOP SECRET" cases, not on some lowly trade violation case.

Sitting on the steps to the statue of Eros, at Piccadilly Circus, Josh waited. The tourists were out in force, snapping photographs. It was 11am and perhaps one of the worst of places to rendezvous; he felt completely exposed. If he was being used as bait for a company Op he wasn't aware of, then this would be a prime time to get tagged by a hostile surveillance team. His senses were up high as he kept his wits about him, and without drawing attention to himself, he kept a sharp watch on the tourists.

His source was said to meet at 11am. It was blatantly clear they didn't know what they were doing; they hadn't even set up a recognition signal. So, Josh had no way of determining who the source was, except through a direct approach.

Another fifteen minutes had passed by and still no contact. He purposely remained sitting in the same spot, to make it obvious to the whistle-blower he was waiting and not a tourist—tourists came and went as there wasn't really much to see. So, somebody waiting for someone else would hopefully stand out, easily enough for an amateur to spot.

Finally, a woman, dressed in smart attire, walked in Josh's direction. He knew this was it. She approached but kept a short distance between them. She pretended to be interested in the statue, but Josh could sense without looking that she kept glancing at him. He waited. He was trained to let the source make the first move—make first contact—just in case it wasn't a real source. It was also a psychological step. If the source made first contact, they would feel in control and wouldn't feel pressured. It gave them free-will. A freely willing source was always better than one that had to be coerced. He waited further, allowing her to make the first move.

"Beautiful statue, don't you think?" The lady directed her comment to Josh.

He looked up at her. "It is if you like statues." Josh played along.

"I'm waiting for someone," she continued.

"Me too." He continued to allow her to make the moves, as she hadn't fully identified herself as the whistle-blower.

"Perhaps we're meeting the same person. I'm waiting for someone for GeneRobotix." She laid her cards on the table and gave Josh the sign to fully establish contact.

He stood up. "I'm also waiting for someone from GeneRobotix. I'm from the Department of Trade and Industry," he said, adopting his undercover role.

She looked relieved. "My name is Rachael, Rachael Banks. I work in the accounts department at head office in GeneRobotix."

Already she was singing like a canary, but Josh wanted to move to a more secure location. Open spaces with little cover were dangerous, in spite of the crowd cover by the tourists.

"Do you want a coffee Ms Banks?"

She hesitated. "Um…okay."

Josh could see she was nervous, most informants were. Although whistle-blowers were protected by law when it came to revealing company secrets—if it was in the public's interest, or a threat to national security or economy—some met with dire consequences; public disgrace, and even suspicious death. It was now his job to ensure she was not only telling the truth, but that she was kept safe.

"I know a nice coffee shop just a short walk from here," he said casually.

He kept the conversation light as they walked to the coffee shop. He was establishing good communication so she felt comfortable with him. At the initial stage of a contact, he liked to keep things casual and light, allowing for a bond to be made from the informant to him. This way they would feel safe to tell more than perhaps they would usually reveal. This made for a better informant.

They entered the coffee shop and approached the counter. "Two filter-coffees please, both with milk." Josh ordered from the lady serving from behind the counter, and passed her some money.

"Take a seat luv and I'll bring em over," replied the lady.

Josh led Rachael to a table in the corner. He sat with his back to the wall facing the rest of the coffee shop patrons, and the shop entrance. He liked to keep everything in his view. At that time of day, it wasn't too busy inside; so, a fairly quiet atmosphere. The lady brought their coffees over and placed them on the table. Josh pushed one over to Rachael.

"So, Rachael, what do you want to tell us?" Josh put his hand inside his jacket pocket and started a hidden recorder.

"I work in accounts. I've worked at GeneRobotix for just a year now. I mean—some of this, what I'm about to tell you.... I'm violating my Non-disclosure Agreement. I can be fired, maybe worse, I don't know. But I can't not say anything, it's just not right."

Josh noted her hands were shaking and she kept fiddling with her fingers: she was scared. He needed to reassure her. "I understand Rachael," he said calmly, with a sincere smile to put her as ease. "Take your time."

She relaxed a little and continued to reveal what she knew. "It's a business transaction; a deal between GeneRobotix and another company working for China. I'm no expert on politics, but China is not on our most favourite list to be doing business with. But it's not just that...it's what GeneRobotix is selling them."

"Go on?" Josh was attentive, and careful not to interrupt her flow while he recorded every word.

"We make bio-genetic, bio-robotic products; advanced technology. Some of the things that are invoiced for are brain implants; microchips that can be inserted subcutaneously to interrupt nerve impulses, to and from the brain. I've heard from others in my department, people who've worked there many years, of experiments: experiments on people. But it's all kept quiet, and if anyone says anything they would be in serious trouble. Apparently, the government knows about it, but I'm not so sure."

"Do you have anything to substantiate that?" asked Josh.

"Just what I've heard," she replied.

"Okay. So why have you decided to come out and tell us this now?" Josh was trying to ascertain her motive; in case she was just a disgruntled employee wasting his time.

"It's not right!" she angrily raised her voice and clenched her fist. "I know the people in China are treated badly, and if the Chinese government gets their hands on this technology—," Rachael paused, a look of serious concern dawned across her face, "—they're sure to use it to suppress their people even further. And I don't want to be a part of that."

Josh was satisfied her motive was honourable. "Okay. But I've already checked on GeneRobotix regarding their product manufacturing. Those implants you mention, have been declared for use in paralysis and traumatic brain injury patients, and mental health. What evidence do you have to suggest otherwise?"

"Last week, there was a meeting between the CEO: Mark Radnus, a Chinese government official, and a lady. I was asked to sit in on the meeting with my department manager, in case they needed financial data. The Chinese official made an order for one million of the new GRX-5 chips. They're to be delivered by the end of the year, with further orders when requested. I'm not stupid. I'm sure there aren't one million people in China that are paralysed, or have mental health problems...are there?"

Josh accepted her argument. "There is a partial trade embargo with China. A restriction of trade on certain products, including those you mentioned; if your suggested use of those chips is true. I will need more evidence from you Rachael, something tangible, like a copy of the signed agreement between the signatories: those of GeneRobotix and the Chinese official. I don't suppose you know the government official's name, or their position?"

Rachael began frowning in thought. "It's a name I can't really remember, or even pronounce if I did. And I don't know where he's from, could be the Chinese embassy. But I can get you financial records; I think the initial transaction has gone through. I don't know about the signed agreement though, as that goes through Legal and I don't usually deal with them."

Josh smiled. "Well, anything you can get. Anything that can further help with the investigation will be appreciated."

She leaned back looking pleased with herself; pleased she was doing the right thing by revealing what she knew. She picked up her cup of coffee from the table; taking a few sips. Josh mirrored Rachael's actions—leaning back and sipping his own coffee—to continue the bond.

He wasn't surprised by what she was revealing. Since becoming a government spy, a number of very incriminating documents, of twisted goings-on with corporate businesses, had passed under his watchful eye. Usually, these businesses would set up non-profit organisations, or philanthropic foundations they could funnel money through. Some would even set up a complex web of shell companies; the greater the web the better: obfuscation by distancing was their deceitful tactic.

Josh placed his cup on the table. "You said earlier, there was a company working for China. I'm assuming an intermediary company facilitating the deals. But it seems to me like the Chinese are going straight to GeneRobotix?"

Rachael shook her head. "No. The lady, the lady with the Chinese man, she's the representative. She spoke very well. A pretty woman who I think was some kind of a lawyer. Anyway, she seemed to speak lawyerish, lots of legal jargon. Her name is Sofia, Sofia Du Bois."

Josh's interest in the case suddenly jumped ten-fold, upon hearing the given description and name Rachael spoke of: Sofia

Du Bois. It wasn't a common name by any means. Somehow Sofia, and by extension View Corp, was involved. There was truly more to this case than he first believed. It wasn't by coincidence he was assigned it, and Josh's estimation of Harris's hidden warning was correct. This opened a new door to his personal investigation. But why had he been given the case by Harris in the first place, and what does he really know? Deep in thought, Josh took another sip of coffee.

CHAPTER 7

CLICK! JOSH PRESSED THE "Stop" button on the audio recorder. Now sitting in his car, in a multi-storey car park, he had finished listening to the secretly recorded meeting he had just had with Rachael in the coffee shop. It shone new light on View Corp and scepticism on the organisation's motives. Harder to think about though, was Sofia's involvement. It seemed no matter what she was involved in, he couldn't help but have feelings for her. But these feelings were corrupting his objectivity.

Josh had arranged a special means of contact with his newly acquired asset: Rachael Banks. He had her cell number and she had the number to the "company's" secure redirection messaging service. This was a method that kept Josh's cover identity in play—as a Department of Trade and Industry official. It was an identity he had set up as his cover-persona with the "office".

After leaving the coffee shop, they went their separate ways. Rachael was now on her way back to GeneRobotix. She had made an excuse of visiting her doctor to get away for part of the morning. Before parting, Josh convinced her to look through the company's financial records and legal documents, to obtain more information he could use. He had also asked her to find any addresses or phone numbers linked to Sofia. He needed to find her, and the boy.

Controlling assets was a difficult part of the spying game; one had to push them along to get the intelligence needed, but not push them too hard that they would back out. The fact that

Rachael was a volunteer asset made all the difference; she was operating through her own choice and coercion wasn't needed. The only nerve-racking part now was the waiting, waiting for her to re-establish contact once she had something concrete. It was difficult to know if she would back out at the last minute, or follow through on her word.

Sitting patiently, waiting for Rachael to contact him, Josh began mentally analysing everything that had gone on for the past few days—from the pre-planning of Operation Sting Bolt to where he was now sitting. He was purposely searching through the trail of thought—pictures in his head, and adding suppositions and conclusions. He was searching for anything that may assist in furthering his investigation, any minor detail that was overlooked.

BEEP-BEEP! Some time had passed when a text message came through on his mobile, it was Rachael: "Hi uncle, meet me for lunch. I have some food."

She had encrypted the message and Josh knew she had information; hopefully it was what he needed. He started the engine and headed off to their pre-arranged rendezvous in a park, not far from the GeneRobotix building.

It took fifteen minutes to reach the park. Josh pulled into a parking bay just off the road and stepped out of his car. He looked around—scanning the area for any unwanted guests, and once satisfied began making his way into the open area. The well-kept grassy park was occupied by a few dog-walkers and joggers, other than that it was quiet. Rachael was nowhere to be seen, so he walked to a bench and sat down.

"Where is she? She should be here by now," he thought.

He sent her a message saying he was waiting, but in his mind, he couldn't help but think something was amiss. Maybe she had backed out, or worse, been caught with taking company documents. He decided to give himself ten minutes as a cut-off time; enough time for Rachael to turn up before he would personally visit GeneRobotix. He continued to watch patiently from the bench, in the direction of the road where he had parked, and the likeliest place she would come from. He watched the traffic zipping past, waiting for one to stop.

Ten more minutes ticked on by and still no sign of Rachael. Josh anticipated something was wrong. He stood up and marched swiftly back to his car. He gave one last look up and down the road for her, before driving away.

The journey was short, three minutes tops to reach GeneRobotix—a large expensive looking corporate building extending back from the road. An ambulance was waiting outside the main entrance foyer. Josh pulled into a "Visitor" parking bay and stepped out. As he walked towards the entrance, two paramedics came out wheeling a covered body on a gurney from the building. They wheeled the body to the back of the ambulance, opened the rear door and pushed the folding gurney, along with the body, inside.

Josh promptly walked over to make an inquiry. "Who is that?" he asked one of the paramedics.

"I'm sorry but I can't give out details. You'll need to speak to someone inside, or go to the hospital," replied the paramedic, who then closed the back of the ambulance and walked off.

Through the glass doors into the building's foyer, Josh spotted security watching him with great interest. Josh walked across the stylish marble pavement, through the heavy glass doors and into the building to reception.

"Can I help you sir?" asked the uniformed security guard.

"Yes, I..."

"Oh Josh, you made it!" a loud voice interrupted.

Recognising the voice, he turned instantly. There she was, standing by a lift door, dressed in an expensive corporate suit. Sofia looked as beautiful as ever.

"Yes, I hope I'm not late. I got held up with another meeting," Josh replied; following along with Sofia's bogus storyline.

"It's okay, Mister Brannon is meeting with me. He just needs to sign in," she said to security.

The security guard nodded, taking Sofia's orders. "Sign here please sir."

Josh walked over and picked up a pen off the reception desk; he quickly filled-out his details in the "Visitor's Register". The security guard handed him a visitor's pass, telling him to wear and display it at all times whilst in the building. Josh took the pass and clipped it on his jacket. He felt a little out of place in casual wear, but that didn't matter now, he was inside.

He walked over to Sofia and looked at her fully in the eyes. He wanted to see how far she had gone, how much she had changed since the last time he saw her. He could see from a person's eyes how deep in darkness they were; how many lies they've sown or truths they've covered up. He didn't need to look hard, Sofia's eyes revealed all. She was in deep, and it showed.

"So, how are you Josh?" she asked out loud, continuing the pretence in front of security that she was expecting him.

The lift door opened; both Sofia and Josh entered the lift together. She pushed a button, closing the door.

"You shouldn't be here Josh!" Sofia immediately threw away her façade. "Why are you here?" she demanded to know. She looked worried; her confidence gone.

"Where's the boy?" he questioned.

"We don't have time right now. I need to get you out of here or you'll cause us problems." Sofia was clearly mixed up in something dark.

The lift journey was too short to get everything out into the open; neither answered each other's questions and Josh, apparently, was in the way. The lift doors opened and Sofia snapped back into her character role—wearing her façade again.

"Ah Sofia, I was just looking for you in your office. And who is this?" A man was standing directly outside the lift.

"Mister Radnus...um...,this is a colleague of mine. Here to collect some paperwork and he'll be leaving. I'll just quickly see to him now and will then come to your office directly."

Sofia was nervous and it stood out like a sore thumb. She wasn't trained for undercover work, which is what Josh figured she was trying to do. Whatever she was up to he knew she was in danger: she was a fish out of water. And he could sense that Mark Radnus—the CEO of GeneRobotix—knew what she was up to, but was staying silent.

"Your name?" asked Radnus, staring directly at Josh as though analysing his deepest thoughts and behaviour.

"Brannon, Josh Brannon. Come to collect some financial records for the Chinese deal."

Josh wanted to help Sofia keep her cover, but whilst trying to feel Radnus out at the same time. He purposely dropped the hint about the financial records that he knew Rachael had unsuccessfully tried to acquire. The records she had paid the ultimate price for: her life.

The covered body being wheeled out on the gurney, Josh became aware it was Rachael as soon as he saw it. He didn't need to see the physical body to know. He knew she had been found out and that Radnus was involved in her "termination" of employment. Josh could see the corrupt evil underside of Radnus's personality that he was failing to hide from him. Sofia could also see it, but was too affected to keep her cool. Josh on the other hand had dealt with snakes before, and had no problem in handling them.

"I was waiting for Rachael Banks from accounts to contact me but she didn't, so here I am," Josh smirked.

He carefully watched Radnus's reaction while referring to Rachael and the financial records. He already knew that lies would come out of Radnus's mouth, Josh just wanted to see what hidden truths, if any, would be sandwiched between those lies.

"I'm sorry to say but Rachael had an accident. That was her being taking away in the ambulance. I'm afraid she passed away. Very unfortunate. She was a bright girl," answered Radnus.

"What happened?" pressed Josh. He was purposely pushing the boundary for a reaction.

"Just one of those unfortunate accidents. She was somewhere she shouldn't have been." Radnus was saying more than he thought with his threatening undertone.

"Well, nothing worse than an employee being somewhere they shouldn't," Josh snidely remarked.

Sofia was quiet, not knowing what was going on with this girl "Rachael". And not knowing made her more nervous, as she didn't know how to cover her tracks with Josh being there.

"Let's go to my office Josh and I'll sort you out with the paperwork. I'll see you shortly Mister Radnus." Sofia took charge again.

"Nice meeting you...Josh Brannon," said Radnus deliberately, while keeping strong eye contact for a moment or two before walking off, as though trying to make some point.

Sofia and Josh looked at each other. "Lead the way," said Josh smiling, as though he had just won the first bout with Radnus. Sofia gave a subtle smile, rolled her eyes, and walked with him to her office.

Josh closed the door. "Nice office."

"Why are you here Josh?" Sofia had calmed a little.

He put his index finger to his lips, signalling for her to be quiet. He was certain if Radnus was as devious as he suspected him to be, there was a possibility the whole building had internal surveillance systems. Instead, he wrote a note while making small talk: "Meet me at my place tonight at 7". Sofia nodded. He smiled and she blushed; an affection rekindled between them, making things awkward again.

"You should go now," she said.

Josh nodded. "Be careful," he whispered.

Sofia gave Josh some papers to add authenticity to their ruse—basic legal documents that wouldn't attract attention with security, or Radnus, if stopped. He left Sofia's office and walked back to the lift. He noted the CCTV cameras positioned in the hallway as he waited. The doors had biometric entry security scanners. The building was as secure as they come for any biotech company and would be difficult, but not impossible, to penetrate. The lift arrived and Josh stepped inside. Just as the lift door was about to fully close, a hand appeared through the remaining gap, causing the door to automatically open again. A woman stepped into the lift and pushed a button. The door closed and the lift started its descent.

"I know who you are," said the woman hastily. "Rachael confided in me. And I don't think her death was an accident."

"Who are you?" he asked.

"I'm Rachael's head of department, in accounts. This is what she wanted to give you before she died."

The woman nervously handed over a sealed brown envelope with the word "Uncle" scrawled on the front in blue ink. Clearly Rachael was panicked as she wrote it. Something had had her scared. Josh took the envelope and mixed it in with the paperwork Sofia had given him. The lift came to a halt on the lobby floor and opened.

"What's your name?" asked Josh.

"Look, I don't want to get involved. I don't want to end up like Rachael. You need to go or security will get suspicious."

Josh quickly pulled out and handed the woman his fake business card, then stepped out of the lift. It seemed everyone there was desperate to get rid of him and wanted him gone, which meant the opposite, that he needed to dig further and uncover the dirty secrets of GeneRobotix and its CEO—Mark Radnus.

The door closed and the lift began ascending with the woman still inside. Josh started walking towards the exit, carrying the documents from Sofia and Rachael.

"Excuse me sir!" the security guard called out.

Josh looked over, half expecting to be grilled about what he was carrying.

"You need to hand in your pass," the guard continued.

"Sure," nodded Josh, with a little relief he wouldn't have to cause a scene. He turned and approached the desk, unclipped his visitor's pass and dropped it on the register. He smiled at the guard and walked out of the building back to his car.

Sitting inside, he opened the brown envelope given to him by Rachael's department head, and pulled out pages of company financial statements. Scanning down the records, he knew Rachael had found something for him. She highlighted an account number in yellow. It was the only one that had no description of where the payment had come from, but was one of the largest payments on the statement—one hundred million pounds. Rachael had also managed to get a copy of the company invoice relating to that transaction. He looked at the name on the invoice: "Wang Holdings", obviously a holding company used as a front for the Chinese government. But what he didn't understand was why View Corp, and in particular Sofia, seemed to be brokering a deal between GeneRobotix and the Chinese.

Scrutinising the invoice and payment further, Josh quickly calculated in his head that the first batch of one hundred thousand GRX-5 microchips Rachael talked about, cost one thousand pounds each. He was no expert in microchips, but that was a considerably high price to pay, even if they were advanced. Something else was going on here. He believed Sofia had the answers he needed but he couldn't contact her directly, knowing that she could be being monitored. It would be too much of a risk for her. For the time being he had to find other avenues of inquiry.

Josh waited, watching from his car, any employees leaving through the main entrance. He was looking for a particular type of employee, not necessarily someone with a low-level position and low pay, but one who could easily be corrupted. He had a good eye for corruptible people. He needed a factory worker, or someone who worked in the warehouse despatch department, who would have access to what he needed. He checked his watch: 15:05hrs. He drove off, following the public road around to the rear of the building and pulled up—parking so he could observe the warehouse despatch.

Watching patiently for an hour or so, Josh singled out his target. Looking through the wired perimeter fence with a pair of binoculars, he identified a fat man in his mid-fifties. He was a gross man, always swearing and playing the joker with the others; taking cigarette breaks when in all probability he should be working. He was your typical factory worker that had been employed in a company for years, without hope of promotion or anything more. He was the type of guy that worked for a pay, just to survive from month-to-month, and therefore susceptible to backhand deals when an opportunity would arise. Well, Josh was that opportunity.

"GeneRobotix, Sarah speaking, how can I help?" The cheerful voice of a young sounding woman answered the phone, after Josh dialled the number for GeneRobotix main reception.

With a naturally sounding pretext, Josh replied. "It's Ross in sales, put me through to despatch, I need to check on an order, thanks." He answered in a polite but direct manner that would gain her compliance.

"Just putting you through now," answered the receptionist.

Josh knew a big company like GeneRobotix would have a high number of staff, and the receptionist wouldn't know everyone. It was always an educated gamble when using a pretext to find out information. The key to a good bluff was always confidence and control of the situation.

He picked up his binos and looked through to the warehouse despatch. His target was sitting and smoking yet another cigarette.

"This is despatch," a male voice spoke on the phone.

"I want to speak to that fat lazy old cigarette smoking joker at the back." Without knowing his name, Josh used the characteristics of the man he was watching to get him to the phone.

"Oh Darren, yeah, hang on I'll just get him."

Josh watched as a skinny young lad walked out of the warehouse into the backyard area, and approach the fat man Josh had his eye on. The lad spoke to him who then went inside. A few seconds later, Josh could hear the phone being picked up on the other end.

"Yeah, Darren speaking, what d'ya want?" the man rudely huffed.

"Darren, there's a problem with a delivery lorry outside on the main road. He's a foreign driver and I need you to direct him into the loading bay, thanks," and Josh immediately hung up.

He didn't give the man any time to ask questions, just gave him the direct order and a problem to sort out. It worked. Josh watched through the binos as the fat man—Darren—reappeared in the backyard, moaning away. He opened the gate and walked in Josh's direction. Without even noticing him, the man stomped right on past, still moaning about having to do some work.

Josh wound down his car window. "Darren!" he called out.

The fat man suddenly paused, turned his head, and stepped backwards a few feet. "Yeah, who are you?" he rudely replied, looking in through the window at Josh. He was further annoyed by being stopped.

"I'm an opportunity Darren. Are you interested?" Josh dangled the carrot.

"What opportunity?" The man's eyes grew large with interest.

Josh's character evaluation was spot-on. The man didn't batter an eyelid when the word "opportunity" was used. Obviously, the fat man was used to "opportunities" coming his way.

"I need something from in there," Josh gestured, pointing his eyes in the direction of the warehouse, "and you can get it for me."

"What do you need?"

"A chip; specifically, a GRX-5."

"What's in it for me?" the man asked quietly. He began furtively looking around; his criminal intent showing itself.

Josh pulled out his wallet. "Fifty for a little inconvenience of your time, that's all."

"Make it a ton and you've got a deal," said the fat man greedily.

"You drive a hard bargain Darren," said Josh, just to make him feel he got the better deal, and to make him more cooperative. "It's a deal."

"Gimme ten minutes," and the man, ignoring why he was out there in the first place, walked back to the warehouse.

Josh waited and watched for fifteen minutes or so. If he was wrong, the man could alert security and they would call the police. Not only his cover would be blown, but also that of Sofia's. But Josh was smart and perceptive. The man reappeared from the warehouse into the backyard. He opened the gate and walked towards Josh. He walked up to the car window and Josh wound it down.

The man pushed his hand into his trouser pocket and pulled out a small see-through plastic bag. It contained a tiny computer chip. "Here it is, the GRX-5. A popular chip." He said it like he was a salesman.

Josh took five twenty-pound notes from his wallet and reached half way to the man. The man reached with the chip and they both exchanged, taking that which they wanted. The sale was done.

"Good doing business with you," smiled the man, while pushing the notes into his pocket. He didn't hang around but turned and walked back; whistling like he had just won the lottery.

Josh pushed the bag into his pocket. He started the engine, made a U-turn in the road, and drove away. He checked his mirrors to make sure he hadn't been tagged by anyone, then drove for home. There was no need to go to the office for debriefing, as Harris had given him specific orders to only report anything of real value, and what "real value" meant in whose eyes was open to interpretation. So, he was taking this opportunity to run his own show. He got what he wanted—a GRX-5 chip, now he was eager to get home. He was eager to plan his evening with Sofia. He not only wanted answers from her, he just wanted to see her again.

CHAPTER 8

CLOSING THE DOOR, JOSH had returned to his flat. He removed his jacket and holstered weapon—hanging them over a chair. He pulled the plastic bag from his pocket and took a seat. Sitting on the sofa, he held the bag up to the light. He began inspecting the minute disc-shaped microchip through the plastic covering. It was really nothing much to look at, being so small. And how the thing worked was far beyond his knowledge. It seemed incredible though, with what Rachael had suggested, that such a tiny object could be inserted into a body to manipulate a person's thinking and behaviour. He was fully aware the Chinese government was a regime that sought absolute control of its people, that it was stepping up its population surveillance programmes, but this was another step too far.

He slipped the chip inside his wallet for safe keeping. He wanted Flash to take a look at it in the morning, to see what his thoughts would be. It would be right up his alley.

Leaning back and yawing deeply, he was starting to feel weary. The late-night stopover at Jonesy's workshop and early morning start was beginning to catch up with him. "I just need a short nap," he thought, as he lay back on the sofa, resting his head on the arm, and closed his eyes. The real world quickly disappeared as he sank into a deep sleep.

Knock, Knock! Knock, Knock!

The knocking on the door suddenly woke him. He looked at his watch: 19:00hrs; he slept longer than he wanted. He stood up from the sofa, rubbing his eyes awake, and walked to the door. He looked through the peephole to confirm his visitor, unlocked the door and opened it. Sofia walked in.

"I wasn't sure you would come," he said.

"I said I would," she replied.

She walked into the living room while Josh looked out into the passageway, to make sure she wasn't followed. He closed and locked the door and joined her. He turned off the light and walked over to the window. Looking down at the street, he waited, watching closely for movement in the shadows of the early darkness. He watched for a couple of minutes, then walked away from the window and turned the light back on.

"I checked to make sure I wasn't followed," she said.

Josh nodded. "You came alone?"

"Just me. No bodyguards."

He smiled. "So, how are you?" He didn't need to ask how she was; he could see. She looked tense and on edge, but he wanted to ask her anyway. He wanted to hear her voice again.

She walked over and put her arms around him, squeezing tightly whilst resting her face on his chest. Surprised by her move, he slowly responded in kind—wrapping his arms around her. He knew she just needed comforting. He held the embrace for as long as she needed, and once he felt her slowly releasing her hold of him, he let go.

"I'm sorry. I just needed to...," and she stopped herself, looking shyly away.

"It's okay, I understand." Secretly, it was something he had desired to do for a long time.

"So, how are you?" he asked again softly.

Sofia looked at him. "Can I get a drink?" She dodged the question.

"Sure. Tea, coffee?"

"Do you have something stronger?"

"Apple juice?" he said smiling, knowing that her "stronger" meant alcoholic.

Completely comfortable in his presence, she returned the smile. "Apple juice will be perfect."

Josh went to the kitchen, took the apple juice from the fridge, and poured two glasses. He returned and handed one to Sofia, who was now sitting relaxed on the sofa. He took a seat at the other end; his body angled with one knee resting on the seat between them. She was looking around the room, at the sparseness of it.

"You haven't exactly made it a home Josh. No photos?"

"It isn't home really; just a place to eat and sleep."

She gave him a disappointed look. "A home is important Josh. It's where you have belonging, where you welcome your loved ones, your family, and your friends. Never permit yourself to not have a home." She sipped on her juice, after giving him a mild reprimand for being too disconnected about life.

He smiled, recognising her words of truth. He knew Sofia was a romantic, a bright flower among the dark weeds. He desperately wanted to be the water to help her grow, but even he knew he was contaminated, that he would eventually cause her petals to fall. He was a realist. A pessimist.

"What's been happening with you Sofia?"

He suddenly changed his tune with her—like switching from night to day. Too much was going on he was in the dark about. He needed answers from her and was sure going to get them. Surprisingly though, the simple question he asked was too much for her. She started looking stressed, as she began mentally prospecting her mind for where to begin. She had a mishmash of thoughts in her head and Josh knew she was having trouble focussing.

"Start from when I left you at the bunker that day; four months ago." He helped her to direct her own thoughts.

She calmed, now she was back on track, and began collecting her thoughts while staring into her juice. She went on to explain. "Well, we thought we'd made good in-roads by releasing you from the Time-fold that day. It was the furthest we'd gotten so didn't know what to expect. Professors Montague and Balantyne began analysing the causal factors and implementing changes to the Radio Frequency Adjuster. I left a few hours after you and that was the last I saw of them. They spent all their time in the laboratory—the bunker; never leaving."

Josh butted in. "I went to the bunker recently. It was destroyed. The structure had collapsed and I discovered a body. I believe Montague and Balantyne are both dead."

Looking deeply concerned, Sofia sat up. "I know. They were important to us."

Josh continued. "And that's when I met the boy—me, as my younger self again. He went back to the bunker, but I never did when I was him. Something has changed Sofia, drastically changed! What?"

His serious stare was piercing through her as he waited impatiently for a response. She became reticent in answering, making him suspicious. So, he had to be forthright, lay his cards on the table to get her to reveal her hand.

"Look Sofia, if I'm to help you, you have to come clean with me! I know you hold back and that possibly you don't trust me because of who I work for, but I need to find the truth. I need you to be honest with me. We need to share what we know."

Sofia relaxed, sitting back against the sofa again. He had pulled down whatever barrier she was holding up. In truth, he was on her side, even though he knew she was holding back on him. Still, he was a good judge of character and knew from the beginning she was a good soul, in spite of whatever secrets she was keeping from him. She was protecting her cause and he knew he would do the same.

"How did you know about the boy and where I live?"

"You vote, don't you? Electoral registers are semi-public records. I'm a lawyer remember; I looked you up." She raised her eyebrows and gave him a cheeky look.

"Remind me not to vote next time will you," he grinned. "What about the boy? How did you know he would be here?"

Sofia sighed heavily, becoming serious again. "We are at war Josh. Not with bombs and bullets, but with pseudo-politics, science, and technology.

I want to be honest with you I really do. But the only way for me to do that, is to let you know that I can't tell you everything. I have to keep some things secret.

Like it or not, you work for the government. And there are those in positions of power and influence, not only in the government, that are not favourable to the survival of the people of this country. And it's not just our country. It may sound crazy to you, conspiracy tin-foil hat crazy, but there are people trying to enslave and destroy humanity. This is bigger than me, bigger than both of us."

Josh accepted her loyalty to her group—View Corp—but he also had a job to do; and more importantly, find out what was happening to him and why. He still had many open questions that needed answering, such as who killed his friend Mac at his old flat—a score still not settled. So, in spite of her unwavering devotion to View Corp, his own loyalty and personal integrity would come first. Therefore, his only option would be to interrogate Sofia for answers. But unlike a forceful extraction of information he would use on a terrorist, hers would be a more gentle and honest approach.

He began revealing what he knew with a hope she would do the same. "I experienced déjà vu recently, another Time-fold. I was on a job, a house raid. I recognised someone I know...knew, an old school friend of mine. He was killed in that raid. Problem is, he shouldn't have been alive anyway. I mean, he had already died back when we were kids, at school. He was dead long ago. It was him without a doubt; all grown, looking older, but it was him. He was dead and buried back then but what, came alive again? Like that experience at school never happened, like his death never happened. What do you know about it?"

Sofia frowned in thought. "He must be a facsimile. I don't know Josh. That's my only explanation."

Accepting for now, her short but plausible answer, he parked that particular line of inquiry for another time. Had professors Montague or Balantyne been alive, he would have been able to ascertain a better, more valid answer.

Josh held back from her that someone else had been in the house during Operation Sting Bolt, someone who had been whisked away by a team he suspected of killing his colleague, Malik—because he was an unwanted witness to their snatch. Not the framed narrative that some "terrorist" had managed to get the drop on him—that was rubbish. And that Sergeant Crofts was almost certainly involved. These suspicions he kept to himself.

"What's your involvement at GeneRobotix?" He changed the subject and watched carefully her response.

Immediately Sofia's face dropped. "The company has something we need, and in exchange, we are brokering a deal with the Chinese government."

"Did you know Rachael Banks?" he asked.

"Yes, she works in accounts."

"Worked, worked in accounts. She was killed today remember? She came to us with concerns about GeneRobotix, concerns about its trading practices. She paid the ultimate price. Mark Radnus is dangerous Sofia and I don't have to tell you that, I've been seeing it in your eyes. You need to get out of there."

"I know, I know...but I can't. I need to see this through." She answered like she was caught between a rock and a hard place.

"Do you know what those over-priced chips are for, that the Chinese government wants so badly?" He wanted to know if she knew exactly what she was helping to trade.

"I know what they can do. Yes." She was feeling grilled and began shifting around on the sofa.

Frowning at her blunt answer, he was beginning to get irritated. She didn't even try to lie. The idea that she knew but was still willing to facilitate the deal irked him greatly.

"So, you want to deal with two devils at the expense of a population's freedom! You know the Chinese will step-up its population control programmes with those chips you're helping to sell them?"

"Look Josh, I know you're concerned but there's no need. We have plans that will stop that, but will still get us what we need. We have to deal with both devils as you put it."

He backed off a little after she allayed his concern. "So, what is it you need from Radnus that's so important you're willing to risk your life for?"

"I can't say. All I can say is that there are more important things than one's own life. Deep down Rachael Banks knew that. She knew something was wrong and even though she didn't know what would happen, she gave her life for what she believed was right. Heroes are ordinary people that do extraordinary things, not sit and watch the devil pass on by doing evil. She was courageous, she is a hero."

Sofia made an exceptionally good argument and Josh conceded she was right. But as a result of her reasoning, he couldn't help but feel inadequate. Upon reflexion, he knew he was no hero, just someone doing his job. He had never fought for any cause. Her light of truth shone on his inadequacies as a fellow human being. But Sofia smiled at him, she knew otherwise.

"What?" he asked, trying not to show disappointment about himself; his own character.

"For someone who works in British intelligence Josh, you're not being very smart." Her smile widened.

Josh perked up, grinning at her character dig of him. He enjoyed her humour. She was honest and funny in a way that was sincere and caring.

"I see how you feel about yourself," she said seriously, "when I talk about heroes. You don't think you're a hero?"

He was beginning to feel put on the spot, feeling awkward. "A hero saves lives, I take them. That's what I do. A hero stands up for what they believe, I hide in the shadows."

Sofia gently shook her head at his self-criticism. "You're right, those are heroic acts. So is silently pursuing the truth while standing in the shadows. I see you Josh. You don't see yourself well enough. You are not who you see because you close your eyes to who you really are. But I see you...I see who you really are."

The truth she spoke pierced through to him. It made him thoughtful about his choices, his decisions, and his actions. It was as though she was stretching out her hand, reaching for him, and gently pulling him back onto a road he had slipped from.

"I've finished my juice." Sofia broke his thoughts.

He hesitated. "Yeah—sure, you want another?"

"Not really," she replied. "Just bringing you back from nowhere-land."

They both smiled, saying nothing, just looking into each other's eyes. They knew how they felt about the other but refrained from saying. It was a moment of enjoyment that words couldn't describe.

"Tell me, the boy, is he safe?" Josh broke the moment of intimacy.

Sofia gave out a slight chuckle. "He is."

"Why did you laugh?"

"You look alike, you and the boy. He could pass for your son."

It was one thing he never thought about—having children. Maybe the rough upbringing he had had put him off.

"Sofia, what can you tell me about View Corp? Who's in charge now that both Montague and Balantyne are dead?"

"Stephen and Miles were never in charge. They were important to us, their work was important and still is, but that's the extent of their involvement. We can still continue despite their set-back."

"Who's in charge then?"

"We have a committee; we don't have one person. It's a group made up of intellects, visionaries, true leaders; leaders that don't seek power to suppress but to lift people up. Its self-appointed purpose is to bring back true humanity."

"Are you on this committee?"

Sofia laughed. "No. I wouldn't be here, or be helping Radnus make his despicable deals with the Chinese if I were."

Without openly revealing his position on the matter, Josh was further convinced about View Corp. That it wasn't a terror organisation but an underground network wanting change, real change; not artificial promises made by politicians before the elections—only to be broken.

"Sofia." Josh sighed. "You know I'm going to continue investigating Radnus and his company. I will have to make a report. It'll blow your cover."

She nodded. "I know. We were expecting that. We've almost finished our end of the deal, and with the first shipment of chips due to leave, Radnus will meet his end of the agreement and we'll be done. Can you give us...give me, a little more time?" Sofia paused; watching and waiting for his response.

He didn't hesitate. "Okay, I'll delay. But I want something in return," he insisted. "I need to know where that first shipment will be going. I need the transport documents. I want to know how, where, and when exactly these chips will be moved. I cannot let these chips leave the country."

Sofia began smiling again, her eyes shining brightly with admiration for him.

"What is it?" he asked, frowning from curiosity.

"And you said you were no hero," she praised.

He thought about what she was referring to and the conversation earlier, then smiled. They both relaxed—sitting back, resting into the comfort of the sofa, neither of them saying a word. They sat quietly for a few stolen moments, sharing a peace between them without the need for utterances, or thinking of anything else but the other. The comfortable silence allowed them to experience the strengthening of their bond. But as captivating and as beautiful as it was, the stolen moment had to be given back; reality was claiming back its time.

Sofia turned to him, and spoke with disappointment in her voice. "I have to leave."

This was the inevitable moment he knew would come, but was consciously trying to stretch their time together. "Sure—okay." The reluctance in his voice to let her go so soon was obvious. Reality and time were once again in control. "How can I reach you? I need your phone number."

Sofia leaned forward to the living room table, picked up a pen and wrote her number on an advertisement flyer. "You can reach me here."

He nodded and both stood up together. Sofia slowly walked to the door, followed by Josh. He brushed past her to open it. He poked his head out into the corridor, to make sure it was safe. He then looked at her and spoke quietly.

"I'll give you the whole day tomorrow to finalise your deal, but I want the transportation details first thing. I'll text you in the morning so you have my cover number. Store it under your phone contacts as "Sales Call" to avoid any suspicions. If you feel unsafe at any time, ring twice and hang up, I'll come for you. I'll answer if you ring more than twice."

Sofia nodded. "You see. I am right. You are a hero."

She leaned towards him, put her arms around his waist, and began hugging him again. He lifted his arms, wrapping them around her like a reassuring warm blanket; feeling her body against his, and gently stroked her soft hair. Sofia looked up, looking into his eyes. A fervent bond ignited between them—their bodies in magnetic embrace, their thoughts and minds as one, an intense connection pulling them closer. It was an embrace they both desired, as their lips touched, and they softly kissed.

Standing in the open doorway of the flat, they looked at each other. Their moment gradually subsided. Duty called. Duty was to keep them apart, just as it had done so since they first met.

"I'll hear from you tomorrow," she said tenderly, her beauty further radiated by the kiss they had just shared.

"For sure," replied Josh protectively; a gentle look on his face reserved only for her.

With that, Sofia turned, walking away along the corridor. As soon as she had left his sight he closed the door, going back to the living room. He looked at the advertisement flyer on the table and picked it up, looking at the number Sofia had written. He began reminiscing his evening with her. His brief moments with Sofia were the most memorable. Nothing compared to how he felt about her. After many years of meaningless relationships and one-night stands, he had finally and completely opened up, allowing himself to love another. Sofia was the heroine, that had found, and saved his lost heart.

CHAPTER 9

It was 7am the following day and Josh had just returned from his morning run. He turned the radio on to listen to the local news while stretching to cool his body down. The headlines had just started.

"Good morning Britain. It's exactly seven o'clock and here's Brian for your early morning news headlines."

"Good morning. Government ministers are in talks about whether they should be allowed to have second jobs. The Prime Minister is proposing to ban MPs from acting as paid political consultants, following revelations that party members have been breaking lobbying rules by accepting payments.

Late yesterday, police sergeant Allan Crofts was found dead in his car, believed to have committed suicide. Police were alerted he was missing and his body was later found in a secluded area. He died from carbon

monoxide poisoning. He leaves behind a wife and two
children.

The Chinese government has continued to...."

CLICK! Josh turned the radio off.

Crofts's body had finally been discovered and clearly a cover-up was in play, but why? A gunned down police officer would usually have the full force of resources allocated to tracking down the perpetrator, but not in this case. Josh could only reason that Crofts was tasked that evening with the sole duty of taking him out. And whoever assigned him with the task had great influence in hiding Crofts's failure. It also meant Josh was known to whoever organised the hit, so he had to watch his own back more carefully.

Without further thought of Crofts or his bereaved family, Josh stripped off his running gear to take a cold shower. The cold water flowing over his body was unbearably necessary; necessary in waking his senses. It helped to sharpen him up for whatever the day would throw at him. Five cold minutes and he turned the water off: goosebumps covering his body. He stepped out from the shower to dry himself. He could feel his finely tuned body, sharp wit, and laser focus. He was feeling ready.

Afterwards, he made himself a full breakfast, like he did most mornings. He made sure he ate well first thing—plenty of protein—as he never knew when he would get another chance.

Ready for work, he picked up his phone and as promised sent Sofia a text message, passing her his number. He waited to make sure it went through: "Message Failed". The returned text message indicated a problem. He wondered if it was the signal or that Sofia's phone was switched off. "Maybe she's on her way to GeneRobotix," he thought, so would give her extra time before sending another.

Meanwhile, he needed to plan his day. Harris hadn't been in contact and Josh certainly wasn't going to check in. As long as he possibly could, he wanted to keep Sofia and View Corp out of any reports he would need to make. Of the case he was on, all he had so far was a whistle-blower's suspicious death and some financial records; records linking GeneRobotix and a possible Chinese shell company to a possible trade violation. There was nothing conclusive that would hold up in any court of law. He had to get his proof that Radnus was knowingly selling microchip brain implants—implants the Chinese government planned on using against its own citizens, in violation of international human rights laws.

Josh speed-dialled a number on his phone; it started ringing.

"Yes, Flash here!" There was an abruptness in his voice.

"Flash, it's Brannon. I need a favour."

"Oh, hi Flash! Good morning Flash! How are you today Flash?" He was already in a bad mood and the day was just getting started. Flash sighed. "Sorry Josh, been up all night. What do you need?" He relented after blowing off some steam.

"No problem," replied Josh. "I want you to check on a holding company for me: Wang Holdings, and an account with the Bank of China." Josh gave him the account number on the financial records passed to him by Rachael's department head. "Give me anything you can find."

Flash began yawning. "Sure. I'll have it for you later today. I need some sleep first."

"Sorry Flash, but I need it right away."

"Well, maybe I can get Tomblin or Alice onto it for you," he yawned.

"I need you to do this one, it's important, if you get my meaning." Josh was insistent, he only trusted Flash.

"Okay, sure." Flash was too tired to argue.

"I also have something I want you to take a look at, something that's right up your nerdy little alley I know will interest you. I'll be there as soon as I can. And Flash, get some coffee in ya," and Josh hung up.

He picked up his keys and wallet—still with the microchip inside, and reached for the GeneRobotix documents on the table. He pushed them inside his jacket. Leaving the flat, he headed downstairs to the parking lot. As he got into his car, he checked his phone. He sent a new text message to Sofia, only for it to be returned as before: "Message Failed". It was coming up to 9am and he knew she would have her phone on by now. As with Rachael, he was sensing something was wrong.

Josh drove to HQ to meet up with Flash. For the whole journey, Sofia had been on his mind, and it was starting to become a problem. He never had this problem in the past, he never really cared about anyone else before, but she was different.

He drove through security and parked up. He got out of his car and entered the building, heading for T-Branch. As he walked along the corridors, he kept an eye out for Harris—ready to duck out of the way. He pushed open the door to T-Branch. The techno-nerd specialists were busy doing what they do—playing with their secret gadgets, and trying to solve the problem of how to stay on top in the spy-world. He looked over to Flash and walked over.

"How's the coffee?" he asked, looking down at a frothy machine-made cappuccino, sitting on Flash's desk.

"It's terrible," sparked Flash, but took a sip anyway. He was still a little touchy from tiredness.

"I checked your fictitious company: Wang Holdings. I assume you knew it was a front. It's registered under the name 'Li Wang' which is our equivalent of 'James Jones'. You really couldn't get a more common name than that. It doesn't have any tax filings or other directors listed. The only thing of interest, is an accountancy firm listed as the registrant. The firm is here in London: Smith and Son, another dodgy name if you ask me. But it does have recent tax filings so seems to be operational."

Josh wrote the address of the accountancy firm down on a piece of paper. "What about the account number?"

"It's definitely a legit Chinese bank account. I was able to deposit a small sum through our Labyrinth system. I'll need more time to find out who the owner of the account is though.

The sneaky Chinese cyber-warfare unit have been at it again. They've put up a new nationwide firewall surveillance and security system. They're intercepting everything—tracking all connections in and out of the country. I can penetrate it without them isolating our I.P. location, but I'll need to "borrow" a few computers to piggy-back off of. May take a while," explained Flash.

"'Borrow'? You mean hack," corrected Josh.

Flash looked disappointingly at him. "You're such a cynic. I don't like to use negative terms, it spoils my karma," he said, then swallowed another mouthful of coffee. "You said you have something for me to look at?"

Josh pulled out his wallet, removed the plastic bag holding the GeneRobotix GRX-5 chip, and handed it over. Flash squinted from the smallness of it; giving it a cursory inspection before dropping it into the breast pocket of his white lab coat.

"I'll run it through the system and let you know what I find."

"Thanks Flash. I'll buy you a coffee," and Josh immediately left.

"Yeah, thanks," said Flash to himself, and gulped down the last of his cappuccino.

Josh stepped outside into the parking area after leaving T-Branch. He sent a third text to Sofia: "Message Failed". It was time to pay another visit to GeneRobotix. He needed to modify the plan he had made with her last night, as things seemed to have gone sour. He had to start pushing for answers. Being soft was delaying momentum in the case, aggressive moves were now needed.

Josh jumped into his SQRV—all special inventory and weaponry inside checked and signed for. He was feeling fresh and ready for anything; focussed and with purpose. He had his target and nothing was going to stop him from doing what was needed. He pressed down on the accelerator, driving past security and sped out into the London streets.

He drove fast as usual. The short burst in and out of traffic had him arriving at GeneRobotix in quick time. He had entered the building and was standing in the lobby area by reception; surveying everything that was going on.

Security was busy calling someone to ask for Sofia, and then put the phone down. "Someone's checking for you now Mister Brannon."

Five minutes passed and still there was no sign of Sofia. Josh's patience was disappearing fast; he needed to make sure she was unharmed. He turned to security, about to make demands to locate her, when the lift arrived on the lobby floor. Josh turned to see who was inside; putting a temporary hold on his temper. The lift door opened and Rachael's department head walked out. She walked directly up to him.

"Good morning Mister Brannon. Ms Du Bois isn't here today. Is there anything I can help you with?"

She sounded robotic, like a commercial ad selling cars, like she was reading from a script. Josh knew it was for the security officer's benefit who was listening in. He would likely be reporting straight to his senior, and to Radnus. She had to behave as though she hadn't collaborated with Josh—by handing over confidential material, and that she was also unaware that Rachael, as a whistle-blower, had contacted him.

"Sorry, I didn't catch your name," replied Josh craftily in front of security. This was an opportunity to get her name; she was unwilling to reveal it in the lift yesterday. He had her in a nice tight spot that would force her to answer.

"I'm Jennifer Baxter, head of accounts," she reluctantly replied; her eyes and body tense.

"Do you know where Ms Du Bois is as she's not answering her phone? I need to go over some important records with her concerning the Chinese deal." Josh was spelling it out as plainly as he could without alerting security.

"Well, she didn't turn up this morning, so I'm afraid I can't help you any further."

She was trying to cut the conversation short so Josh would leave; trying to get rid of him. But he wasn't having any of it. He didn't care about ruffling people's feathers.

"She said she would be here today. Perhaps I could wait in her office?"

"I'm sorry Mister Brannon but that won't be possible."

"Perhaps you can help me then. She was going to get me the details of the first shipment. I need to add the costs of the storage and shipping to our bill."

Jennifer plainly understood Josh's cryptic conversation, and what he really needed—the location and means of transportation for the first shipment of GRX-5 chips to China. The security officer had seemingly disengaged with their conversation, and carried on working on a crossword puzzle.

"I'll go and fetch the information for you. I'll be right back," and Jennifer headed back up inside the lift.

Whilst waiting, Josh began devising a contingency plan in his head—a plan B, in case Jennifer lost her nerve and bottled out. He knew she wasn't strong like Rachael. So, with security preoccupied, Josh began mentally noting the security measures of the building: security cameras, bio-security locks, the fencing—all the physical security that would prevent any professional criminal from gaining access. It was never enough though. He knew security was only as good as the weakest link, and that was usually in human form. A weak mind, corruptibility, ego, and support of a cause, were the usual ways to exploit human behaviour to gain access. Corruptibility had already helped him to solicit the microchip.

Whilst he was busy making his assessment, the lift door opened, with Jennifer reappearing with some documents in hand. She walked directly up to Josh; glancing over to see if security was watching. He was still busy. She was nervous; she was trying too hard to look normal and it showed. With a trembling hand, she passed Josh the documents.

"I believe this is what you need Mister Brannon. Everything's there. Please say hello to Ms Du Bois…Sofia, for me."

"Thank you, I will," replied Josh, sensing her fear and unusual body language.

Leaving, Josh walked through the glass doorway out of the building to his car. He opened the door and sat himself down, watching the immediate area around him as he did so. He closed the door. He looked down at the papers Jennifer had just given him. The first was the manifest of the initial consignment of GRX-5 chips—one hundred thousand pieces. Stapled to it was another form detailing the storage location—a dockyard. It also had the name of the ship they were to be transported to China on, as well as the time the ship was due to leave port. He looked at the third piece of paper which wasn't stapled but loose: "THEY KNOW" was written in blue ink. Josh immediately looked up; he heeded the strong warning.

Starting the engine, he proceeded to drive away. As he joined the main road, he was quick to notice a tail. Looking in his rear-view mirror, a black Mercedes was following him, two cars back. He could make out at least two male occupants. In usual circumstances he could call for backup—alerting the Quick Reaction Force to take them out—but an opportunity had helpfully presented itself. He had a plan.

As far as he knew his cover identity was still intact, that whoever was following him likely believed he was nothing more than an investigator for the Department of Trade and Industry, and not a highly trained government intelligence operative. This would give him an advantage if, and only if, his cover was solid. Not slipping into complacency though—as he was still unaware of their skills—but whoever these men were, they were in for a surprise.

Driving at normal speed, he pretended he hadn't noticed the tail. He navigated through the busy streets and headed out of the city; taking care not to lose them. He was leading them to a quiet location that would suit the purpose of his plan, a place where cries for help would go unheard.

"Jonesy, you alone?" asked Josh with his phone to his ear.

"Mister Brannon, good to hear from you again, and so soon. I received your prompt payment for the car; most generous of you. How can I be of assistance?" replied Jonesy.

"I need to hire your workshop for a few hours at most. Any problem?" Josh kept checking the Merc was still following; it was.

"No problem Mister Brannon. I'll clear my schedule for you."

"I'll be there soon," and Josh hung up.

The journey was longer than it could have been, as Josh had been careful not to lose the amateurs following him. He pulled up to the entrance of Jonesy's yard and checked his mirror. He watched the Mercedes stop further up the road; some distance off on the roadside, but in view. They had direct line of sight of him, as he casually drove inside the yard and stepped out of his vehicle. He purposely gave off the impression he was unconcerned and not aware of them. He walked into the workshop where Jonesy was waiting.

"I'm all ready Mister Brannon." Jonesy was holding a stockless Mossberg 590 sawn-off shotgun. Josh hadn't mentioned about the people following him, but Jonesy knew that whenever Josh called, trouble wouldn't be far behind. He was always prepared.

"I need these two alive," said Josh. "I need you as bait in the office."

"Will do," obeyed Jonesy, and as he walked into the office, sharply racked the slide of the shotgun back—loading a cartridge into the chamber.

Jonesy turned the radio on to attract their guests. He was no stranger to this type of work. He had himself a few trophy wounds of his own; collected over the years. He plonked himself in a swivel chair behind his office desk, resting his shotgun across his lap, out of sight.

Josh waited in the workshop. He positioned himself behind a large metal container full of car parts. It would provide excellent cover from fire if things didn't go as planned. The metal door to the workshop opened and two burly men walked in. Both men, somewhere in their mid-forties, looked like pit-bulls, gangster hard men. They both wore a three-quarter length black leather coat, and sported a studded earring in their left ear—they almost looked like twins.

The plan was working, as they both walked to where the noise of the radio was sounding from—the office. Josh watched, preparing himself for the inevitable. He knew these two wouldn't lie down and concede without a fight; which is just what they were about to experience. They stepped into the office, one after the other, and Josh quickly followed up from behind.

As Josh swiftly entered the room, one of the thugs turned his head. Josh immediately kicked the back of the man's knee, causing him to buckle and loose his balance. The second thug turned and reached inside his coat for a weapon, but Josh lunged forward with his elbow, planting it hard on the man's jaw. CRACK! His jaw broke from the impact but he remained standing; mouthing a muffled noise of pain. The first man was recovering his footing, so Josh swept in with a hard blow to his stomach; into his solar plexus. The man's muscle and fat helped cushion the blow, but still, he felt the effect of the hard punch to the nerves.

Both thugs had met more than their match. Jonesy remained seated, watching the show with enjoyment, his shotgun pointing at them in case things turned in their favour. The man with the broken jaw continued to remove his weapon—a pistol, in spite of the pain. Jonesy pointed and fired a round—blowing the man's hand off. His pistol fell to the floor; a detached bloody finger stuck in the trigger guard. Josh punched him hard again on his already broken jaw. He fell to the floor, unconscious. Josh pulled his 9mil ready to fire, but the first man put his hands up in defeat. He knew they had been licked.

"Harry Slater." The thug spoke in a husky cockney accent. "Been a long time."

Josh looked at Jonesy and Jonesy looked at Josh. "Looks like my past has finally caught up with me Mister Brannon," shrugged Jonesy. "Mister Brannon, meet brothers Bazza and Bernie Hill from the East End."

The thug—Bazza, looked directly at Josh; ignoring the pistol barrel pointing at him. It wasn't the first time of having a gun shoved in his face. "Fair fight Mister Brannon, I'll give you that. Mind if I check on my brother?"

Josh nodded. "First take your coat off and remove your weapons. Throw them to the floor." He kept his 9mil trained on Bazza's large stocky body. He was built like a rhino.

Bazza slowly removed his coat, revealing a holstered pistol. He threw his coat on the floor as ordered and slowly removed the gun, throwing it on top of his coat.

"Step back against the wall," ordered Josh.

Bazza did as he was told, allowing Josh to kick the coat and weapon over to Jonesy. He also kicked over Bernie's bloodied pistol, still with finger attached.

"Take your trousers off."

Bazza undid his belt and button, unzipped his trousers, and let them fall to his ankles. He levered his shoes off with his feet, kicking them to one side, then stepped out of his trousers; keeping his socks on.

"Now take your shirt off."

Bazza took off his holster, letting it fall to the floor. He unbuttoned his shirt, removed it, and dropped it on top of his trousers. He was now standing in just his boxer shorts and socks. Josh was satisfied Bazza had no more concealed weapons.

"You can check on your brother now."

Josh was assessing if somehow, he could get answers from the brothers without resorting to force. Clearly Bazza cared for his brother despite being a hardened criminal, so there was a slim chance he could get through to them. If his brother died, Bazza would clam up, wanting revenge. If that would be the case, Josh would have no other option but to do things the hard way.

Bazza walked over to his brother, who was still unconscious on the floor. He looked in bad shape, with a pool of blood originating from the shredded stump where his hand should be. Bazza began prodding and pushing his brother, trying to bring him round; he was wasting his time. Josh could see the pallid look of Bernie's face and knew he was dead. His death was now going to make things harder.

CHAPTER 10

WITH JONESY STANDING GUARD, holding his shotgun, Josh had restrained Bazza to a heavy metal container in the workshop. He was sitting on a chair in just his Union Jack boxer shorts; his arms tied with rope behind his back to the container. Bazza was a hefty brute and quite powerful, which meant Josh needed to double up on restraints. Using his equipment from the SQRV, he tied a set of plasticuffs to Bazza's wrists and ankles—securing them tightly together.

"What now Mister Brannon," asked Jonesy. He lowered the shotgun now that Bazza was powerless.

Josh looked directly at Bazza, a firm engaging look to get his full attention. "Bazza, I'm sure you know the score of what's coming. You've probably done similar things to others. So, I'm not gonna stand here and bullshit you. I need some answers. And you're gonna give em to me. It's that simple."

Bazza got the message loud and clear, but the desired effect of it bounced off his thick skull. "You killed my brother Mister Brannon, and that don't sit well with me. We had our differences me and him, but we were still family. So, you dish out what you have to, and I'll take what's coming. If you kill me—well, what more can I say."

With those last words Bazza looked away; staring down at the floor. Josh knew he was preparing himself for what was about to come. Looking at his body, Josh could see he was going to be a tough nut to crack. Bazza had multiple scars—old knife and bullet injuries—across his body. He was used to pain and likely numb to it, so a different tactic was needed.

Josh knew torture wasn't the best method for extracting information. Experience had taught that someone under torture would say anything to stop the pain; in other words, lie. He always found the best way was reasoning. Anyone could be reasoned with if you found the right button to push; even a thug like Bazza. Find the hook that would elicit a favourable response, then dig in on it, until the person gave up what information was needed. It took longer, but the intel was usually more reliable.

"Keep an eye on our guest Jonesy. I'm going to check their car."

Jonesy raised his shotgun as a sign he understood. Josh walked out of the workshop along the road to the Hill Brother's Mercedes, still parked on the roadside. He pushed the button on the car remote—retrieved from Bernie's coat pocket—unlocking the doors. He then drove it back into the yard.

The Merc was a top of the range model, which suggested business had been good for the Hill Brothers. Crime seemed to be paying well; materialistically anyway. But right now, with one brother dead and one tied up, the odds were no longer in their favour. Josh began searching the inside. He opened the glove compartment and his attention was immediately drawn to a fat white envelope. He pulled it out and opened it. It was stuffed with fifty-pound notes, a similar amount to that found in sergeant Crofts's car. He closed the envelope of cash and slipped it inside his jacket.

He finished searching the interior and moved outside to check the boot. He opened it and was faced with the reality of who the Hill Brothers actually were. Inside were the tools of their trade: a shovel, plastic bags, plastic sheeting, duct tape, and a selection of saws—for cutting up bodies. These items, Josh was fully aware, were intended to be used on him. The Hill Brothers were as repulsive as a pair of cockroaches feeding on a rotten corpse. Josh accepted killing as part of his job—to protect others, but just to kill for a pay cheque, that was beneath contempt. He now realised he wasn't going to get anywhere with Bazza, by being reasonable.

Just as he was about to close the boot, he noticed a plastic card half hidden under the sheeting. He picked it up and turned it over. He suddenly froze inside. It was a photo ID card, an ID card from GeneRobotix. But what caused him to freeze was who it belonged to. He was looking at the photograph of a woman, a woman familiar to him, and he silently read her name: "Sofia Du Bois." His left hand clenched into a solid ball, as his whole body began tightening up at the idea the Hill Brothers had harmed her. A boiling rage was starting to bubble up inside of him, a rage he had to quickly contain. He had to control his emotion. He smoothly suppressed and put a lid on his anger; knowing that if he can't get what he wants from Bazza, he will unleash more pain on him than an eternity in hell.

Focussed again, he kept hold of the ID and closed the boot of the Merc. He walked to his SQRV and opened the boot. He pushed back the panel covering the tools of his own trade, took out a small black case and slammed the boot closed. Carrying the case, he walked back into the workshop.

Bazza and Jonesy were talking like it was old times, but stopped as soon as Josh returned. He placed the black case on a workbench in plain view, so Bazza could see it, but not know what it contained. That was for Bazza to guess at, for what it was for, and to imagine the worst. Josh was playing a psychological game with him.

Leaving the workshop, Josh beckoned Jonesy into the office with him, out of earshot to Bazza. "Tell me about the Hill Brothers. What's your involvement with them?"

"Hmm, bit of a long story Mister Brannon." Jonesy was rubbing his stubbled face while trying to think of a place to start. "I worked for the Petersons; been with them a long time. They were a family in the East End; into prostitution, gambling, the usual stuff...."

Josh interrupted, "Yeah, I know all that. I checked your background, who you worked for, and the deal you made for anonymity. But what about them—the Hill Brothers?"

"Well—him and his brother, they were taken on as enforcers by the Petersons. They would do anything; no scruples. I've done some bad things in my time, but even some gangsters have a line they won't cross. They had no line. Women, elderly, even kids. Anyway, once the Petersons got put away, they went freelance; thugs for hire. You won't get far with him Mister Brannon. He's as stubborn and hard as they come," revealed Jonesy.

Josh considered the unthinkable, of how he could extract information, but if Jonesy was right, it might be best to try his alternative method first. He knew that whoever paid Crofts also paid the Hills. The fact that the Hills followed him from GeneRobotix, it didn't take much to figure out where the money had come from. He just didn't know about Sofia, if she had been harmed or not. And from what Jonesy had just revealed, he knew the Hills were just low-level criminals at the bottom of a large pyramid—disposable cannon fodder.

Josh stepped out from the office and walked over to Bazza, who was sitting quietly and watching intently. He removed the stuffed envelope of cash and held it out for Bazza to see.

"I know who paid you to take me out, but what they didn't tell you is who I am. I don't work for the Department of Trade and Industry. Your employer short-changed you and your brother. Your employer threw you under the bus Bazza. They knew you wouldn't succeed just as the police officer before you failed."

Josh watched Bazza closely as he spoke the truth to him. He watched his subtle but noticeable physical reactions. He could tell from the responses what Bazza had been told, what he knew, and what he didn't know. He was unconsciously telling all without realising it. Josh just needed to ask the right questions and check the immediate responses. So far, he had partly confirmed his DTI investigator cover was still intact. Bazza reacted like he had no idea Josh was anything else but that. There was still a possibility though that Radnus knew he was a government spy, and purposely omitted to inform the Hill Brothers. He also picked up the sign that Bazza didn't like the idea of being duped by his employer. This was the hook Josh was looking for.

"Had your employer told you the truth Bazza, you would have probably asked for more money. And come better prepared. Your brother may even still be alive right now, and possibly our positions would be in reverse—you standing here, and me sitting where you are right now." Josh plainly laid it all out.

"You won't get anything out of me," insisted Bazza, not realising he was already spilling the beans.

Josh put the envelope of cash down on the workbench and picked up Sofia's ID. He held it up to Bazza's face. "I found this in the back of your car. This lady, Ms Sofia Du Bois, she's my target. I hope you killed her for me. Please tell me she's dead Bazza?"

Bazza gave off a subtle expression of pleasure and not disappointment. This sign of pleasure told Josh he hadn't killed her, otherwise Bazza would be disappointed: disappointed at having done Josh's work for him. Sofia was still alive!

"Where is she Bazza, where's Ms Du Bois?" questioned Josh.

With a mulish smug look on his face, Bazza spoke without thinking. "I wouldn't tell you even if I knew," he replied, believing he had successfully given nothing away. But he was as stupid as they came. He didn't realise that what he unthinkingly said, was in fact an answer, that he knew nothing. He certainly wasn't the "brains" of the brothers' outfit; if the pair had any at all.

"Okay, so you don't actually know where she is. How did you come by this ID card?"

Bazza looked confused. "I didn't say I don't know where she is."

"You said you wouldn't tell me even if you knew!" paraphrased Josh aggressively. "So you don't know!"

Bazza looked annoyed. "That doesn't mean...."

"I get it Bazza, don't worry," Josh rudely interrupted, "not everyone is important. I get it that you and your brother are bottom of the food chain. I understand that now. I think I'm done."

Josh pretended to be finishing up with him, but was secretly waiting for an anticipated reaction. Bazza's ego had been beaten down and he was desperate to regain his feeling of self-importance. He was angry and pulling at his restraints. Jonesy stood by in case he managed to break free.

"We only deal with organ grinders, not monkeys!" ranted Bazza, while jerking heavily on the rope and trying to stand. "You av no idea what you're talking about!"

Josh rebutted aggressively. "They didn't even tell you who I am! That tells you how important you are! You're not good enough to know!"

"Fuck you! Nobody fucks with us! We're important enough to speak to the main man!" Bazza was wound up and fighting to get free; he wanted to tear Josh apart.

"Why would Mark Radnus want to speak to you two, he's got more important things to do? He would hire another idiot to do the deal with you! You're lying to make yourself look good! No 'main man' would respect you two chumps!" Josh kept up the aggressive attack on Bazza's ego.

"You're wrong!" yelled Bazza. "When he gave us the girl's picture, he was happy to av us get rid of ya!"

Again, without thinking just reacting, Bazza blurted out what Josh wanted to know. His trick worked. After Josh ceased attacking his character, Bazza was quick to realise he had been tricked into revealing the fact that Mark Radnus had hired them, and gave them Sofia's ID. Josh had all he wanted to know, and knew Bazza wouldn't be privy to anything more. The Hill Brothers were just sacrificial lambs to be used for the dirty work, and then themselves to be done away with. He had finished with him.

Josh called Jonesy to go into the office once again for a private conversation. "I've got what I need to know. I'm done. You can cut him loose once I've gone."

"Sorry Mister Brannon but I can't do that." Jonesy was shaking his head. "He knows where I am now, and people will pay good money to find me. He'll grass me up as soon as he gets outta here, and I need to protect my family. He knew once he saw me, he aint gonna leave the way he came in. Besides, it'll be good to get him off the streets. I'll clean up here now Mister Brannon; there's no charge. Looks like five grand in that envelope and the Merc will fetch a nice price. That'll do nicely."

Josh said nothing about Jonesy's intention. They walked out of the office and Josh picked up his black case and Sofia's ID. He left the envelope of money sitting on the workbench—Jonesy's "clean-up" payment. Josh walked out of the workshop without even giving Bazza one final look; he was a mountain of dead meat sitting in a chair. After putting the case away, Josh got into his car. He started the engine and began moving off. BANG! The sound of a shotgun blast went off inside the workshop. Jonesy had begun "cleaning up".

Driving back towards London, Josh had to change direction—his plan's direction. He needed to find Sofia and shut down GeneRobotix. He was about to overstep his assignment instructions, of which Harris would most definitely have something to say about; likely jump up and down like a whining prostitute tricked out of her earnings. He didn't care though. His integrity was worth more than his job and a pay cheque.

He knew that breaking his code—compromising his personal integrity, would weaken him. It's a concept the easily corruptible and criminal cannot see. Allowing oneself to be morally bought for power or money, would eventually make one weaker, not stronger. As soon as one accepts the coin of the Devil, the Devil has control over them to do its bidding; just as with Sergeant Crofts.

Joining the M25, he headed east along the motorway. The documents Jennifer had passed him gave him a new target location—the London Gateway deep-water port, situated on the River Thames. The document also gave the cargo ship's designation the GRX-5 chips were to be shipped to China on: the "SHENG LEE". It was due to sail early the following morning, so luckily time was on his side.

BEEP-BEEP, BEEP-BEEP! BEEP-BEEP, BEEP-BEEP!

Josh switched his Bluetooth on to answer the call coming through. "What have you got Flash?"

"I've got some interesting news for you on this chip Josh!" Flash was excited. "It's effectively an AI brain implant. The US military's Defense Advanced Research Projects Agency has been experimenting with similar chips, to change a person's behaviour, BUT—the one you gave me is five generations beyond DARPA's. This chip is highly sophisticated!"

"What can it do?" asked Josh, as he manoeuvred at speed left and right across the motorway lanes, over and undertaking vehicles in his way.

"It seems to be able to interface with the brain and nervous system. It can receive and transmit electrical signals remotely. I haven't been able to test it fully, but to hazard a guess, I would say you are looking at the state-of-the-art in mind-control technology."

"Thanks Flash. Let me know if you come up with anything else."

"Sure, will do. This is fascinating stuff Josh, but to be honest...it's kinda scary," and Flash hung up.

Flash's words of warning had Josh thinking. No one in the "normal" world would ever believe any organisation, let alone a government, would be willing to create and use such apparatus on their citizens. But here he was, a single operative investigating the planned abuse of hidden powers upon a whole population. Did he feel like a hero as Sofia had previously suggested? No. It was simply a duty to one's fellow man to keeping them safe.

He pulled off the M25 motorway onto the A13. A short drive further had him driving past Stanford-le-Hope and into the London Gateway docks. He approached the main gateway and parked off to one side. He stepped out of his car and walked over to security. Entering the kiosk, a security officer looked over.

"Yes mate?" enquired the officer.

"I'm from the Department of Trade and Industry, come for an inspection. Can you inform your manager so I can gain access," requested Josh, in a formal tone of voice.

"Do you have some ID sir?" asked the officer, adopting a less casual manner than before.

Josh pulled out his wallet and took out his cover ID card, placing it onto the counter. The security officer knew the drill on surprise inspections and phoned through, giving his senior Josh's details on the ID.

"Someone will be with you shortly sir."

Josh waited ten minutes before a security vehicle pulled up. Two men arrived, one wearing a suit and the other dressed in security uniform. They entered the kiosk and both looked over at Josh.

"Mister Brannon?" asked the suited man. He was looking a little tense and ready for an argument.

"Yes, that's correct."

Josh held out his hand as a friendly gesture, to break down the man's defensiveness. The man took his hand and Josh gave a friendly shake, putting him at ease. He had a way of making people comfortable in his presence, especially when he needed them to be.

"I'm Mark Maro, security manager here. How can I be of assistance?"

"I assume you checked my ID Mark?" questioned Josh.

"Yes, I did. And I was told to make everything available to you."

"Good. I'm here on an inspection. Can we talk somewhere a little more private?"

The security manager looked puzzled. "Let's go outside."

Josh and the security manager stepped outside, away from the kiosk and the other two security personnel.

"Are you ex-military Mark?"

"Ex-police," he replied.

"Good. You'll understand what I'm going to say then. As a government official, I am officially binding you to the Official Secrets Act of what I am about to tell you. That means, you cannot disclose to anyone what I am about to discuss with you here. Do you understand?"

Josh waited for a response. The security manager nodded in agreement.

"What I'm about to tell you must be kept strictly secret. I'm not here on a routine inspection, but investigating a serious trade breach between a bio-tech company and China. I have a shipping manifest of a cargo to be sent to Qingdao, China. The ship is called the "SHENG LEE", and is due to sail early in the morning. I need to inspect the shipment without anyone knowing."

Although surprised, Mark nodded. "Well, I'll have to find out if the container has been loaded already. There's that possibility. If it has, you will need to get permission to board the ship for an inspection.

The Chinese get a little twitchy when it comes to customs and port authorities. Let me take you through and I'll get what information you need," said Mark, and waved for his colleague to join them.

Following the security manager's vehicle, Josh drove through the gateway into the dockyards, to a two-storey office building. Carrying the documents relating to the cargo of GRX-5 chips, he continued to follow Mark into the building, to a corner office.

Sitting with a computer at his desk, Mark held out his hand. "Let me take a look at the manifest."

Josh handed over the paperwork and watched the monitor as Mark typed in the container number.

"Looks like you're in luck. The container is still waiting to be loaded. It's in the container stacking yard. What do you want to do?" he asked.

"I want you to delay loading and I want to inspect its content."

"Okay. I'll radio the shuttle carriers on the quayside to leave it where it is. We can go and take a look."

Mark picked up the manifest and led Josh back outside to his security vehicle. They drove a short distance to the automated stacking yard, where all the piled containers were waiting to be lifted onto the awaiting cargo ships. On foot, they walked past the mountains of stacked metal containers, until Mark identified the one they were looking for. It was perched two down from the top of a stack. Mark radioed for a shuttle carrier driver to come over, then ordered him to bring it down.

Once the shipping container had been placed on the ground, Josh approached the door panel. The serial number on the container matched that on the paperwork; given to him by Jennifer at GeneRobotix. The handles of the container were locked with steel padlocks, and a special electronic security seal. The strong wire of the seal passed through two metal rings—welded, one on each door—and was designed to alert of any unauthorised tampering. Anyone gaining access would have to break the seal.

Turning to Mark, Josh needed a solution to gain access. "I need to get inside without going through the doors. And I need it to be clean and untraceable."

Surprised by the request, Mark raised his eyebrows. "I think you need Houdini, but I think he's still dead."

Josh puzzled momentarily and came up with a solution. "I know the next best person, but I need you to give him access."

Mark agreed, and they both went back to the office, to set up the special entry for Josh's guest.

Around an hour and a half later, the darkness of evening had set in. Josh had ordered himself a meal from the canteen, the first since breakfast. He didn't know how hungry he was until he ate that first bite. After which, the meal disappeared in seconds as he wolfed it down his gullet.

Mark appeared in the canteen doorway, "Your guest is here." He then stepped aside to allow him in.

"Mister Brannon, been a long time. How are you?" said Jonesy, walking into the canteen.

Josh stood up from the table and gave Jonesy a nod. "Did you bring your gear?"

"Got everything I need Mister Brannon. Just show me the 'can' that needs opening."

All three headed to the car park.

"I think we should go in mine," suggested Jonesy, "I've got all my gear inside."

He pointed to a black Mercedes parked by the door. Josh looked at Jonesy disapprovingly, knowing he was driving around in the Hill Brother's Merc.

"New plates Mister Brannon; all legit," whispered Jonesy, as they walked over to it.

Josh opened the car door and got in. The interior smelt of chemicals and looked sterile clean, like it had just been driven from a motor dealer's showroom floor. Jonesy had covered his tracks well. Likely, he had removed the VIN—Vehicle Identification Number—and replaced it with another. His sinister professionalism showed to high standards.

Jonesy drove the three of them to the container under the direction of the security manager. It was dark out. The stacked containers blocked out most of the artificial light coming from nearby flood lights, so Jonesy pulled out a light from the boot. He walked up to the outside of the container and began inspecting it; analysing the locks, the sides, edges, and joins.

Josh and Mark waited, watching Jonesy scrutinizing the metal shell. He probed the container's door hinges with a screwdriver, tapping gently. He looked around the stacking yard, walked over to a mobile metal frame staircase, and wheeled it to the container. He pushed it flush against the side and climbed the steps. Standing on the roof, he shone the light around, inspecting the top. A few minutes of inspection, Jonesy came back down.

"We take the top off," he recommended.

Mark spoke with surprise, "Are you sure? These containers are solid. They need to be. The cranes pick them up by the roof."

Jonesy turned to Josh. "It'll be like opening a can of beans Mister Brannon. And once I put the lid back on, no one will know you've taken a few," he assured. "Gonna need to borrow one of those big cranes though," and he pointed to a container shuttle carrier.

"Get it done," commanded Josh.

Jonesy grabbed his tools, taking them up onto the container roof, while Mark arranged for the shuttle carrier to be positioned overhead, at Jonesy's instruction. He also requested heavy duty chains be looped over the shuttle carrier's lifting assembly.

Shooting sparks from an acetylene cutting torch began flying into the air and over the edge, as Jonesy went about his business. Half an hour later, he called for the driver of the carrier to lower the lifting assembly. It was lowered, and instead of clamping it onto the container itself, Jonesy attached the dangling chains to the roof section he had just prepared. He climbed down with his gear, then gave the thumbs up to the shuttle driver, who engaged the carrier's lifting assembly. As the mechanical giant lifted, the chains tightened and the container roof smoothly came off.

"There ya go Mister Brannon." Jonesy was standing with arms folded, looking proudly at his work. "Like I said. Easy as opening a can of beans."

With the help of Jonesy's floodlights, Josh and Mark climbed the staircase and looked over the edge, down inside the container. It was half filled with boxes from floor to ceiling. Josh reached in and pulled up one of the boxes, resting it on the edge. He read the stencilled description on the box: "GeneRobotix GRX-5 Component, 1000 pieces". He quickly estimated at least one hundred boxes containing one thousand pieces each, making up the first shipment of microchips in the China deal. He had his evidence. He now needed to inform Harris, to get him up to speed and stop the shipment.

"There's something at the front, by the door," said Mark. He was standing up and leaning over the edge.

Unable to see, Josh climbed on top of the boxes and lowered himself down into the container. Mark followed suit. They were standing over what appeared to be some kind of metal containment pod, resting on a platform. It had oxygen tanks attached to the outside, with tubes running inside the pod. A digital unit fixed to the outside displayed a number of life-sign metrics: oxygen level, temperature, heartbeat, and brain activity. Mark looked completely bewildered at what they had discovered, but Josh nervously suspected what he would find, or rather, who he would find. He just hoped he wasn't too late. The pod was locked from the outside.

"Need a hand Mister Brannon?" Jonesy was peering over the top, holding a screwdriver.

Josh reached up and grabbed the tool. Pushing hard, he jammed the screwdriver into the seam of the pod opening, then began levering it up and down, forcing the lock to break. He dropped the tool, rested his palms on the upper half of the pod, and pushed upwards. The pod hatch opened, and Josh's eyes widened as he looked inside. For those first brief moments, all he could do was stare. His stomach turned, as he looked down at the tubes and electrodes attached to Sofia's pale still body.

CHAPTER 11

"WHAT THE HELL IS going on?" questioned Mark. He was looking intensely at Josh and began pressing him for an explanation.

Josh ignored Mark's emotional concerns to focus on what was important. He remained silent, staring at Sofia, seeing if the apparatus she was connected to could be turned off without proper medical intervention. His worry, if he disconnected her from the pod's tubes and sensors, was that he might kill her. He needed expert guidance. He couldn't contact Harris now as he didn't trust him. And the fact that Sofia is a part of View Corp made things more problematic. He also had no other contacts within View Corp.

Josh turned to Mark. "Remember what I said Mark; Official Secrets Act applies here too." He then looked up at Jonesy, who was looking down over the edge of the container, getting an eyeful. "You too Jonesy."

"Haven't seen a thing Mister Brannon," replied Jonesy, tapping a finger on his nose—a sign of secrecy.

"What do we do now, she needs medical attention?" said Mark. "And if this is some kind of human trafficking, I'm not sure I can keep my word on staying quiet, official secret or not. I have a duty to report this."

"It's not human trafficking," replied Josh.

Mark looked confused, "Then what is it?"

"An experiment," and Josh leaned in to get a closer look at Sofia's head.

He softly put a hand on each side of her head and gently turned her face away from him. A wire was coming from the base of her skull, covered by a strip of surgical tape to keep it in place. Josh pulled off one side of the tape and moved the wire slightly. It had been fed directly into the back of her head through the skin—possibly into her brain, but he was no doctor to know for sure. He knew now that he couldn't disconnect her without putting Sofia's life in danger, that his only safe option was the local hospital. He replaced the tape and moved her head back into its original position.

"Mark, I need you to arrange for a critical care unit. Let's get her quickly to hospital."

"I'm on it," said Mark with relief, and pulled out his phone and started dialling.

"Mister Brannon," Jonesy spoke up, "I think it's best for me to leave now."

Josh knew what he meant, that he couldn't get caught up in a police investigation that could expose his real identity—his criminal past and becoming a state supergrass. Josh simply nodded, and Jonesy's head disappeared fast from over the top of the container.

"The medical unit is on its way," said Mark, while putting his phone away. "I'm not sure if they're gonna believe all this though. I've seen some strange things during my time in the police force, but nothing like this." He was shaking his head in disbelief.

Josh was looking at Sofia's pale face, he then turned to Mark. "I need to align our stories, make sure they dovetail so my investigation isn't compromised further. I need your assurances."

Mark shrugged his shoulders. "Well, what do I really know? A DTI investigator needs to look inside a container on an official investigation. I was instructed to assist and we came upon this. Not much else to say really. And I'm assuming I'm right in thinking you don't want your disappearing colleague mentioned?"

"It would certainly make things easier if he was kept out of this," replied Josh. "But it sounds like you have the facts of it all. And if anyone wants further information just direct them to me." He then turned his attention back to Sofia, waiting quietly for the ambulance.

Some minutes later, blue flashing lights appeared at the dockyard in the distance, getting brighter as they neared the container stacking yard where Josh and Mark were waiting. A critical care paramedic unit arrived, accompanied by a uniformed police unit. Two paramedics and two police officers stepped out of their respective vehicles. Josh raced over to meet them.

"What have we got?" asked the lead paramedic.

Josh immediately identified himself. "I'm an investigator from the Department of Trade and Industry," and flashed his cover ID. He then pointed to the container. "A lady needs immediate medical attention. We need to get her to hospital ASAP. She's connected to what appears to be some kind of life support unit that I believe is actually harming her. We need to get her off it."

"Show me the way," said the paramedic, as he grabbed an emergency medical pack from the ambulance.

Still lit up by Jonesy's floodlights, Josh escorted the paramedics over to the container where Mark was standing by. Both police officers followed, but so far kept out of the way to let the paramedics do their job. The container doors were now fully open, to allow access to the pod and Sofia. Now that Josh's clandestine investigation had been compromised, there was no need to hide, so they broke the security locks on the doors.

The paramedics approached the pod and began their assessment. They carefully looked at Sofia, talking between them and exchanging their thoughts on the connection tubes and wires entering her body. They looked at the pod's life-sign gauges to assess her current condition. Josh and Mark watched, along with the two police officers. After their initial inspection the lead paramedic spoke to the group.

"We're going to have to transport her to hospital inside this thing. Her life-signs look good so it seems like it's keeping her alive. But we're just concerned about the wire going into the back of her head. Anyone know what this thing is, or what happened to her?"

Mark looked sideways at Josh for a response. He was still somewhat in the dark himself and had no definitive answer.

"Okay, so how do we move her?" asked Josh, while avoiding the question.

"Well, it's a self-contained unit so we just need to unbolt it from the platform it's on. Then we will need to lift it into the ambulance and stabilize it," replied the paramedic.

Josh took charge, directing Mark to get dockyard maintenance to assist in unbolting the pod from its platform. As the surprised maintenance man worked at unbolting the pod, the paramedics made space in the back of the ambulance. Once everything had been prepared, Josh, Mark, and the two police officers took a corner each and lifted the pod from the platform. At the guidance of the paramedics, they carefully moved Sofia and the pod to the back of the ambulance. Using straps, the paramedics secured the pod in place and connected their own life-sign monitoring equipment to Sofia.

The lead paramedic looked at Josh and Mark. "We're going to have to radio ahead to get this lady's medical information. Anyone know her name...address...next of kin?"

Josh answered, "Her name's Sofia Du Bois, that's all."

"Well, it's an unusual name, so it's a start," said the paramedic, and closed the rear door of the ambulance. He looked at Josh, "Will you be attending?"

"Yeah, I'll follow you."

"Before you leave sir," one of the police officers interrupted to speak to Josh, "I'm going to have to accompany you in your vehicle while my colleague follows on behind. Just a formality until we can establish what's happening here."

"Sure, let's go," ordered Josh.

Jumping into the back of the police car, Josh was driven back to his own vehicle, parked up outside the office block. He, and the officer he spoke with, swiftly changed cars. Josh started up and quickly pulled off after the ambulance that had continued on to the exit, escorted by Mark. The ambulance, with blue lights flashing, was passing through security. Josh quickly caught up, and Mark, who was standing by the security kiosk, waved them through. Josh was now in convoy behind the ambulance, with the escorting officer sitting beside him, and the police car with the second officer following on behind.

Heading west along the A13, the emergency convoy had an almost obstruction-free passageway. The hour was late that, with minimal traffic on the roads to slow them down, allowed for good progress. Josh drove close up behind the speeding ambulance, to enable him to follow it safely through the red stop lights. His extremely close driving had his police chaperone sitting uncomfortably silent. Trying to appear calm, the officer had his body continually braced—legs stiff, pressing his feet hard into the floor and body into the car seat. His colleague, in the speeding patrol car behind, kept a more comfortable distance.

The convoy turned off South, onto the M25 motorway, across the Queen Elizabeth Bridge and the River Thames, then taking the fastest route to the nearest accident and emergency hospital with a neurology department. Josh followed the ambulance as it drove into the hospital grounds. It pulled up outside the A & E entrance where a team were standing by. The paramedics had radioed ahead so the hospital emergency team were prepared. Josh pulled into a parking bay close by; it was night and the car park was all but empty. He flicked his headlights off and both he and the officer left the vehicle; both running over to the ambulance.

The emergency team had already begun to remove the pod from the back of the ambulance. They slid it onto a scissor lift trolley and slowly lowered it to the floor. The team, two males and one female dressed in scrubs, quickly wheeled the trolley into the hospital through the emergency entrance. Josh followed closely behind. Passing through corridors, the pod was wheeled into the emergency care ward, into a special unit.

The nurse turned, and using her body, obstructed Josh and the officer from entering. "I'm afraid you can't go in. You'll have to wait outside," she ordered. She looked at Josh, "Are you a relative?"

"A friend," he replied. "Can you let me know how she's doing?"

"As soon as we do the preliminaries, I'll let you know. Does she have any close relatives? She doesn't seem to have any online medical records. We need to check for allergies or adverse reactions to drugs."

"No living relatives I'm aware of; her father is deceased. I don't know about allergies."

"Okay, I'll need you to register her at the desk," and the nurse pointed up the corridor. "A doctor will come and see you when ready. You can wait up there." The nurse turned and walked into the restricted area, closing the door behind her.

"Let's do what she says and then I need to ask you a few questions Mister Brannon." His chaperone—the police officer—spoke up.

Escorted by the officer, Josh walked up the corridor and approached the reception desk. A nurse passed him a form on a clipboard to complete, regarding Sofia's admittance as a patient. He took the clipboard, a pen, then sat down. Carefully, without revealing too much about his case, he filled in the form. There were more blanks and "Not Known" comments on the form than answers. He suddenly came to realise that he didn't really know that much about Sofia, that he had barely scratched the surface in understanding her secret life.

He took the "completed" form and handed it back to the nurse receptionist. She looked down at the notes then looked up at him.

"Is this all you have?" she enquired, raising her eyebrows.

"Yeah."

The nurse looked disappointed, "Very well, take a seat."

Josh now needed to get the two police officers off his back, which meant pulling some strings. Both officers were standing close by, watching him intently. They were eager to start their interrogation, as so far, they had kept their distance, until Sofia was out of harm's way. Josh took out his phone and dialled the "office", instructing Control to intercede. He looked over to the officers, passed the controller their police identification numbers on their epaulettes, then hung up.

Both officers walked over to Josh, his chaperone with his notebook open, ready to take notes.

"Mister Brannon, we need to ask you some questions about the lady brought in tonight. Um…let me see now…a Ms Sofia Du Bois," he hesitated on the name while checking his notebook.

At that precise moment, before Josh could say anything, the officer's mobile phone started ringing. He instinctively answered it, allowing the interruption of his questioning. Josh noted a change in the officer's mood, knowing what was being discussed. The confused officer began questioning his new instruction, but was clearly out-ranked by the caller. The call ended abruptly, leaving the officer a little disgruntled and in the dark. The officer closed his notebook, put it away and turned to his colleague.

"We need to leave."

The second officer looked likewise confused. "We still need to find out what happened here."

"Not anymore. We've been called off this one."

"By who?"

"Inspector Knowels; the order came down from the Super. Looks like Mister Brannon's got some influence."

Josh remained quiet, allowing the officers to get over their moment of protestations, and accept their order.

"Well, good night, Mister Brannon." The officer gave a single nod, then began walking back along the corridor, in the direction they had entered. His colleague joined him, still protesting as they left.

Now that Josh had rid himself of two of his problems, he could focus on Sofia. He approached the reception desk and enquired on her progress, just to be told to sit and wait. In his profession, he wasn't accustomed to waiting, but knew he had no choice if he wanted to see Sofia well again. Bursting in on the medical technicians treating her, just to get his answer, wouldn't be helpful. He reluctantly plonked himself in a plastic seat resting against the wall, and folded his arms.

Time was ticking by, and still no word on Sofia's progress. 2am was slowly approaching and Josh could feel the heaviness of his eyes. The tiredness setting in began causing thoughts of failure, failure to protect her. He began thinking he should have pulled her out of GeneRobotix when he had the chance. He knew the danger she was in but allowed her to stay. The tiredness was causing irrational thoughts to set in. It was preventing him from seeing that Sofia had gotten herself involved with GeneRobotix long before he was involved. He also couldn't see that he had just saved her from whatever danger lay in wait for her in China. All he could think about at that tired moment, as his eyes slowly closed, was his failure to act.

"Excuse me...excuse me."

Josh flicked opened his eyes and looked up. A man was standing over him dressed in green scrubs and wearing a surgical cap.

"You're here for Ms Du Bois?" he asked.

Josh quickly checked his watch: 07:30hrs. He had slept soundly through the rest of the night. He hadn't even been disturbed by the hospital staff shift change, or the early morning cleaning crews. He rubbed his gritty eyes and stood up from the plastic chair—his "bed" for the past five-and-a-half hours. His body ached; the side of his neck hurt from the awkward position it had been resting in, as well as having a numb backside.

"Are you here for Ms Du Bois?" repeated the man.

"Yeah. And you are?" asked Josh slowly.

"I'm Doctor Franklin; a surgeon. I've just come out of theatre with Ms Du Bois. Are you a relative? What's your connection to her?"

"I work for the government. Sofia...Ms Du Bois, is involved in a case I'm working on."

"Are you the one that found her?" asked the doctor.

"Yeah. How is she?" Josh was eager to know.

The doctor sighed. "Well...in all honesty, I'm still not sure really. I've never come across anything like this before. I managed to disconnect her from the apparatus she was connected to, but I've had to induce a coma until I can figure out how to proceed further."

As Josh looked at the doctor's scrubs more closely, he focussed on the blood stains. "Is she alright?"

"She's alive, but on life support," answered Franklin. "What can you tell me about her condition?"

"Just what you see Doc." Josh wasn't going to reveal anything that wouldn't help Sofia's situation. "Why did you put her in a coma?"

"Well, the contraption was indeed keeping her alive. And we were able to transfer life support to her from one of our own machines. But—but the problem is, the wire into her brain. Or rather, not so much the wire, I was able to disconnect that, but what it's connected to...."

"I'm following Doc." Josh knew what was coming, but still wanted to hear what he had to say. He wanted to hear it from the lips of a medical expert.

"She has an implanted electronic chip in her upper spinal-cranial area, which appears to have a neuro-connection to her brain. My educated guess, is that it's being used as some kind of interface between the brain and nervous system. I can't remove it as I don't know why it's there. I don't know enough about it to make a valid decision right now, as to whether it's safe to remove.

I have requested a second opinion from a neurosurgeon from The Royal London Hospital. Once I confer with him, I can make a better decision. In the meantime, I'm keeping her under observation in the critical care unit."

"Can I see her?" asked Josh.

"Yes, certainly," and the doctor requested a nurse show Josh the way.

The nurse escorted Josh through the hospital corridors to the intensive care ward. Following her into a room, he looked around at the unconscious patients connected up to various life support machines. She showed him to the corner space near the window. It had a blue screen surrounding the bed which the nurse pulled back, to make way. She stopped and held the screen for Josh to step inside. Josh stepped past the nurse, who then put the screen back and left, leaving him alone with Sofia.

He forced himself to face her. Like the others in the ward, she too was connected up. Sofia was lying flat on her back, tubes and wires connected to her body, like she was a part of some piece of machinery. And the more he looked at her, the greater the sinking feeling he felt inside. He felt helpless, helpless to save her. For him, killing and destruction was easy, but to help another, or create something good and worthwhile, that was hard.

He stepped closer to the bed, and looked at her deathly pale face. He slowly extended his arm and reached for Sofia's hand, touching it gently. She felt cold. The sinking feeling inside of him dropped even more. He reached with both hands to cover hers, trying to warm it up. He took hold of the blanket that was covering her body, and pulled it up further. Slowly, he began to realise that the intimate truth they shared was beginning to vanish. He couldn't console himself, and a single tear rolled down his cheek.

"I'm sorry," he whispered to her, "I should have been there for you...I should have been there."

He gently rubbed the back of his fingers over a part of her cheek that was still bare; a part that wasn't covered by hospital apparatus—between the tubes, wires, and tape. He felt her soft cold skin on his fingers. It was more than he could bear. Inside, he was feeling completely useless. If there was any way he could change the outcome, he would.

After watching her for several minutes, his internal lamenting gradually changed to frustration; frustration and the idea of powerlessness. Thoughts were shifting in his head. He wasn't completely aware of it, but he was beginning to lift his own spirits. The more he thought about the actuality of it all, the more he became aware of its truth. Frustration quickly turned to hate, to suppressed anger. His attention suddenly switched. A powerful feeling inside surged back, a feeling of intenseness he was accustomed to. He had flicked his internal biological switch from being effect to being cause: from weak prey to deadly predator. His deadly focus had switched, switched to the rightful target, to GeneRobotix and Mark Radnus.

CHAPTER 12

I⊤ TOOK JOSH OVER an hour to drive back to his flat from the hospital. He was irritated. The early morning rush hour traffic was at its height, which had caused him immense frustration. But that wasn't the real source of his frustration. His last memory of Sofia lying helpless in the hospital deeply impressed on his conscience, and he was burning to right his wrong of not protecting her. His motive to resolve the case flipped from government interest to deeply personal.

He prepared himself for the day ahead: cold shower, heavy protein breakfast, strip and light clean of his Sig Sauer 9mm pistol. Sitting on the couch putting his weapon back together, all he could think about was Sofia's pale face. "What had she gotten herself into? Why was View Corp working with Radnus and GeneRobotix?" he thought.

He leaned back and began carefully inspecting his thoughts of the past several days, from Operation Sting Bolt—including the facsimile of his friend Liam—, the recently destroyed bunker and the boy facsimile, taking out sergeant Crofts, and his new assignment investigating GeneRobotix. A lot had happened in a short space of time. The more he looked the clearer things became. He flicked back and forth through the pictures in his mind. Suddenly he became aware, he realised that every happening came back to him. He was the link—the common denominator. All paths, past and present, led back to him.

BEEP-BEEP, BEEP-BEEP! BEEP-BEEP, BEEP-BEEP!

Josh picked up his phone from the table and looked at the display, it was the office. He pressed the button to take the call.

"Brannon," he answered.

"Brannon, I need you to come in right away," instructed Harris.

"I'm in the middle of the assignment sir."

"That wasn't a request; I need you in," insisted Harris, and terminated the call.

Josh sensed an underlying panic in Harris's voice. Something was up and he wanted to know what. He picked up his 9mil and slid a loaded magazine up inside the pistol grip—CLICK! He pushed the weapon into its holster, down the left side of his body, and stood up. He put his jacket on, grabbed his keys, and picked up Sniffer, before walking out of the flat to meet with Harris as ordered.

KNOCK KNOCK KNOCK! Josh knocked on Harris's door with a heavy hand.

"Come in!" shouted Harris.

Josh opened the door and walked in, closing it behind him. Harris was in his usual spot, sitting at his desk full of paperwork. Josh wondered if he had ever seen any action beyond ink on paper.

Harris looked up. "Brannon, the case you're currently working on has been put on hold for the time being. I'm assigning you to another. I need a report of your findings so far, on my desk by this afternoon."

"Why's it being shelved?" questioned Josh. He knew something was beginning to smell rotten.

Harris furtively looked away. "We have other priorities come up and I'm short of people."

He couldn't hide his lying, which made Josh even more suspicious. He knew that in order to get more information out of Harris he was going to have to push him.

"You're wrong, and making a big mistake sir! This case is high priority!" argued Josh.

"Brannon, just follow orders!" snapped Harris. He hated his authority being undermined, especially by subordinates. "There's nothing more to do," he hastily added.

Josh calmly looked at him. "And how would you know that sir, when I haven't submitted any reports yet?"

Harris was looking like he had just been checkmated. He remained silent, looking guilty as hell knowing that Josh didn't believe him. Although specifics hadn't been revealed, Harris was beginning to fail at hiding his true agenda and he knew it. "That will be all Brannon," he said quietly, and picked up a piece of paper from his desk and began reading—or pretending to.

For a few seconds more, Josh remained standing, while looking contemptuously at him. He then turned and walked out of the office, with a hidden smile. Unbeknown to Harris, while giving him a bit of a hard time, Josh had been surreptitiously scanning the paperwork on his desk. He knew where the order to take him off the case originated; a name Harris failed to hide in a recently dated communication on his desk: Sir Charles Godfrey—the man Josh met with Sergeant Crofts during Op Sting Bolt.

One thing Josh knew—during investigations—was that the closer one got to the truth, the harder those seeking to hide it would fight back. He had scraped away the dirt and was beginning to hit rock. Now the big boys were stepping in to stop him. But why they put him on this case in the first place was still an unknown, a mystery. Why put someone on a case you don't want them to investigate? Unless the opposite is true; telling someone to stop but knowing they won't. Either way, and regardless of any order, he wasn't going to let this case go. There was more to it than what he was seeing, and he wasn't easily dissuaded.

Josh stopped by T-branch to catch up with Flash. The "white-coats" were gathered in an office together, in some kind of briefing. Through the window, Josh watched Flash sitting at the back, trying to hide his yawning. Clearly the meeting was going well. The head of the branch was standing out in front of the group, pointing to a board with written figures. Josh had no time to waste and stormed in.

"I need to see Flash on a pressing matter," interrupted Josh.

The group instantly looked round, appearing somewhat relieved to have an interesting intermission. The chief nerd upfront took exception to the intrusion, but even he knew operations took precedence over budget meetings. Without seeking permission from his senior, Flash happily sprung from his seat, joining Josh outside the office. They headed to the corner, to his desk.

"What else did you find out on the chip Flash?" Josh jumped straight in.

"Well, as I suspected, its sole purpose is bio-control. It appears to collect and store chemical and impulse data from the brain and nerves. The chip is a brain-computer interface that helps translate brain-cell activity into raw data. The microchip records activity of the brain and translates the brain signals into digital data. The digital data can then be transferred and processed on a computer that would have a machine learning algorithm to decipher it, and then translate those brain signals into commands. Now, once you have the digital commands, you can simply write your own program.

Josh, this stuff is serious. Install this on someone and you turn them into an organic robot. The uses for this technology are endless. You could turn an ordinary housewife into an assassin without them knowing. Just a quick command download, and a head of State's closest friend could become their fiercest enemy." Flash didn't mince his words.

"Can it be removed?" questioned Josh.

Flash pondered for a second or two. "Anything that's inserted can be removed. You just need to know how, and in what sequence. Kind of like removing a chip from inside a computer." Flash smiled at his analogy without thinking about the reality of it.

"A human is no computer Flash," said Josh seriously. His sound distinction between man and machine resonated profoundly on Flash's conscience, removing his smile.

Josh was deeply concerned of the consequences if Sofia's chip was abruptly removed. He was still waiting for the neurosurgeon's phone call on how he planned to proceed. So, in the meantime, Josh was desperate to scrape up as much information as he could; information that could help in the surgeon's decision.

"Well...you know who created it," answered Flash, "Maybe just ask."

Simplicity of solution was what Josh liked, and Flash's answer was the same as his own—a simple solution. He knew the creator and already had limited access.

"Thanks Flash."

Josh quickly left T-branch and headed out of the building to his car. He thought about Harris's instruction, to get his report written up and placed on his desk before noon. It was an order he was about to disregard, as he got into his car and drove out from the compound.

As he was driving, he dialled a number on his phone. Although she didn't know it yet, he was making her his newly acquired informant. His new informant—Jennifer Baxter—answered her phone.

"Hello, Jennifer speaking."

"Jennifer, it's Josh Brannon, I need to meet with you."

"How did you get my number?" she whispered harshly.

Josh ignored her question. "I'm on my way. I'll be there in half an hour."

"I told you; I don't want to get involved."

"You are involved Jennifer and Sofia's life is at stake here. Now where shall I meet you?"

She paused in answering and for a moment Josh thought he had lost her, but then she spoke.

"There's a park not far from here, Rachael and I used to visit during lunch. It's at...."

Josh interrupted, "I know it. See you there in half an hour," and he hung up.

He knew he would need to be firm with Jennifer to get her cooperation. She wasn't willing like Rachael. Jennifer was scared and rightly so. He just hoped his firmness was enough to force her to meet with him.

He raced to the park he had arranged to meet Rachael at, before she was murdered. He hoped Jennifer wouldn't meet the same fate, not because he cared about her, he didn't, he needed information. To him, she was just an asset now, someone to be used. That was the cold and hard truth of it. He was out to see his assignment through—to the bitter end.

Josh was waiting in the park, sitting on a bench watching the road for Jennifer to arrive. He checked his watch: 12:25hrs. He began half expecting a call from Harris about his report, something that was going to be late, very late.

A maroon car pulled up on the edge of the park. Josh watched intently. The door opened and Jennifer stepped out. She looked around and spotted Josh sitting on the bench. She began walking directly towards him; over the grass and not along the pathway. She approached and Josh stood up. She had a blank expression that made him wary, one that appeared as if she didn't fully recognise him. He instinctively knew something was wrong.

Right up close, Jennifer reached into a bag she was carrying, and pulled out a large kitchen knife. Almost immediately she began lunging at him with it—trying to stab him. Josh quickly moved and danced his body from side to side—dodging the knife blade thrusts. As another thrust came at him, he skilfully took hold of her wrist and arm, twisting it into an arm-lock hold. Usually by now, an attacker would have dropped the knife from the pain of the hold, but Jennifer kept on fighting. Josh forced her to the ground, face down in the grass, but still she fought against him. She never screamed or yelled, just acted out violently. He pulled the knife from her hand and threw it aside. In spite of her unusual strength and persistence, Josh was managing to subdue her.

An elderly couple walking their dog, who witnessed the attack, quickly shuffled over. Josh looked up at them.

"Are you okay?" asked the old man. "We saw what happened. Do you want us to call the police?" The man's wife looked worried.

"No, it's okay," replied Josh, "It's just a domestic. We're going through a divorce. I just wish our marriage could have lasted as long as yours."

His imaginative deception worked. The couple smiled and accepted the lie.

"Well young man, 'talking' is the secret to a happy marriage," said the old lady quivering. Her husband smiled, took her arm, and they continued to walk their dog.

Josh looked down at Jennifer, her struggling had slowed considerably; likely due to the rapid exertion of energy she had just expended in such a short space of time. He already suspected the cause of her unusual behaviour. He pushed her hair aside to reveal the back of her neck. There was a fresh cut in her skin, a surgical cut just below the base of her skull. It made complete sense. She was a subject of an experiment at GeneRobotix. He knew she had been discovered by Radnus, and had been implanted with a GRX-5 chip. She had been programmed to kill him.

Now he was landed with another problem. He had no idea what else she had been programmed for; perhaps to kill herself after she had killed him. He needed to de-program her somehow, but couldn't risk taking her back to his flat. He needed to remove or destroy the chip. He came up with a solution after he spotted a nearby garden display; a potential solution that would hopefully be immediate.

He lifted Jennifer off the ground and walked her to the display. It had a set of colourful lights mingled in with flowers and plants to make it look pretty at night. He set her face down on the ground next to it. He put his knee on her back to keep her in place, as she began struggling again. He reached for an electrical cable and pulled it from the display lights—bearing the copper wires inside. He picked up a small twig from the ground, and with it, pushed one bare wire onto the other, creating a spark. He pushed Jennifer's hair to one side again, and in one swift simultaneous move, took his knee off her back and pushed the live wire into the back of her neck. Her body convulsed from the electrical current. Josh immediately pulled the wire away and waited. Jennifer began moaning and groaning, her body limp at first but slowly gained strength. After a gradual increase of consciousness, she began to sit herself up on the grass. She looked hazily at Josh and sighed deeply.

"W-what happened...how did I get here?" she asked, looking around the park in confusion.

"What do you remember Jennifer?" asked Josh.

She screwed her face up from concentrated thought. "Uh—um, our phone call; I remember you calling me at work. I was upset."

"And after that?"

"I don't know. I felt strange. It felt like I had taken a back seat or something; watching my body move. I wasn't fully aware of what I was doing but could still move. I could feel my body, but I wasn't in control of it. It was like a dream," she recounted.

"What else do you remember before that, before our phone call?"

Jennifer screwed her eyes up in an effort to think. "Um...just working as usual."

"Have you been to a doctor lately, or had any procedures done on your neck?" Josh was trying to get her to remember.

"Err...I felt ill yesterday at work, had to see the doctor. I passed out in his office. He said I just had a blackout caused by stress and gave me some pills. It wasn't anything. I felt a pain on the back of my neck afterwards, but he said I just took a bit of a fall and was nothing to worry about. What's happening to me...what's going on?"

"I believe your illness was caused, caused so that your doctor could implant you with a microchip made at GeneRobotix—a chip that overrides your ability to self-control, to make you do what they want. The microchip was inserted into the back of your neck at the base of the skull, which is why when I looked, you have a small surgical incision.

They know you've been passing me information Jennifer; likely your phones and computers have spyware. They just needed to insert the chip and wait for me to contact you. Once they knew we were to meet, and where, they flicked a switch. My guess is, they would have had you kill yourself, after you killed me with the knife."

Jennifer suddenly put a hand over her gaping mouth, after realising what she had done. "Oh my god, I'm so sorry! I remember now...I had a knife. I attacked you. I would never do that." She was shocked at her behaviour.

"It's okay, it wasn't you in control. But you're in danger now. You can't go back to work as they will know they've failed. They will want to 'clean up' their mistake."

"By 'mistake'...you mean me, don't you?" she asked anxiously.

"I'm sorry Jennifer, I can't sugar-coat it. And I don't want you to end up like Rachael. Do you have somewhere you can go for a few weeks? A relative, or friend your company doesn't know about?"

"I have a friend up north. I can see if I can stay with her for a while."

"That's good," replied Josh. "And get rid of your phone."

Jennifer tried standing, but felt a little dizzy. Taking her by the arm, Josh helped her to the bench and they sat down together. She began to cry, the shock of everything suddenly hitting her hard. It was a reality no one could have imagined, and only something a 'conspiracy theorist' would come up with—but this was reality.

It wasn't long before the old couple walking their dog came by again; heading in the opposite direction. They looked over at Josh and Jennifer sitting on the bench together—Jennifer crying. They looked at each other then looked over smiling; believing their advice was working, and perhaps they had helped to fix the "marriage". Josh let them believe their fantasy and attempted a genuine smile to keep them happy.

"Jennifer, I need to know who your doctor is."

She wiped her eyes. "No, he's not my doctor. The company employs him. He works in the laboratory."

"What can you tell me about him?"

"His name is Anthony Faust. He's paid very well, much more than everyone else. He's been with the company for years. I don't know where he lives but the Payroll Department would know. I can ask...." She then burst into tears again, after realising she couldn't go back to ask.

"Describe his features to me; is he German?"

She sniffled. "He's in his early fifties, going grey. He has a bit of a belly. I don't think he's German, he sounds English. The girls in the office call him "Feisty Fausty", he can get quite angry."

"So he has a temper. What about his car, what does he drive?"

"Um...a black Mercedes, it's a company car. He parks it in the executive parking at the front of the building."

"What hours does he work?"

"He's there early morning, before the day staff arrive, and is usually there till late, after the night shift have started."

Josh was making a mental note of everything Jennifer was saying. "He has no family then? No wife?"

"No. He's always eyeing up the girls, but not in a nice way."

"Thanks Jennifer, you've been very helpful."

She managed to smile a little. "How is Sofia? I really like her."

"She'll be just fine," replied Josh, keeping his answer brief.

He didn't want to pass Jennifer any information on Sofia's condition, or whereabouts, as he knew she couldn't be completely trusted. It was no real fault of her own, or that she would intentionally betray anyone, it was just her weak personality that made her a potential liability. She was a weak link.

"What now? What are you going to do?" asked Jennifer nervously.

Josh glared directly into her frightened eyes. "Whatever I need to!"

CHAPTER 13

DISOBEYING ORDERS WAS NO problem for Josh. He could easily discern right from wrong, according to his own survival viewpoint, regardless of orders. In his estimation, shelving the GeneRobotix assignment was next to genocide of the Chinese population. Stopping the Chinese government from acquiring the GRX-5 chips was crucial, and he was damned if he was going to let Harris stop him.

Josh looked down at his phone; it was ringing again. It was another call from Harris. And once again, Josh ignored it. He was ignoring his orders by continuing on the assignment and failing to submit his report; but he didn't care.

It was getting late as Josh continued his surveillance of GeneRobotix, waiting for his new target to appear: Dr Anthony Faust. He had set himself up, parked well away from the building so as not to be seen by security, but close enough to identify Faust once he leaves.

Earlier in the park, Jennifer had given him some useful identifying information of Faust, before they went their separate ways. She was now driving north to her friend's place to lie low for a few weeks; cutting all ties with GeneRobotix at Josh's advice. It had to appear to Radnus his plan had worked, even just for a short while, that she had killed Josh with the blade and turned it on herself. Josh now had a window of opportunity to make use of.

In Jennifer, he had managed to find a way of deactivating the microchip implant, and as crude and painful as it was, it worked. But he had no way of knowing of any side-effects, since it was still hardwired into her brain, and could still be damaging to her. He needed a better solution for Sofia, and he still hadn't heard from the surgeon. And as much as he wanted to focus on her, he had to look at the bigger picture.

Darkness had settled in nicely, giving Josh that comforting feeling he enjoyed: one of being protected by the shadows. The GeneRobotix night shift had already arrived and were likely at their posts, assembling and testing bio-tech products of potential harm. Perhaps they knew, or maybe didn't know, that they were helping to manufacture a product that could imprison the minds of millions. Perhaps they didn't care, for it wasn't to be used on them, or so they hoped, just like the unsuspecting Jennifer Baxter.

The GeneRobotix building at the front was lit up by security and street lighting. It was enough to allow Josh to see movement from the distance he was sitting at. Occasionally, he would use his special night vision binoculars for a close-up view—a T-branch product designed with an advanced image video recording function. There were three cars parked directly outside the main building, one of which was a black Mercedes. This he suspected, was likely Faust's company car that Jennifer had mentioned. Had Josh been able to get closer he would have placed a tracker on it, but couldn't risk being seen.

He checked his watch: 23:10hrs, as a figure appeared, coming out of the building through the main door. Josh lifted the binos to his eyes, ready to take a photo if the opportunity lent itself.

WHOOSH!

A sudden surge of thought impinged on him once he had focussed on the figure through the lenses. Déjà vu flashed in his mind, sucking up his attention. Fortunately though, his control over it had improved, allowing for a faster recovery time. He refocused his attention and sight onto the cause of the déjà vu—a man.

He watched the man, who fitted Jennifer's description and wearing a white lab coat, walk to the black Merc. It was his target—Dr Faust. Why he had caused the Time-fold reaction, Josh didn't know. All he knew was that there was an inexplicable connection between him and Dr Faust. Evidently, GeneRobotix was involved in more than just creating harmful mind-control products and breaching UK trading laws. There was something more sinister going on. It was now making sense that View Corp was involved with GeneRobotix, but why this was the case was still unknown.

Josh continued to observe the Merc with Faust now sitting inside. Its white reversing light illuminated in the dark and the car reversed out from the parking bay. It then drove forward, heading for the exit to leave. Josh started his engine and waited for the Merc to drive on. As soon as the Merc had all but left his sight, Josh switched his headlights on and pulled off to follow.

The lack of other traffic on the road, to use as cover, made the surveillance difficult. Josh followed behind as best he could, keeping a safe distance. So far, the follow seemed to be going well. He knew that if any problems would arise, it would be as soon as Faust drives onto even quieter roads. That would make Josh's car stand out like a sore thumb.

The Mercedes began indicating left and drove into a petrol station just off the roadway. Josh followed and watched as the Merc pulled up in front of the kiosk. He then drove to the furthest petrol pump, pretending he needed fuel and waited. Staying hidden in his car and watching the Merc through the passenger window, Josh reached for his binoculars, resting them in his lap, ready to take a photograph of Faust if the opportunity arose. The Merc's car door slowly swung open. Josh waited, not making any sudden suspicious moves, to see if Faust would look directly over at him. If he did, it could mean that Josh's cover was blown. Dr Faust stepped out of his car, totally ignoring Josh, indicating a high probability the surveillance hadn't been compromised.

Faust, with his back to Josh, walked over to the kiosk's night window to purchase cigarettes. Preparing himself for a sneaky photoshoot opportunity, Josh picked up his binos and placed his right elbow on the steering wheel for stabilisation. Looking through the lenses at the doctor's back, he waited for the precise moment for him to turn around. Faust finished paying and turned. Josh instantly pressed the button on the binos to begin automatically taking a series of photos of him. Satisfied he had snapped some good clear images, he put the binos down and waited for the doctor's next move.

Faust returned to his car and drove back onto the roadway. Josh started his engine and slowly pulled off; making sure he had given the doctor plenty of distance before sitting on his tail again. He followed the Merc for ten minutes or so when he started to get a feeling in his gut that something was wrong. Although there was no sign of compromise, he couldn't help but sense Faust knew he was there. To Josh, it was too obvious he was tailing him, and so needed to make the quick decision to either abort the surveillance or confront him.

As soon as he had decided to intercept Faust's car and pull him over, a black SUV pulled out fast from a side road, sped up and began tailgating Josh's car. Its headlights shone full beam into his rear-view mirror; blinding him. The vehicle, being driven aggressively, bumped the rear of his car, jolting it forwards. Josh quickly dropped to a lower gear and sped up fast with the SUV in close pursuit; both vehicles overtaking the doctor's Mercedes.

Josh's training and innate ability to escape danger kicked in fast as he pushed down on the accelerator. The engine revs of his SQRV were screaming in a high pitch range. He sped through a red light at a junction, simultaneously broke hard and dropped to second gear, while making a sharp left turn; the SQRV tilting hard right but sticking like glue to the road surface. He pushed down fully on the accelerator again, screaming the engine while making it back up the gears with quick changes—still with high revs and pushing the engine to its limit. The pursuing vehicle hardly lost an inch as it stuck with him throughout. From the way the SUV was being driven he knew the driver was a professional. But Josh still had a few tricks up his sleeve.

For several minutes he kept the SUV on his tail, preventing it from overtaking while leading it to a dual-carriageway, away from any built-up area. He fully opened his driver's side window, slid his hand inside his jacket and pulled out his 9mil. As they sped along a straight piece of road, he pushed his left leg up to hold the steering wheel steady and with both hands cocked his weapon. The dual-carriageway was approaching fast. Josh had no idea how many hostiles were in the pursuit vehicle so had to plan for the worst. He had to assume there were four; fully armed and skilled like himself. His plan had to be surprising, aggressive, and above all else, deadly.

The single carriageway turned into the dual road, and as he anticipated the black SUV bolted to overtake. Josh kept to the left and slammed on his brakes, hard enough to suddenly let the SUV leap ahead. As it dashed forward, Josh pointed his pistol out of the window and fired a well-aimed shot at the SUV's front left tyre. The tyre exploded upon the bullet's impact. Josh broke further to let the SUV, now weaving uncontrollably, to pass on ahead. Flopping sounds from the blown tyre quickly changed to a grinding noise as the tyre disintegrated and the bare wheel rim dug in on the road surface. Josh followed the SUV along as the driver tried unsuccessfully to maintain control. The speed they were driving at was too much for it, causing it to suddenly flip and roll. Josh kept with the tumbling ball of metal as it finally settled on a grass verge. The SUV landed on its roof at the left edge of the road, smashed beyond repair.

Josh now had the advantage and needed to keep it that way. "Surprise" and "aggression" of his plan had been achieved, now came the "deadly", if it hadn't already been achieved.

He pushed down hard on the breaks of his car and as soon as it stopped, he leapt out—leaving the engine running with headlights on full beam to illuminate the area. He raced towards what had looked like a new Audi SUV, but now was just a mangled clump of metal. Five metres short of the crashed vehicle, he knelt on one knee, pointing his weapon into what could barely pass for a window. One wheel of the vehicle was still turning, and smoke was beginning to plume from the engine block.

Looking into the wreckage, Josh made out just two occupants, both oriental males. The driver was dead, his body just as mangled as the wreckage surrounding him. He then heard a groan coming from the other side, the passenger. Josh moved tactically to the other side and knelt down, looking through the buckled window at another mangled body. The passenger inside still had a pocket of life left inside of him to slowly draw a weapon—a Chinese made NZ85B 9mm pistol. Josh easily knocked it from the man's limp hand. Still strapped in his seat and hanging awkwardly upside down, the man said nothing.

Keeping his weapon pointed—ready to fire, Josh rapidly searched the passenger, running his free hand over the man's torso, arms and legs. The man moaned in pain as Josh touched his twisted leg. Running his hand over the man's lower leg again, he could feel his tibia had broken and had pierced the skin. Ignoring his dire condition, Josh continued frisking the man's suit jacket. He felt the man's wallet through his outer clothing and removed it. He flipped it open, revealing a Chinese diplomatic ID card, but Josh instinctively knew he was MSS—China's Ministry State Security.

Looking at the MSS agent, he didn't have long to live. Josh knew he couldn't apply heavy means to extract information from him; that would only hasten his death. But just from the fact they were there—that the MSS agents had attempted to take Josh out—was enough for him to know he was on the right track.

He fleetingly wondered if his true identity was known to the Chinese. Chinese intelligence was good at gaining information, it was their specialty. They certainly knew of him, but as what, a British intelligence officer or an investigator for the Department of Trade and Industry? And if the Chinese knew he was British intelligence, would they have alerted Radnus? He just had to continue his cover as a DTI investigator and let it play out to be sure.

Josh looked back along the road for any headlights of approaching vehicles—for unwanted witnesses. A couple of cars had already passed by on the opposite side of the dual-carriageway, but the central barrier had favourably covered the spectacle of the crash. It seemed so far, there were no witnesses.

Luckily for Josh, the scene looked like an everyday Road Traffic Accident, so there was no need to clean up. Apart from any evidence of a bullet being fired, an accident investigator would likely believe the MSS agents had had a blowout and lost control. The tyre Josh shot out was obliterated and the chances of the bullet being found were bordering on negligible. He just needed to make sure he replaced the agent's wallet and weapon, so it didn't appear he had drawn it in defence.

The only loose end left was the all but deceased passenger, who was letting out the odd groan here and there. Would an autopsy detect that he finally died of suffocation and not of his wounds? Josh couldn't be certain of that, but he also couldn't leave him as a potential witness. He had to risk eliminating him. Josh pushed his 9mil into its holster and reached out to cover the MSS agent's nose and mouth with his hand. Just as he was about to block his airways, the agent let out one final breath. Josh checked for a pulse; he was off the hook; the man was dead.

Before leaving, Josh checked the wreckage and bodies where he possibly could, for any intelligence. They were both clean apart from their official identification purporting to be diplomats. The Chinese agents had come out clean—no intel. Josh managed to locate their mobile phones; both Government Issue. The driver's had been smashed in the accident but the passenger's was still intact. Josh checked the phone over carefully, knowing it would have built-in spyware. He smashed the front and back camera lenses on a sharp piece of metal poking out from the wreckage, in case the phone was the type that automatically took photographs—remotely sending images back to the Chinese. Access to it was difficult. The phone was security protected with a bio-metric fingerprint and voice recognition system. He could get around the fingerprint protection—using the dead man's finger, but not the voice recognition. His only option now was to remove any power sources so the Chinese couldn't track it, then take it back to T-branch for stripping and analysis. He pulled it open and removed the battery.

Carrying the MSS agent's deactivated phone, Josh rushed back to his car—the engine still running. He glanced along the dual-carriageway before driving off the grass verge onto the roadside. It was clear—no traffic, so Josh put his foot down; speeding away from the "accident".

As he drove, Josh dialled the control room at HQ. The connection was instant. "Verify: One, Five, Three, One."

The control operator's voice pattern computer system immediately verified Josh's identification code. "ID verified. Go ahead Brannon," replied the operator.

"I need a location check on a black Mercedes, VRN: Lima, Foxtrot, Two, One, Whiskey, Sierra, November. Last seen heading North on the A406 North Circular." Josh relayed Faust's vehicle details and vehicle registration number to Control.

"Roger that, checking now," replied the operator. "The vehicle just passed Junction 7 on the M11 heading North."

"Roger. Give me a location update feed on this target," ordered Josh.

"Roger. You should be receiving your feed now. Confirm?"

Josh checked his phone. He pressed on a map app and an icon appeared; representing Dr Faust's black Mercedes. "Received, thanks, out," and Josh terminated the call.

Judging from the icon, Faust was travelling fairly fast and Josh had plenty of ground to cover to close the gap. He pushed down on the accelerator, speeding along the North Circular and eventually joined the M11 motorway heading north. The motorway was relatively clear of traffic, allowing Josh to hog the outside lane at a steady one hundred and twenty miles an hour. And it wasn't long before he was passing the junction of the M25 London Orbital Motorway.

Every few minutes he checked the map icon for the position of Faust's car. Josh was easily closing the distance between them and had gained much ground in a short space of time. Luckily, so far, the speed he was travelling hadn't attracted the unwanted eyes and intervention of traffic police.

He checked the app again. Faust had turned off, leaving the motorway at Junction 8, and entered London Stansted Airport. Josh quickly contacted Control, to check for flight bookings under the name of "Dr Anthony Faust". A name search produced no results, indicating he was either just meeting with someone or using an alias to leave the country.

Josh reached for the binoculars he had used to take photos of Faust, and while juggling between buttons on the binos and keeping his car straight, uploaded them to Control to utilise. Now he needed to condense a thirty-minute drive into ten.

Twelve minutes later Josh arrived at Stansted Airport. The icon on his phone—Faust's Merc—had been stationary since it first stopped at the airport. He drove to international departures, guessing that's where Faust would be. Josh parked up and walked into departures. The terminal was less busy due to the time of night, so would make it easier for him to comb through the passengers. He walked up to an armed police officer standing by the entrance.

"I'm Brannon. My company called ahead. I believe you're expecting me."

The officer nodded, "Yes sir, come with me to security."

The officer escorted Josh inside, taking him through the concourse to the airport's security control room. The officer opened the door and stepped inside. Josh followed. Inside the room were two airport security officers, sitting in front of multiple CCTV monitors stretched across the wall. One turned around, the older of the two.

"My security manager has already left, but I've been told to assist. We received the photo of the man you're looking for, but so far, we haven't found him. Unfortunately, there are some camera blind spots, but the check-in and security gates are well covered."

"What about the car?" asked Josh.

"We've located it in the short-stay parking. One of our guys is watching it. Can you give us more info?" All three looked at Josh.

"He's a person of interest; child human trafficking suspect," lied Josh. With them believing that, he knew they would put in the extra effort of finding Faust. "How many men do you have on shift?"

"Er—this time of night, besides the guys checking passengers through, eleven. I've got eleven mobiles on the ground."

"Right. Share that photo with those eleven; the more eyes the better. Get one of them to check with boarding, and cover the exits best you can. Anyone spots him, I want to know first."

"Sure. I can only send the photo by text," replied the security officer.

"Okay, let's get it circulated," ordered Josh.

"Anything more I can do?" asked the police officer.

"Stay here until we can make a positive ID. Then I'll need you to assist."

The security officer sent the photo out to the officers in the terminal, and radioed each to confirm they had received it. He then continued to monitor the airport CCTV system, swiftly moving the cameras—zooming in on possible suspects. Everyone had their tasks, but still, nothing was coming up. Time was ticking by and Josh was beginning to get twitchy. He knew Faust had slipped through the net. The time delay in catching him was getting wider and wider. It was beginning to become obvious.

The office phone started ringing. The security officer picked it up, listened briefly, then turned to Josh after hanging up. "That was security at private jet hangar number one. There's a possible sighting of your man. Unfortunately, he's already left on a private jet."

Josh needed to confirm the identity for himself. "Okay, let's check the CCTV recording."

The security officer stood up. "Hangar one has a separate system. I'll take you over there."

A short drive to Hangar 1, all three: Josh, the security, and police officer, made their way to the customs and security office. The officer who had phoned through with the possible identification of Faust was waiting for them. He had the recorded CCTV video footage set up on the security monitor, ready for them to watch.

"Okay, let's take a look," said Josh.

All eyes were glued to the screen. The officer began playing the recorded footage of the passengers leaving. Josh felt a sudden sinking feeling inside his stomach, as he watched the video of Faust, clearing to board a private flight. He had left in a hurry and without any luggage.

After checking with staff in air traffic control, it was confirmed that the flight was already in the air heading for Germany—the city of Munich. It had just cleared UK airspace, flying over the English Channel. Faust was out of reach.

"What now sir?" asked the security officer.

"You can stand down," replied Josh, disappointingly. "You can stand your men down."

Josh looked again at the screen, at the paused image of Dr Faust. He gazed at the image in distant thought. He didn't know why, or know from where, but his recognition of Faust ran deep in his mind. Faust was somehow a part of his personal quest to find his truth, but he had let him slip through his fingers. Faust had escaped: but only for now!

CHAPTER 14

THE FOLLOWING MORNING, JOSH had been summoned to see Harris. He was waiting outside his office; full report in hand of his findings concerning his assignment—GeneRobotix. He had typed it up after returning from Stansted Airport, in the early hours of the morning, and had only managed to get a few hours of sleep. His eyes were stinging from tiredness.

It felt like being back at school, waiting outside the headmaster's office to receive his punishment. When his colleagues passed by, they would give him a sideways glance; they didn't want to be associated with him in case they too would have their names written in Harris's "bad book". It had clearly gotten around that Josh had gone "rogue" for the day—disobeying Harris about dropping the GeneRobotix case. Now he seemed to be in the doghouse with everyone. It was interesting to see how fickle and cowardly "friends" could be, once one was caught up in trouble: suddenly withdrawing their support. The old adage about "knowing who one's true friends are when in trouble" came to light for Josh. It showed who he could really trust.

"I hear you're in the shit again Josh," said Mohammed; stopping by on his way to the gym.

Josh looked up from his seat. "Well, when you stir a big pot of shit, some of it sticks," he replied.

"Come by the gym afterwards if you want to release some steam. We can wipe some of that shit away."

Josh raised one corner of his mouth; a slight smile of gratitude. It was all he could muster under the circumstances. Mohammed gave a reassuring nod and continued on his way. Not everyone had abandoned him and it was always good to see who his true friends were. One good loyal friend was worth more than a thousand fake ones. Mohammed stayed true. He didn't allow other people's prejudices to reduce his loyalty and friendship. He was willing to be seen with Josh. It just went to show it's not about colour of skin, religious beliefs, or anything superficial. It was about the person inside; the real being and their demonstrated humanity towards their fellows, no matter what. That was the true test of a friend.

"Brannon!" Harris's raised voice sounded through the door.

Taking a deep breath, Josh stood up. He opened the door to Harris's office and walked in. It felt like walking through the door to the gallows. He knew he was a condemned man as Harris was always looking for a reason to get rid of him. It looked like he now had one. Josh just had to somehow convince Harris of the importance of the case, without making him feel he had made a grave mistake in shelving it. Harris's ego wouldn't allow himself to be wrong; his ego was the problem Josh had to overcome. Both had to be big enough to set aside their differences, for the greater good of saving the Chinese people from their own despotic government.

"Morning sir!" In spite of his exhaustion, Josh gave a hearty greeting; he needed to stay on top of his game.

"Sit down Brannon," said Harris coldly. "I've asked Marion from Human Resources to sit in on this meeting."

"Righto sir."

Josh took a seat across from Harris and the HR lady. She had a notepad and pen at the ready and barely acknowledged Josh's presence. Her eyes were fixed downwardly on the notepad, like she already knew what was coming and couldn't confront looking at him. It dawned on Josh that a decision had already been made in his absence; that they were now just going through the formalities to avoid breaking any employment laws.

"How are you doing Brannon? Are you fit and well?" asked Harris insincerely.

Josh knew what was coming but went along with it. "All good sir," he replied.

"I must ask; do you want a representative with you during this meeting?"

"No."

Marion had begun writing on her pad; getting everything down for the record.

"Brannon, this is a formal disciplinary addressing your recent disregard for orders in the field. You were specifically ordered yesterday to stop investigating case number IG/43, and to submit your report. You blatantly disregarded those instructions and took it upon yourself to continue the investigation. Do you have anything to say?" Harris happily laid the charges out.

"It's all in my report sir."

Josh placed his report on Harris's desk and slid it across to him. The report contained everything about GeneRobotix and the trade deal with the Chinese, the GRX-5 chip and its purpose, and the suspected murder of the whistle-blower—Rachael Banks. What the report failed to mention though, was Sofia and View Corp's involvement, as well as the slight disagreement he had had with the two Chinese MSS agents. He also left out the details of sergeant Crofts's death and the Hill Brother's pathetic attempt on his life. Josh's report was solely geared around exposing GeneRobotix, Radnus, and Dr Faust.

Harris ignored the report lying on his desk, not even giving it a single glance. His mind was already made up. He looked at Josh, like a cowardly pack of hyenas would at a cornered crippled prey, salivating at the moment of final strike. Harris had Josh exactly where he wanted him. And Josh knew, that no matter what he said, it would fall on deaf ears. This was the final step onto the gallows trapdoor before the lever was to be pulled; dropping him through the floor with a snap of death. He had nothing to lose now, being that the outcome had already been decided.

"For the record sir, the discontinuation of this case is a bloody mistake; a mistake made from either incompetent leadership, or complicity in working with the Chinese government to suppress its people. I hope it's the first reason, but I suspect not. My formal recommendation, sir, is to continue investigating this case. To shelve it because of any prejudice or dislike for me is foolish, and I hope you're no fool sir. I urge you to reconsider, not for me, but for the millions of decent ordinary Chinese under a tyranny they don't want."

Josh looked sternly at Harris whilst giving his final words. Marion lifted her head, after scribbling away in short-hand at what Josh had vehemently voiced. His reasoning and honesty had gained her full respect.

"Thank you Brannon," said Harris uncaringly. "I have to advise you; I am putting you on two weeks unpaid suspension from your duties as of now. You are required to hand in your weapon to the armoury and any other company equipment, including your phone. You are not to disclose any information on this case to anyone; you will not continue on this or any other assignment during your suspension. Franks is waiting outside; he will escort you out. That will be all."

Harris leaned back in his chair, openly showing his smugness at having finally gotten rid of Josh, albeit for only two weeks. Josh momentarily considered the unthinkable; wanting to introduce Harris's arrogant face to his fist. Instead, he stood from his chair and quietly walked to the door. He had other plans on his mind.

Before leaving, Josh looked down at Harris. "Be nice to have a spot of holiday sir. Thanks very much," he said, smiling.

From the cocky remark, Harris's face suddenly looked like it had been trodden on. He just couldn't seem to keep Josh down and it irked him no end. Josh walked out of the office to be met by Franks who was standing quietly by the doorway.

"Franks," greeted Josh, with a friendly nod.

"Brannon," replied Franks, with a bland expression.

"Well, I guess it's a trip to the armoury then."

Franks nodded, "That's right. And the Quartermaster."

"Well, after you then," and Josh gestured with his hand for Franks to lead the way.

Franks escorted Josh to the armoury, passing a few of their colleagues on the way. Their looks said it all; the word on his suspension had already circulated. Josh and Franks were standing by the armoury window—a small opening through a caged room.

Smithy appeared. "Alright Josh. I've heard all about it. Gossip travels fast you know."

"Yeah, I know."

"Sorry to have to do this. Gonna need your weapon and ammo."

Under the watchful eye of Franks, Josh pulled out his 9mil. He removed the loaded magazine and placed it on the window counter. He pulled back the slide on the pistol—locking it in place and placed it next to the magazine. Smithy picked up the weapon and checked it.

"Spare mags?" asked Smithy.

Josh removed a further two full magazines from his holster and placed them on the counter. It was beginning to feel like an uncomfortable defrocking ritual. Stripping him of his weapon was like being stripped of his dignity.

Smithy took all three magazines and the pistol. "Have a good holiday Josh," he winked.

Franks butted in, "Quartermaster's store next."

Under orders, Franks escorted Josh to the QM's store to hand in his equipment: shoulder holster, knife, and phone. He was then escorted from the building to the parking lot. Franks stood by as Josh got into his own car; making sure he left to begin serving out his suspension. Josh started the engine. He drove out from his parking bay and passed through security. As he drove out into the street, he smiled to himself, smiling about the one gadget they didn't find out about, that they didn't confiscate: "Sniffer"—Flash's device.

After a tiresome journey Josh arrived home. He checked his watch: 10:34hrs. He was thoroughly exhausted. He made himself a mug of tea and plonked himself down on the sofa. Random thoughts drifted in and out of his mind as he began to relax a little. He blew on his tea to cool it down and took a couple of sips. He put the mug on the table, rested his head on the back of the sofa and within a few minutes drifted off to sleep.

"Sofia!"

Josh woke suddenly; startled by a dream about Sofia. He checked the time on his watch again: 12:30hrs. Two hours had passed like it was two minutes. He checked for messages on his phone; nothing. Sofia's surgeon hadn't contacted him at all about her condition. Josh picked up his phone to call the hospital.

"Dale Valley Hospital," a receptionist answered.

"I'm enquiring about a patient admitted two evenings ago: Sofia Du Bois."

"Are you a relative?" asked the receptionist.

"A close friend, I was the one that brought her in. I spoke with Doctor Franklin; he can vouch for me."

"Okay, let me check the computer. Ah…here we are; it says she was discharged by Doctor Franklin the same day of her operation."

Josh was met with complete surprise. "Discharged; I don't understand?"

"Umm…the record says she was released to another medical team for transfer…er…at ten-thirty that morning. I don't have any other details."

"Is there a transfer form; a name?"

"Let me check transfers…yes, here we are, a 'Doctor Faust.'"

Josh tensed up, gritting his teeth. "Is Doctor Franklin in today?"

"Yes, but he's in surgery. Can I pass on a message?"

"No," and Josh hung up.

He sprung from the sofa and darted into the bedroom. He pulled open a cupboard door and reached up to a shelf. After pushing some old blankets out of the way, he grabbed a metal lock-box, placing it on the bed. He reached for a key from the side-cupboard drawer and unlocked the box. He flipped the lid open and removed a Glock 19 handgun—an untraceable gift, courtesy of Jonesy. Josh selected a magazine from the box and began loading it with 9mm rounds. After pushing in the last round with his thumb, he slotted the mag into the gun. He pushed the weapon into a holster and inserted it into the waistband of his jeans; flapping his jacket over the top to conceal it.

He strode into the living room, grabbed his car keys and left the flat. He ran down the stairway to the car park, where he noticed something attached to his car windscreen. Josh approached with caution; ready to pull out his weapon. A piece of paper had been placed under the wiper blade. But instead of immediately removing it, as any ordinary person would, he left it in place and made a thorough sweep of the parking area—making sure he wasn't being watched. He then checked beneath his car for devices. Once everything was cleared, only then did he remove it. Using the sleeve of his jacket, to preserve any fingerprints, he unfolded the paper and read the handwritten message: "KNOW YOUR ENEMIES".

He wondered what it meant; who had put it there. It was an added problem to his list; his home had been compromised. But he didn't have time to play someone's cryptic game; he needed to find Sofia once again.

After getting into his car, he put the note inside a folded piece of paper he took from a notepad; dropping it into the door's side-compartment. He then started the engine and quickly headed out of the building.

Driving as fast as he could, through the dense London traffic, he made his way to the Dale Valley Hospital where he last saw Sofia. He slotted his car between an old Mini Cooper and Volkswagen Golf in the carpark, before walking briskly to the hospital's main reception.

Josh immediately interrupted a receptionist's conversation with her colleague. "I'm looking for Doctor Franklin, the neurosurgeon."

The intensity in his voice instantly grabbed the receptionist's attention. "Is it concerning a patient?" she replied.

"Yes, it's important. Is he here?"

"Let me check for you."

The receptionist picked up a phone and dialled. Speaking loudly, Josh listened in to her quick conversation. She put the phone down and returned her attention to him.

"Doctor Franklin is busy right now. He's just come out of surgery and needs to prepare for his next operation. Can I pass him a message?"

"No. I'll come back," replied Josh and walked off.

He had overheard the receptionist's phone call, saying Dr Franklin was cleaning up. Josh walked out of reception and asked the first nurse he bumped into, the way to the neurology department. The nurse pointed and Josh, taking her direction, headed along the corridor while following the overhead signs. He reached the neurology department and watched the various hospital staff weaving in and out of the rooms. He spotted a doctor dressed in scrubs and tagged along, following him to the surgery unit.

"Excuse me. You're not supposed to be in here!"

A loud voice spoke out from an open side door. A fat middle-aged nurse appeared from a recovery room, glaring at Josh, and looking stern. She darted over to block him from going further, putting her large body between him and where he needed to go. Josh put out one hand and brushed her aside like she was nothing; a feather blown by a strong hurricane. She protested loudly, causing the heads of staff to turn to see what was happening. She followed Josh, still protesting, as he searched the ancillary and staff rooms of the department for Dr Franklin. Each time he opened a door he called out Franklin's name.

"Yes!" Finally, a voice responded to one of Josh's calls. He walked into the men's changing room, followed by the persistent nurse who ignored the "Male" sign on the door.

"I'm sorry Doctor Franklin. I tried to stop him!" The nurse was irate, standing up to Josh like she wanted to fight him.

"That's okay. I'll speak to Mister Brannon. You can leave now Nurse Jackson."

Dr Franklin calmed her down and continued washing his hands. The nurse gave Josh a dirty look as she walked out of the men's room.

"What do you want now Mister Brannon? I thought you got what you wanted. I have to say it was against my better judgement but when threatened...well...."

"I'm sorry! What are you saying?" quizzed Josh, a little confused at what Franklin was talking about.

"What?" Franklin stopped washing his hands and turned to Josh, looking somewhat baffled himself. "The other day...removing Ms Du Bois against my professional opinion," he continued. "Are you okay?"

Franklin was looking at Josh, like he was some kind of mental patient that had just broken out of an institution. And Josh, he was feeling like he had stepped into something else, something it seemed that he should be aware of, but wasn't.

"That's what I'm here about; Ms Du Bois!" Josh was beginning to raise his voice. "I phoned and was told she had been removed. I want to know where and by whose authority?"

Franklin frowned heavily. "Well...by you, of course," he replied. "Are you sure you're okay?"

Josh was more confused than ever. Their conversation seemed to be on different subjects, different wavelengths altogether. He was beginning to lose his cool but quickly steadied his anger and channelled his thoughts.

"Doctor Franklin, WHERE—IS—SOFIA?" Josh articulated his words slowly, with an intensity that gave a clear warning, that if not answered satisfactorily, something unpleasant would be inflicted upon the doctor.

Franklin heeded the loaded message and looked nervous. "I don't understand what you're saying. You came back for her. You took her with you. What do you want me to say?"

"So...you're saying...I came back and took Sofia, Ms du Bois, from the hospital?"

"That's correct. The same morning after I operated. You left and then came back," answered Franklin, still looking at Josh as though he had lost his marbles.

"I need you to show me the hospital's CCTV footage. I need you to clear it with security!" demanded Josh.

"Okay. Let me finish up here and we'll go."

Once Franklin had dried his hands, both he and Josh stepped out of the men's room into the corridor. Using an internal hospital phone on the wall, Franklin contacted reception to inform security they were on their way to the security office. They walked together silently; both of their confusions needing to be straightened out. Franklin was beginning to worry he was entertaining the delusions of a crazy person. And Josh, he was beginning to think he was a crazy person.

Franklin knocked on the security door. It opened. Two security staff were waiting; standing by to restrain Josh if needed. Nurse Jackson had already stopped by, to overly inform them—with her wild exaggerations—about how Josh had "thrown" her to one side and "crashed" through the ward "screaming his head off". Luckily, they knew Nurse Jackson well enough to know better than to take action based on her word.

At the instruction of Franklin, one of the security officers began searching for camera footage on the Digital Video Recorder. He brought up the video footage on the monitor, from the date and time Josh had brought Sofia into the hospital. As the video played, Josh and Franklin reviewed the events of two nights ago; watching the A&E staff wheeling the pod through the doors late that evening—the pod Sofia had been encapsulated in.

"Okay, show me the time when Ms Du Bois was transferred," ordered Josh.

The officer pushed the fast-forward button, zipping the video footage through the night to just before ten-thirty the following morning, when Sofia was reportedly transferred. The officer pushed the "play" button and they all began watching the monitor. Josh watched intently. The multi-camera view on the screen showed the various camera positions around the hospital entrance: all camera recordings playing at the same time.

"There!" snapped Franklin, pointing at one of the camera views.

The security officer clicked a button to put the view in full frame—taking up the whole monitor. Josh watched as it played.

WHOOSH!

Suddenly Josh's focus waned considerably; his perceptions deeply dulled. His attention bounced from the screen directly back into his head. Something powerful had sucked in his thoughts, as though the millennia of time had been violently pulled into the void of a black hole. Déjà vu struck him hard. Something he saw, but instantaneously forgot, had triggered a new and powerful Time-fold experience, one that was difficult to pull away from.

"Mister Brannon? Mister Brannon? Are you alright?" called Franklin.

Hearing Franklin's muffled voice in his head gave Josh a familiar marker, a beacon to follow that would pull him out of the mind void.

"Mister Brannon? Are you alright?" repeated Franklin.

Franklin's voice slowly pulled Josh back to the present, helping him refocus. He was back.

"Yeah...yeah, I was just thinking." Josh pretended like nothing had happened.

Dr Franklin wasn't easily fooled though, looking at Josh with scepticism. He was still trying to figure him out as to whether he was nuts or not.

Josh put his attention back onto the monitor, to watch the video. However, during the Time-fold episode, the video footage had continued playing past the crucial moment that appeared to have been the trigger.

"Play it again," demanded Josh.

The officer wound back the footage and pressed play, allowing it to play at normal speed. The first striking image that came into camera view was that of a hospital bed, being wheeled towards the exit by hospital staff. Josh knew it was Sofia. He knew it to be her by instinct alone, despite not being able to see her face. A few seconds later, following behind, two males came into view. They had their backs to the camera but Josh sensed something. He sensed something unbelievable he couldn't reconcile.

"Show me the facing camera!"

The security officer clicked on another camera angle—a camera facing inwards at the hospital exit that recorded the front of people leaving. He rewound the footage again and pressed play. This time Josh was able to see faces. He watched again as the hospital bed was being pushed out. This time he could clearly see Sofia's face; she was connected up to a life support machine. He continued watching as the two males entered the frame. Josh recognised Dr Faust straight away, as he did when he saw the back of him from the other camera angle. But what he wasn't prepared for, what he couldn't accept, was the male accompanying Faust.

"Pause it!" snapped Josh.

The security officer quickly paused the video. Josh froze, staring deeply at the image of the accompanying male on the screen. The more Josh looked, the harder it took for him to swallow the truth of who he was looking at. Franklin stood by, somewhat vindicated by the image. Both looked at each other, then looked back at the screen—and the clear image of Josh walking alongside Dr Faust.

CHAPTER 15

AFTER A DEEP AND private conversation with Dr Franklin, Josh managed to convince him to not mention anything of what had happened. Luckily with what Franklin had dealt with, regarding Sofia's operation and the implanted chip, he had become easier to convince that things were not always black or white; that there are many shades of grey. However, there were limitations on what Josh could or would disclose to him. The idea of another "Josh Brannon" identity walking the streets, and why, would fly in the face of reason. Franklin would most certainly call for a psychiatrist to section him under the Mental Health Act. Josh was also having a hard time convincing himself of the strangeness of having a duplication of himself walking around. And it made it even tougher to swallow, knowing that this other "Josh Brannon" was collaborating with Dr Faust.

Before leaving the Dale Valley Hospital, Josh obtained a copy of the CCTV footage on computer disc, showing Sofia's removal. Dr Franklin had also provided him with a copy of the transfer form: written on it was Dr Faust's signature and the location she was transferred to—a psychiatric hospital in North London.

Driving into the psychiatric hospital grounds, Josh looked across at the main building—a grandiose old manor house. It had several stone steps leading up to the main entrance; the entrance flanked by two impressive pillars on both sides. There were extensions and out-buildings set back behind the manor house, hidden away. The building, probably built in the seventeen or eighteen hundreds for some person of nobility, was showing its age. Cracks and mildew covered the stone walls. The windows were all closed and despite the manor house looking pleasant from afar, the hospital gave off a sinister perception the closer one got.

Josh parked near the entrance and walked into the main reception. It was quiet, not one person on duty. He walked up to the reception desk, a newly built addition that looked out of place. A visitor's book was open and in plain view. He leaned over, rotated the book and began thumbing through the pages, looking for an entry. He dragged his finger down the page looking for Sofia or Dr Faust's name. Nothing had been entered.

"Can I help you?"

Josh looked up to the top of a carpeted stairway. A middle-aged woman was standing, looking down at him.

"I'm with Doctor Faust. I came the other day with a patient—Ms Du Bois."

Josh lied. He knew if Faust had brought Sofia to the psych hospital, then his double—the facsimile Josh Brannon—would have accompanied him. Josh was hoping the hospital staff would recognise him as being the facsimile that came in with Faust, so he could easily gain access. That would make things so much smoother—for them.

"Let me get Doctor Andrews."

The woman walked off. She returned a couple of minutes later and called Josh upstairs. She showed him to an office, knocked on the door and walked in. Josh followed. The room was large with high walls and ceiling, with books covering most of the walls in old wooden bookcases. A wiry looking man holding a book was standing by a large window. His face was gaunt and pale, like he hadn't eaten or seen much of the light of day. He looked like he had an extreme vitamin deficiency. His hair was scraggly and he wore an old pair of wired spectacles, resting halfway down his nose that he looked over the top of.

"That will be all Ms Fletcher," said Dr Andrews.

The lady walked out of the office and closed the door. Dr Andrews stared unpleasantly at Josh, scrutinizing him over the top of his glasses, as though trying to read his mind.

"What do you want?" asked the psychiatrist impatiently.

"Doctor Faust wants assurances his patient is okay."

Josh was playing a risky bluff, hoping he could trick Andrews into either taking him to Sofia, or give him information on her whereabouts. For the bluff to work, he had to keep his conversation very general, to avoid being discovered he wasn't the "Josh Brannon" working with Faust. So far, it seemed to be working.

"I can assure you she's fine! Now I need to get on with my business and stop with these interruptions!" snapped Andrews.

"Doctor Faust wants to be sure," replied Josh. He wasn't letting go until he got what he needed.

Andrews huffed and puffed like a madman. "Follow me!" he snapped again.

He opened the office door and walked briskly out. Josh followed along. They headed down the carpeted stairway, walked past Ms Fletcher on reception, and on towards the rear of the manor. They continued through a connecting corridor that looked as though it had been added since the 1940s. It was like walking into a prison. There were closed locked doors along the corridor, leading into patient confinement rooms. Fingernail scratch marks were visible on the walls next to the doors—an indication of enforced patient detention.

The psychiatrist led Josh to a nearby staff room, where two male mental health nurses were eating and watching TV. As soon as they spotted Andrews, they jumped up like a couple of kids being caught doing something wrong. They both looked worried, but as soon as Andrews gave a hidden signal their demeanour changed. They looked aggressive. Josh immediately detected something wrong and knew he had been rumbled.

Andrews snapped at the two male nurses, "I'm detaining this man under the Mental Health Act!" He pointed at Josh as the so-called mental patient. "Lock him in a seclusion room!"

The male nurses pounced as Andrews quickly stepped out of the way. They lunged for Josh but he was already prepared. He had been harbouring his anger over the past several days—over the loss of Sofia and now his suspension—so was secretly longing for some serious payback and release. The two nurses and Dr Andrews had no idea of what was coming to them.

Both nurses charged Josh at once. That was how they subdued patients; by using an overpowering force. But Josh was no patient; he was a trained intelligence operative with a special set of skills. He picked up a nearby chair and thrust it hard into the legs of one of the nurses, making him trip and fall—one man down. With the second nurse, it was a simple sharp punch to the throat; he began to croak as he gasped for air. Josh wasn't finished but just getting started. The first nurse was clambering up still, his head at waist height as Josh brought his knee up and jammed it hard into his face. The nurse flew backwards to the floor, blood splattered over his white uniform.

Out of the corner of his right eye, Josh caught sight of Andrews coming at him. He had a syringe in his right hand and jumped forwards, attempting to inject Josh with a psychotropic drug. Josh quickly stepped back out of the way, dodging the needle. He then pushed down hard on Andrews's inner elbow with his right hand and simultaneously bent the psychiatrist's arm back with his left, jabbing the needle into Andrews's neck. Josh pushed on the syringe plunger—pumping the drug into Andrews. The psychiatrist panicked and ran off with the syringe still stuck in his neck.

Josh turned his attention back to the two cowardly thugs and lunged at them. He allowed himself to go psychotic. He shut off all reasoning and began working them over hard. It was as though he was watching a killing machine from a distance, outside his body, as it went hammering in full force. The psychotic episode lasted until he was satisfied he had expended all rage. Gradually, he came back to witness the aftermath of his revenge. Both nurses were unconscious, half dead, blood covered their entire faces and uniforms. One nurse had a missing ear—ripped off as he tried desperately to escape. Josh had given them the same treatment they likely gave to their patients.

Calming his breathing, Josh focussed his mind. He approached one of the nurses, who was bent over a broken table, and pulled off a set of keys from his belt. Josh walked out of the staff room, back into the corridor. Using the keys, he opened the doors to the seclusion rooms one by one, looking for Sofia. What he witnessed though, was a failure of mental health and a betrayal of genuine help. The patients in each room were strapped to a bed, heavily beaten, and dosed up to the eyeballs with mind-altering psychiatric drugs. None of the patients were responsive. And two of the female patients looked as though they had been sexually abused; the abusers not cleaning up after them.

Josh could feel his rage gauge beginning to fill up again, especially as Sofia wasn't there. He threw the keys on the floor and began hunting for Andrews. Josh raced back to reception to find Ms Fletcher kneeling on the floor, leaning over the drooling psychiatrist. The drug he had attempted to inject Josh with had done its work. Andrews was comatose on the floor.

Two hours later, Andrews came round. Josh had him strapped to one of the beds in the seclusion room. Ms Fletcher and the two male nurses were locked in another room.

"Where is Sofia Du Bois?" asked Josh calmly, standing next to the bed.

Andrews slowly looked up, focussing his eyes on Josh. His eyes still looked dull from the anti-psychotic drug he had mistakenly taken.

"You — need — to — let — me — go. I'm—going—to—call—the—police," slurred Andrews.

Josh could see he needed to get some life into the doctor before he could have a semi-intelligent conversation with him. He needed to elevate the doctor's adrenalin level. Josh looked around the room and pulled a medical cart over to the bed. The ECT electro-shock machine was already plugged in and ready to use. The doctor watched as Josh, pressing buttons and flicking switches, figured out how to get the machine to work.

"You can't use that on me it will kill me," protested Andrews.

Already his adrenaline was kicking in at the thought of getting electro-shocked. But still it wasn't enough, so Josh continued. He placed both electrodes to the doctor's head, one on each side of the temple. The doctor began shaking his head from side to side to prevent Josh from zapping him. Andrews's fear was driving up his adrenaline, making him more conscious.

"Please, please, I'll tell you anything. Don't hurt me!" he yelled.

Josh put the electrodes down; satisfied he would get a better response now.

"Where's Sofia Du Bois?"

"I don't know. Doctor Faust asked me for a favour, to hold her here while he set up the paperwork to have her transferred. That's all I know."

"Transfer to where?"

"I don't know. He didn't say."

"How well do you know Faust?"

"Academically, we went to the same university; nothing more than that."

"Why did you help him?"

Andrews kept quiet as Josh hit a nerve. He knew what Faust had over him. Faust knew about the psychiatrist's perverted little hotel of a psychiatric hospital, and used it as blackmail. Andrews and his staff were just perverted predators preying on broken people for sex and financial gain. Whilst the doctor was out cold and the nurses and Ms Fletcher were locked up, Josh had a poke around Andrews's office. Looking for files on Sofia, he came across a sordid collection of photographs; photos of abuses that would close the "hospital" for good, and see Andrews and the others jailed for life.

"Where did you go to university together?"

"I met him at the University of Munich, and the Kraepelin Institute of Psychiatry."

From what Andrews was revealing, and the fact that Faust had taken a private flight to Munich, corroborated Dr Faust had links to the city.

"When I was introduced to you, how did you know I wasn't telling the truth?" questioned Josh.

"Anthony, Doctor Faust, told me you would come back for the woman and I was to...." He stopped before incriminating himself further.

"Yeah, you were to get rid of me, I got that. So you saw me with Faust when she was brought here?"

Andrews looked confused at the question. "Well of course. You came together. I must say you weren't as talkative as you are now, but that's probably due to the feeling of inferiority in the presence of a dominant role model called...." Andrews immediately stopped spouting his psychiatric gibberish as Josh pulled out his gun from his waistband.

Josh cocked his weapon for Andrew's to see then walked out of the seclusion room, leaving the door wide open. He unlocked the adjacent room holding the two nurses and Ms Fletcher, opened the door and stepped inside. All three, sitting against the wall on a mattress on the floor, looked up at their self-appointed executioner. Josh raised his weapon and pointed at them.

BANG! BANG! BANG!

One by one, Josh aimed and fired one shot each, just above their heads. Each cowered against the wall, curled up in a quivering ball; a bullet hole in the padded wall next to them as a stark warning. Josh walked out, closed the door so they couldn't be heard, and locked it again. He walked back to the room holding Andrews, who had heard the shots fired, and believing his staff had been executed, wet himself. Josh let Andrews see the gun, then pushed it hard into the psychiatrist's temple; the slightly heated muzzle singeing his skin. Andrews began mumbling and crying. A bullet to the head was less than he deserved and an easy way out. Josh replaced his pistol, pushing it back into its holster and walked out, locking the door behind him.

He walked back through to reception, picked up the phone and dialled the police emergency line. He reported gunshots fired, gave the location of the mental hospital, then hung up without giving his name. He knew the police armed response would be swift in their arrival. And what they would find, upon their search, would be a pervert's trove of photographic abuse spread across Andrews's desk.

Sitting in his car, Josh briefly contemplated the evil he had just witnessed. Knowing he could have easily ended their lives, along with the misery they cause, he wondered why he didn't. He had no answer. He pushed down on the accelerator and drove down the tarmac drive, leaving the sanctuary of hell. Two minutes out and a convoy of police cars raced past him in the opposite direction, blue lights flashing, heading in the direction of the hospital. Knowing he had ended some, but not all of the misery of the patients there, gave him a sense of satisfaction and usefulness.

He made the journey back towards the heart of London. It was strange working for himself and not at the direction of the office, or Harris. Josh was knowingly disobeying all orders of his suspension. But orders that prevented a justifiable cause, in his eyes, were wrong. He wasn't naive to know that when someone resisted a valid investigation, a cover-up was being employed. Harris was corrupt to the very core of his black heart.

Josh arrived at his next stop—GeneRobotix. His target: Mark Radnus. This time there was going to be no pussyfooting around; it was all guns blazing if necessary. Josh marched through the glass doors into the reception area and straight to the lift, bypassing security.

"Hey!" shouted security. "You need to sign in!"

Josh ignored the order and waited for the lift to arrive. The security guard walked over and as the lift door opened, he tried to prevent Josh from entering. Josh grabbed the guard's wrist and arm, twisted it, and pushed him aside. He then walked into the lift and pressed for the floor Sofia's office was located. Stopping at the floor, the door opened. He exited the lift and marched forth towards the executive offices. Reading the nameplates on the doors, he walked up to the one labelled: "Mark Radnus - CEO".

Without knocking, Josh burst into the room, slamming the door closed behind him. Radnus, sitting behind his desk, suddenly looked up—his eyes popping out with surprise at seeing Josh alive. He immediately picked up the phone to call security but Josh stomped over, pulled it from his hand and replaced it on the phone base.

"Where's Sofia Du Bois?" he demanded.

Radnus said nothing, or was just too slow to answer, so Josh grabbed the phone and slammed it hard into the side of Radnus's head.

"I won't ask you twice!"

Josh was making his intentions very clear and still Radnus said nothing; either from arrogance or stupidity, or both. Josh slammed the phone into his head again; a cut appeared with a trickle of blood. Radnus looked stunned. Josh raised the phone for a third time, about to swing.

"WAIT!" Radnus put his hands up to protect himself. He had had enough. "She's with Doctor Faust!" he shouted.

"I know that! Where?" Although Josh wanted to smack him in the head again, he resisted to let Radnus answer.

"Munich!" shouted Radnus.

"Munich's a big place. Give me a location," demanded Josh, still holding the phone up.

"The Kraepelin Institute! He has contacts there."

Josh dropped the phone on the desk and walked off. He opened the door to be faced by a small crowd standing outside. Staff had gathered after hearing the noise of raised voices.

"You should get a new boss, that one stinks," criticized Josh, and calmly walked back along the corridor to the lift; all eyes watching him.

Back down in main reception, the lift door opened. Josh was again met by the security guard he had dealt with on the way in. This time he had two colleagues with him. All three were looking uncertain about what to do, so Josh made it easy for them.

"I'm leaving. Just a misunderstanding. Sorry," and Josh walked by without them taking steps to stop him. All that was needed was a genuine apology, confidence, and a big set of balls. He got into his car and without further difficulties drove away.

All roads were leading to one place: Munich. It was time for Josh to take a well-earned break to the beautiful German city. His suspension gave him the time to get away. He needed to book a flight as soon as possible, as Radnus was sure to contact Faust—something Josh had reckoned on. He wanted to rattle the cage in the hopes Radnus will make contact. All Josh would need then is Flash's device: Sniffer, to hopefully get a number and exact location. His plan was underway.

Josh arrived home. He immediately booted up his laptop and connected Sniffer. Using it to hack the GeneRobotix security system was easy. He focussed on the phone exchange and pulled a mobile phone number dialled from Radnus's office, shortly after their heated meeting earlier. The connection line to the phone number Radnus called had been passed through a phone carrier in Munich.

Using Sniffer, Josh "pinged" the number—sending call signals to the target phone without making it ring—to get a location without alerting the phone user. The returned cell tower signals confirmed the phone's current location to be at the Kraepelin Institute in Munich. Josh now had Faust's mobile number, and once there he could track its location, even if Faust moved. He just had to hope Faust wouldn't ditch his phone by the time he arrived.

After booking the next available flight, Josh cleaned himself up and packed a small travel bag of necessaries. He put his weapon away, knowing he would have to fly without it; he would make plans to source something else in Germany. Wearing a fresh change of clothes, Josh picked up his keys and Sniffer—the only piece of hardware he was certain to get through customs. He walked out of the flat to his car and began making his way to Heathrow Airport, and his flight to Munich.

Never before had Josh made such an effort for another person. His attraction for Sofia was beyond anything he had experienced. Had he been an ordinary person, he questioned if he would, or even could, do anything to get her back. Would he have the fortitude? He didn't know. All he did know, was that right now, he would go through anything to get her back.

CHAPTER 16

IT WAS HALF AN hour after take-off, on the two-hour flight from Heathrow to Munich. The Lufthansa flight attendants were pushing a metal trolley along the gangway, serving drinks to the passengers. Josh ordered water; avoiding the sugary drinks, knowing they would spike his energy level then cause it to crash, making him tired and unfocussed—a state he couldn't afford to be in.

Sitting comfortably in his aisle seat, he looked around at the other passengers, wondering what their lives were like. He looked at a man dressed in a business suit across from him, tapping out some document on his laptop. A young woman sitting next to him by the window, reading a glossy magazine and looking at wedding dresses. And a young couple, sitting quietly in front of him with their child. It was the quiet downtime moments such as these that had Josh thinking of other possibilities, other paths he could have chosen—happier options perhaps.

But was anyone's life really that happy? Just through observation alone, Josh could see the cracks in these personalities. The businessman was stressed. His reddened face showing his high blood pressure, and looking as though he could have a heart attack at any moment. The young woman gazing at wedding pictures looked melancholy. The thin pale band around her empty left finger, where her wedding ring ought to be, was a tell-tale sign of her recent marriage break-up. And the resentful young couple, clearly thrown together from a night of irresponsible passion that bore a child, now having to suffer their lives together.

At the end of the day, it all boiled down to choices. The businessman could choose or not choose to stay in a job that was eventually going to kill him. The sad divorcee could choose to find a better husband, or not. The young couple could choose to make the relationship work, or end it amicably. Choice is always there, even if one chooses to stay in a difficult situation. It was something Josh had realised—no matter what you think or feel, you always have a choice.

An hour later, Josh woke from a shallow sleep to a flight announcement that the plane was about to start its descent. He had purposely tried to get as much sleep as he could before the next leg of his investigation. His military and intelligence training had taught him to always get as much sleep as possible, whenever possible. "A tired soldier is a careless soldier", was a philosophy he pushed on his platoon at the regiment. If you had five minutes spare, get your head down and rest, as you would never know when you would get your next break.

The flight attendants began walking the aisles, checking passenger seat belts had been fastened and luggage was squared away, as instructed by the announcement. Josh fastened his belt. The young woman next to him pushed the magazine she had been looking sorrowfully at into her bag, and began struggling to fasten her belt.

"Allow me," said Josh, offering to help and clipped it together.

She smiled gratefully, the first time during the whole flight, and thanked him. He could have easily made a play for her, being that she was in a vulnerable state. He was good looking, and she would probably be thankful for the needed attention and consolation of her loss. But Josh just wanted to show there was still hope; that all was not lost for her. And besides, the person he once was, he was no longer. He had changed.

The overhead lights went out and the plane began its descent. Looking outside through the small oval window, the city lights began to get brighter the lower they flew. Josh looked at his watch: 20:30hrs. It was still on UK time, so he set it one hour forward to match local German time: 21:30hrs. The ground was levelling out fast as the plane was about to touch down. The first bump of the tyres hitting the runway shook the plane. The landing thereafter was smooth, as the breaks slowed the plane to crawling speed and began taxiing towards the arrivals terminal.

The plane's loudspeaker clicked on to make an announcement, first in German and then in English, telling everyone to remain seated with their seatbelts on until the plane came to a standstill. But people were people, and ignoring the announcement, the passengers began unclipping their seat belts. The businessman Josh had predicted would end up having a heart attack was already standing, with his carry-on bag and laptop, like he was at the starting line of a race. He was huffing and puffing at the slowness of the plane's taxiing as he kept checking his watch.

The plane reached its terminal, the doors were opened and the hustle and bustle began. Passengers were shoving each other to grab their belongings from the overhead storage bins. The businessman was nowhere to be seen, having stormed up the gangway to the front. Josh stood and collected his bag. He pulled down the young woman's bag and handed it to her, earning him another smile. He watched and waited for the disorder to become orderly again. The passengers slowly filed out and Josh followed.

He began wondering if he would get through customs unchecked. Again, he had broken the rules and gone against all government travel protocols. Intelligence operatives were mandated to notify Control before travelling to any foreign country—hostile or friendly. Even holidays abroad had to be authorised beforehand. He was also travelling on his own passport, under his true name and not a cover identity. If he was known in foreign intelligence circles, of which he was clearly known to the Chinese MSS, he could be tagged or snatched. But it was a risk he was willing to take.

Walking down the gangway from the plane to the terminal he sensed something. Not the usual déjà vu sensation he would get from a Time-fold experience, but more of an extra-sensory perception of being watched. He wasn't entirely sure, but one thing he would not dismiss easily was his keen senses. His sharp senses and gut feelings, along with his training, were what kept him alive so far. He continued—behaving as normal, walking to customs and passport control.

The Bundespolizei—German Federal Police—were on duty performing passport and security checks. As Josh queued, waiting with the other passengers, he watched carefully for signs of exposure, without making himself look suspicious.

Next in line, Josh approached and handed over his passport to the official. The man sitting behind the console opened the passport and began checking it. He first scanned it through the computer system then looked up at Josh, comparing him to the passport photo then looked down again at his monitor. Josh was mentally timing how long it was taking for him to be cleared, by comparing his waiting time to other passengers. In relation, if he took considerably longer, he knew something was wrong and possibly his passport had been flagged. The customs official stamped his passport and handed it back. He was clear to enter.

Josh walked through customs without requiring to be searched, or have his bag checked. He followed the flow of passengers to blend in and watch for anyone who might be tagging him. He was satisfied he wasn't being followed despite his senses warning him earlier. He located and entered a nearby toilet, walked into a cubicle and locked the door. He placed his bag on the toilet seat, unzipped it, and pulled out Sniffer. He connected it to his cell phone and "pinged" Dr Faust's cell number with silent low frequency call signals. According to Sniffer, Faust's phone was still situated in Munich. It hadn't moved.

Finishing up in the toilet, Josh continued on, passing through the airport's atrium to the other side. His next step was to find a cheap hotel where he could establish a working base. He walked outside to a taxi rank. Looking up and down the line, most of the taxis were well-polished Mercedes and not what he was looking for. He was looking for something, or more accurately: someone, of a particular class. He walked past the competing eyes of the Merc taxi drivers—all hoping for the foreigner's fare, but to their disappointment, Josh approached the old dented BMW at the back of the line.

"Englisch sprechen bitte?" asked Josh in poor German. His foreign language training was an area he had not mastered at all.

"I speak English," replied the taxi driver; an Arabic man.

"Good. I need a hotel in the city, something cheap."

"I can take you. Get in! Get in!" he said enthusiastically without hesitation.

Josh had found who he was looking for, someone that seemed to know the rough spots of the city. He entered the taxi and they drove off. Josh kept looking back to see if he was being followed. He was still clear but couldn't shake that feeling from earlier in the terminal. The taxi headed south on the A92 autobahn towards Munich city centre.

"You on holiday?" asked the taxi driver.

"Sort of," replied Josh. "Where are you from?" he asked the driver.

"From München…er, Munich."

"No, before, before living here?"

"Iran."

"And your family?"

"Yes. We're all from Iran."

The driver was used to small talk with his passengers, so happily answered Josh's seemingly unimportant questions. But what he didn't realise was that Josh was creating a life-picture of the man and picking out his tiny lies. He wanted to know who he was going to be dealing with whilst on his "holiday". The driver continued happily chatting away.

"Farhad, what's your real name?" interrupted Josh.

The taxi driver suddenly hesitated; now he wasn't being so smooth in his conversation. Josh had thrown a spanner into his automatic flow of polite conversation, and stirred up a reaction to a truth he was hiding.

"What? That is my name...but how do you know?"

"Cut the bullshit. You're an illegal here; you and your family."

The driver became angry. "Hey! You disrespect me and my family. You pay now and get out!"

"Stop sweating Farhad. I'm not interested in your immigration status. But maybe we can help each other," suggested Josh.

The taxi driver calmed down. "How can you help me?" he asked.

"You need money." Josh was blunt about the taxi driver's obvious predicament.

"I have money! I can feed my family. What makes you think I need your money?"

The man was proud, so Josh had to make it look like the taxi driver was doing him a big favour and not the other way round. "I need your help. And in exchange, I will pay you for your valuable time," said Josh diplomatically.

He had turned the situation around. The driver was pondering the proposition without even asking what he had to do in return.

The man was desperate, just as Josh had guessed, but wouldn't admit it to anyone, even himself.

"How much?" The man asked the deciding question.

"One hundred a day; pounds sterling," said Josh.

"Two hundred," the man haggled. Haggling and bartering was in his nature.

"Done," said Josh firmly, knowing he was willing to go to three hundred. "I need someone to show me around and not ask questions; someone that knows the city and how to get certain things. Can I count on you?"

"Yes. You can trust me," said Farhad smiling; smiling at the prospect of making good money.

Josh knew he couldn't fully trust him but he needed a local guide, and not just someone that knew the city. He had to tap into the criminal underworld to get certain equipment he couldn't bring through customs. Usually, the office would set up contacts to supply him with what he needed, but this time he was on his own. He had to make his own contact with an arms dealer, and arms dealers were very twitchy and always suspicious, particularly with strangers. Hence the need for someone like Farhad. Josh was confident he had picked the right person to get what he needed.

Josh opened his wallet and pulled out two hundred pounds and handed it over. Farhad took it without counting and pushed it into his trouser pocket.

"So, what things are you wanting?" asked Farhad.

"You know people, people that have access to certain hardware. I need something small; semi-automatic." Josh said it as a statement and not a question; knowing Farhad could get access.

Farhad didn't look surprised, but was very wary at the request. He wanted to be sure he wasn't getting himself set-up in a police sting operation. Josh sensed the concern and needed to ease Farhad's worry.

"I'm a private investigator, here to find a kidnapped woman caught up with some very dangerous people traffickers." Josh laid it on thick to gain co-operation.

"Hmm...." Farhad hesitated but agreed to help. "I know people. It will cost, but I can set it up."

"Good. Now take me to a cheap hotel," and Josh leaned back in the seat to relax.

A short journey off the A92 autobahn took them into Hasenbergl—a borough in the northern part of the city, considered to be a low-income neighbourhood with some racial tension. Despite a little graffiti daubed on the walls, the area was relatively well kept and clean—typical of German cities. They pulled up outside a block of residential flats.

"Best hotel in München, and very cheap," said Farhad, pointing and smiling away like a salesman.

"This is not a hotel Farhad," replied Josh, looking out the window at the building.

"You can stay. Your own room. You will meet my family and only an extra fifty a day. Very good food."

"Thirty extra." Josh made his final offer.

"Very good! We have a deal." Farhad was pleased with himself.

The set-up was ideal for Josh. He had quickly assessed the situation before agreeing. The five-storey high block of flats stood back from the road, a little less than two hundred metres from the Hasenbergl U-Bahn underground station entrance. The U-Bahn gave him an easy means of moving around Munich, plus a quick escape route if needed. Also, living with Farhad's family would give him better cover than having to book into a hotel. Often hotels would report suspicious behaviour to police, and as Josh was about to embark on a mission that would probably raise some questions, he couldn't afford the added attention. He knew the type of residents in the flats would likely be anti-police; they would stay silent about anything they witness. Josh needed people to be blind to his comings and goings.

"Come come!" Farhad beckoned Josh to step out and follow him.

Josh grabbed his bag and followed along the pathway. The darkness of night covered the drab coloured building that the street lighting couldn't quite illuminate. The poor lighting was perfect for Josh, giving added protection from being seen. They entered the block of flats and proceeded into the lift, taking it to the third floor. Farhad led the way down a dimly lit corridor to a flat door. He pushed in his key and opened it; immediately two young children ran to greet him—a boy and girl.

"These are my children. This is Karim and Manijeh."

The children looked up, smiling at Josh—a stranger in their home. Not having been a father, Josh had had no real dealings with children and wasn't sure how to treat them. One thing he knew though was how not to treat them, as his father had done to him during his abusive childhood years. A woman appeared from another room.

"Ah, this is my beautiful Aisha, the light of my heart and the brains of my family. Meet my wife."

Josh watched Farhad gazing at his wife with a loving smile, and who could blame him. She was dressed in traditional Iranian dress and looked a picture of beauty, her face smooth and unblemished. She had the appearance of an Arabic princess; someone that would be the star of a movie. She was not what Josh had imagined her to be like, based on Farhad's own appearance. He was rough looking, not having aged well.

The children stood by their mother as she looked at Josh, silently wondering why he was there. The silence was beginning to become a warning that things weren't going well, so Farhad spoke up to explain.

"My friend from England is going to be staying with us for a short while my dear."

He spoke tentatively, almost expecting to be chastised. He was right. Josh could see the hidden upset behind Aisha's beautiful exterior. It was time for him to start building bridges between them.

"As-salāmu ʿalaykum," said Josh directly, in a way that Aisha would be sure that he meant what he said—peace be upon you.

She lightened up at the effort he had made to speak Arabic and smiled. "Wa ʿalaykumu s-salām," she replied—and peace be upon you, too.

Farhad's tension suddenly dropped away with his wife now seemingly accepting Josh into their home. He began his loud and lively discourse again, as though nothing unusual was going on; like accepting complete strangers into his home was an everyday occurrence.

"Where did you learn Arabic mister...?" asked Aisha.

"Josh. Call me Josh. I'm afraid I'm a bit of a fraud, as that's all I know," he confessed.

"More than most Westerners," she replied. "Is Josh short for Joshua?"

"Yes."

"A religious name. Are you religious?"

"No. I mean—I don't—I'm not sure." Josh spoke with uncertainty. "If being religious means believing something more than what we see around us, then perhaps, most recently, I could be."

Josh was referring to the unusual occurrences in his life that had some scientific meaning, but did not explain everything. Perhaps there was something more, something that branched into the realms of religion or a spiritual universe. He was no longer one to discount other possibilities, no matter what his limited imagination would seem to allow. And one belief he couldn't forsake, was the belief he could rescue Sofia.

CHAPTER 17

BEING WELCOMED INTO A stranger's home was something Josh had never experienced before. He was touched that on just one evening someone he had never met before had moved him in with his family. The cynical side of him believed it was money motivated, and at first that was how it seemed. But after speaking with Farhad's wife on a deeper and more personal level, Josh discovered a whole new side to Farhad and their life together.

Aisha had revealed their plight in Iran. She and Farhad were young and in love and full of ideas of political change. She was an activist in the country, standing up for human rights and became too outspoken against the regime. The secret police paid them a visit at their home one evening: Aisha was pregnant with their first child—Karim. They smashed in the door and began to forcibly take Aisha, but Farhad stepped in. He managed to convince them to take him in her stead, by saying he had put her up to it. He was taken and Aisha never heard from him for two months.

After many appeals to government officials, she had to eventually buy Farhad back. It cost her five thousand US dollars, money she didn't have. After scraping the money together, she made the payoff, and what was left of Farhad was returned to her. He underwent horrific beatings and torture, the likes of which no one would survive. But he was strong. Farhad had broken bones that were left to mend without setting them properly. The deep whip marks he had on his back are now scars she still cannot face.

Farhad knew that if he allowed them to take her instead of him, she would likely have been secretly executed, along with their unborn child. So, his only solution, was to put himself in harm's way to save her and his child.

After Farhad's release they made a run for Europe. They joined an illegal caravan of migrants and crossed an unguarded part of the border into Turkey. They were unwelcomed by its people, who were fed up with the hordes of immigrants, so continued west into Bulgaria. Living on handouts from the locals, Karim was eventually born on the roadside. They were discovered and taken in by a charity and began the process of seeking asylum. Their application failed; they couldn't afford to pay the corrupt official. Once again, they went on the run. They continued crossing borders, changed their names and settled in Germany—Munich. Now they live in comparative harmony, but always with one eye open; expecting immigration and police to bang on their door.

In light of Aisha's compelling story, Josh gained a newfound understanding and deep respect for Farhad; whom at first he didn't fully trust. One never really knows what another has gone through in order to survive; Josh had complete reality on that. And now he wondered if he was just bringing them more trouble. Somehow though, he would make it right for them, but in the meantime, he needed their help.

It was late and Farhad had just come off his phone; talking to a friend of his. Through a friend of his friend, Farhad had set up a late-evening meeting with an arms dealer, who had access to what Josh needed. Without revealing anything to Aisha, Farhad looked over at Josh, tacitly indicating they had a meeting to go to. But Aisha was far from naive. She knew there was danger ahead, but they needed the money to survive. She said nothing and pretended ignorance.

Farhad kissed his wife and both he and Josh left the flat. They walked back to his taxi and drove off for the meet that Farhad's friend had set up. Enroute, Josh reached inside his jacket and pulled out a fat envelope of cash he brought with him; money that was concealed in his travel bag—something the airport security had overlooked. He counted out five hundred pounds from the wad of notes then slipped the envelope back. He knew black market weapons fetched a high price, but he was going no higher than the five hundred he had just removed. If he couldn't bargain his way to get what he needed, he would take it. He just hoped they wouldn't be stupid enough to mess up the deal he intended on getting.

Driving into a dark industrial complex in Obersendling—south of the city, Josh's senses were on high alert. Both he and Farhad remained silent as the taxi warily rolled forward in the darkness. The only noise being made was the crackling of loose gravel and brick under the pressure of the tyres as it rolled over the top. The complex was a wreck of a place, ideal for illegal transactions. The arms dealer had chosen well. They passed a set of large rusty metal containers along a broken wall.

"Stop by that wall, keep your lights on and engine running," directed Josh. He was strategically checking the area: emergency exits, firing points, and cover from weapon fire. He had no weapons himself, so had to play it safe.

Farhad brought the taxi to a still, keeping the engine running and lights on as instructed. Two men showed themselves, stepping out into view, out of the shadow of a doorway. Josh knew instinctively they were tooled up: why wouldn't they be? He was trading with an arms dealer after all. He had to expect the worst. Josh stepped out of the taxi and began walking slowly towards the two men. He was cautious, shifting and flicking his eyes around, scanning for signs of hidden gunmen in the buildings. He kept close to cover as best he could, just in case they didn't like the look of him and began shooting. Farhad followed close behind as they approached the two men.

Farhad spoke out in Arabic, making a formal greeting of which one responded by finishing the traditional Arabic greet. So far things were going smoothly. The two heavily built men, dressed in jeans and black jackets, scrutinized Josh with incriminating eyes, seemingly trying to assess if he was an undercover with the BKA Bundeskriminalamt—Germany's Federal Criminal Police. Josh knew these two were the monkeys and not the organ grinder. These were the heavies he would have to deal with if the man in charge got greedy.

Partially satisfied Josh was authentic, the two heavies allowed entry into the derelict building. One of them led the way whilst the other waited for Farhad and Josh to pass by, after which he followed along. All four walked into a large dimly lit factory warehouse—the light being produced by a set of carefully placed spot-lights. The large open space was an operational nightmare—no cover and overexposure. Josh was rethinking his plan of extraction if things changed for the worst. Ahead of them was a middle-aged Arabic looking man, sitting at a solitary table in the middle of the open floor. Maybe he wasn't as smart as Josh had first pegged him to be. The leader was also leaving himself wide open, with just a table as cover; not that it would stop a bullet.

By order of the first heavy, Josh stopped ten metres short of the table, with Farhad standing next to him. The second heavy, standing guard over them, kept himself slightly behind Josh; to his right. Josh could sense he had his hand on the grip of a concealed weapon as a precaution. The first heavy continued walking to the table. He walked up to his boss, bent down and whispered to him. He then stood upright and turned round to face Josh and Farhad, placing his hand inside his jacket, making it clear he was also holding some kind of weapon.

Both Josh and Farhad were on full display, being analysed by the leader. And likewise, Josh was analysing him. He was observing the leader's doubt and uncertainty about them, which were bad signs. The man was saying nothing but communicating all Josh needed to know with his demeanour. Josh was already prepared for a quick and violent strike on the dealer and his men, but had to brave it out a little longer; the arms dealer was just being overly cautious.

Farhad broke the stalemate. Once again, he started the customary dialogue, reaching out to the leader. The Arabic words—a shared reality—seemed to calm the situation. The man looked less uncertain and more at ease. He spoke to Farhad in Arabic, both exchanging words in their own tongue. After their salutations the leader turned his attention to Josh, still with a hint of mistrust in his look.

"Farhad says you want to make a deal. I trust him but not yet you. So please excuse me while I keep my men in place." The leader spoke fairly good English.

"I understand," replied Josh diplomatically.

He allowed the leader to have control, or rather let him think he had, so things would run without any hick-ups. Taking out a low-level arms dealer wasn't his mission, he had bigger fish to fry and needed the firepower to do it with.

"The prices are in Euros and are non-negotiable," said the arms dealer.

"Everything is negotiable," answered Josh. He couldn't let the dealer see him as a pushover, or he would lose credibility.

The leader squinted and backed down a little. He also wanted what he wanted, which was money. He was a businessman after all and business was business, a sale a sale. "How much do you have?" he asked.

"That depends on what you've got?" Josh wasn't going to reveal his hand that fast.

The arms dealer was beginning to show a look of irritation at Josh's business etiquette, or lack of it, but refrained from spoiling an opportunity to make his money. He stood up, reached for a suitcase on the floor and placed it flat on the table. He opened it and spun it around for Josh to see its content. Josh walked over to the table and looked inside at an assortment of handguns. He knew the weapons had likely been involved in gun crime and that the man was trying to offload them onto an unsuspecting fool. But Josh couldn't afford to waste time in finding another arms dealer, so would make his choice.

Josh singled out a Glock 19, something he was used to and picked it up. He checked it over: pulling back the top-slide, pulling the trigger, checking for structural damage. It was in good condition. He placed it on the table next to the case. "I'll take this and two spare magazines plus ammo."

The arms dealer tried to not look impressed at Josh's weapon handling skills and pushed the case to one side. "Nine hundred for the Glock and I'll give you the magazines and ammo for an extra two."

"I'll take it off your hands for four hundred—pounds sterling."

The negotiations had started and Josh kept a straight face, but the arms dealer wasn't impressed with the miserly low offer Josh had just made.

"Are you trying to insult me?" said the dealer, raising his voice.

He was already getting heated under the collar and Josh, easily keeping his cool, kept his mouth shut; being careful not to respond to the dealer's criticism. Josh watched carefully. He was fully aware of the mental process the man was going through; the push-pull effect of resisting the lame offer but at the same time wanting to make a deal. The mental tug-of-war in his head was already showing.

The dealer came back with a lower offer. "Seven for the gun and one for the rest. Eight hundred total."

"I'll give you five hundred all in." Josh knew that was his limit and if he couldn't get the final deal, he was going to have to finalise it in other ways.

"Seven for all," replied the dealer, and he took the additional magazines and ammo from the case, placing them next to the gun as a sales teaser.

"Five is my final offer," said Josh firmly.

Both the heavies were half expecting things to go sour and Josh was sensing their tension. Still, he kept his cool and waited for the dealer's response. The dealer picked up the Glock, spare magazines and ammo and placed them back inside the case. Believing things had gone south, Josh was about to take out the thug standing next to him, but then the dealer pulled out an old Sig Sauer P6 pistol and dropped it on the table.

"You can have this for five hundred—pounds sterling, plus ammo."

Josh looked at the weapon, picked it up and checked it over. It was old and scratched up and wasn't something he had used before. He placed it back on the table and looked directly at the arms dealer.

"Done!" he replied.

The arms dealer smiled and the thugs relaxed their bodies. Farhad breathed a sigh of relief as he also believed things weren't going well. Everyone was happy and the negotiations finalised with Josh handing over the money. He collected his gun and ammo and put them in his pocket.

"Perhaps we can do business again," suggested the arms dealer with a big grin on his face.

"Perhaps we can," replied Josh. He now had a contact that could serve some usefulness in the future.

After completing the transaction, and with Farhad finalising the meeting in traditional Arabic style, Josh and Farhad walked from the table back the way they came in, this time, unescorted. Outside, Farhad's taxi headlights shone light on the way; the car engine was still running and had been all the while they were inside. Luckily, they hadn't the need of a fast escape.

"You got a good deal Josh?" asked Farhad.

"Better than I expected."

"And now what?"

"Now, we go home," said Josh.

Driving north, back across the city, Josh began thinking about Sofia. He wondered if he was passing her by without knowing it. Was she in the building they had just driven past or the car that had turned to go in another direction? He wondered how close or how far away he was from her. He wondered if she was awake or still in a coma. All his thoughts were about her being alive, none dare enter his mind that would suggest otherwise.

They pulled up and parked outside the flats—Farhad's home, and headed upstairs. In the hallway, Farhad turned to Josh. "Please do not show that to my family," he said, looking down at Josh's pocket; pointing out the concealed gun.

"You have my word Farhad. And thank you for everything."

Josh smiled; not something he did often. He began to recognise a true friend in Farhad, regardless of their financial agreement. Farhad smiled back. He opened the flat door and they walked in. Aisha had put the children to bed and was waiting up. She had a meal prepared for them.

"Please Josh, go and eat." Aisha offered him a seat at their table.

"Thank you. I just need to freshen up a little."

Josh went into the children's bedroom—Karim and Manijeh had temporarily moved to their parent's room to accommodate Josh's stay. He removed his jacket and the gun from the pocket. He lifted the bed's mattress and placed the gun and ammo on the base; dropping the mattress on top. He then walked out of the bedroom to the dining table and sat down to eat. Aisha and Farhad were waiting patiently for him, so they could all begin eating as one. The silence was comfortable as they ate quietly. It was like being part of a family Josh never had.

Finishing up, Aisha spoke. "The night is very late and I must go to bed. The children have to go to school early. Goodnight Joshua. Goodnight husband."

Farhad spoke Arabic to his wife, wishing her beautiful dreams which made her smile. He was pleased that he could still make his wife happy and grateful for what they had together. In spite of everything, the enforced government interference in their lives, they continued to flourish as a family. She left the room to be with their children.

"Love is a beautiful thing Josh, don't you think?"

"If you say so," replied Josh.

"This woman you are searching for. Who is she?" Farhad was breaking the rule about not asking questions.

Josh sat silently and sipped his black tea.

"Hmm...I believe she is more than just some woman. I believe that you tread a dangerous path for reasons only the heart can explain. I will help you find her. We will find her!"

Farhad's words resonated deeply in Josh. His accuracy of truth and willingness to help struck a deep chord in him. Josh couldn't help but feel humbled by his true friendship and humanity, but was unable to show it. He couldn't help but feel that the illegal immigrant he was drinking tea with was more of a human being than he could ever be. Farhad just smiled, needing no explanation, and let the conversation fade away. He lifted his cup, joining Josh, and together they silently drank tea.

Putting his cup down, Farhad yawned and stood up from the table. "I think I shall go to bed now Josh. My wife will be restless if I am not by her side. Goodnight."

Josh stood. "Goodnight Farhad."

Farhad retired to the bedroom to be with his wife and children, leaving Josh alone. Josh quietly walked to his room and closed the door. He lifted the mattress and picked up his weapon and ammo, putting them on a small table next to the children's crayoned drawings. He was starting to feel he shouldn't be there, that he was putting the family's lives in danger. His bond with them had grown unusually fast, and to use them as he had planned was not something he could do anymore. It was time to leave.

Josh packed his bag and crept from the bedroom into the living room. With bag in hand, he stood pondering as he looked around their home. It was bare of material necessities and a little run-down, but what it did have was more real than any modern TV or stereo system could provide. It was built on the couple's shared life experiences and their unquestionable love for each other and their children. These were what made this place a home. Their family life needed to be preserved, and Josh realised by being there, he was a danger to its survival.

Before leaving, he took the envelope of money he had and counted out a thousand pounds. He laid the notes on the table and placed his empty tea cup on top. He knew Farhad would figure out his reasoning for leaving. Josh turned off the lights, walked out of the flat and quietly closed the door behind him. He took the lift to the ground floor and stepped out of the building, into the cold air of the night. He looked up at the bright stars and condensed vapour of his breath. Oddly, he smiled. He swung his bag over his shoulder and continued walking; entering the entrance to the nearby U-Bahn station. He was on his own again.

CHAPTER 18

JOSH HAD TAKEN THE U-Bahn to Scheidplatz station—further south towards the city centre. He found a cheap hotel within walking distance from the Kraepelin Institute of Psychiatry, where Dr Faust had recently visited.

Feeling tired, Josh entered his hotel room, dropped his bag on the floor and looked around. It was very late, but as always, company protocol needed to be observed before he could relax. He began systematically clearing the room. He walked through the bedroom and bathroom, ensuring the cupboards were empty and windows secure. He moved on to identifying and checking points around the hotel room where someone could hide a covert surveillance device. He knew if he was being followed, a surveillance team wouldn't have had opportunity to fit the room with "eyes and ears", but a hotel voyeur, that was different. A voyeur could have installed hidden video cameras for their own misguided pleasures. Josh couldn't afford to have any recordings of him going about his work.

With no specialist eavesdropping or covert camera detection equipment, Josh had to do things manually. He went around inspecting the lights, plugs, sockets, and switches—all the main power supply sources a camera or bug would be connected to. He checked the mirrors in the bedroom and bathroom, ensuring they weren't two-way; set-up with hidden cameras behind them. Finally, he moved on to checking the surfaces, in and under cupboards as well as the walls and ceiling, for any tiny holes that could be hiding a pin-hole camera. As certain as he could be, he was satisfied the room was clean.

Now, and as much as it went against the grain, he had to get a little sleep. He knew he would be useless to Sofia if he was tired and exhausted; not thinking straight. He needed to hit the pillow and get a fresh start in the morning; to locate his target: Dr Faust.

It was seven AM. The alarm on Josh's phone began sounding for him to get out of bed. He had had trouble sleeping and had tossed and turned for the past hour or so. He reached for the phone, disconnected it from the charging lead and turned off the alarm. He turned the side-light on and tried to rub the tiredness from his eyes. He leaned over the edge of the bed and picked up Sniffer. He connected it up and "pinged" Faust's cell number. It was still in the same position as the night before—the Kraepelin Institute.

Josh rubbed his eyes again and pushed himself to get out of bed. Still tired, he went straight for a shower; turning the cold water on full to shock his body into waking up. He persevered the cold for as long as he needed, then turned the water off. Fully awake, he reached for a towel, dried himself and began shaving.

He needed to move fast, as he didn't know what Faust's plans were and couldn't rely on him keeping his phone; allowing him to be tracked. He also didn't know how deep Faust's involvement went. What he did know, was that his specialist skills were being used by the Chinese government, and like every other country, they were deeply protective of their state secrets: going to any lengths to protect them.

Fully dressed, Josh lifted the pillow to get his gun. He hadn't had time to strip and clean it so quickly did so. He looked over the parts and despite the scratches and overall rough look, it was fit for purpose. He had no oil to lubricate the working parts so had to leave them dry: hoping he wouldn't get a weapon stoppage if he came under contact during a fire-fight.

Holding the weapon—now fully assembled—he inserted a loaded magazine. And without putting a round in the chamber, pushed the weapon into the inside pocket of his jacket. He stood in front of the mirror, checking himself over, to make sure he looked ordinary. His hair looked plain, without any style; his boring colourless and unfashionable jacket was perfect for going unnoticed. He was content with his grey-man appearance. He zipped up his bag and placed it inside the cupboard.

Before leaving, he began arranging the room in a way he could easily identify if someone—with nefarious intentions—had gone inside once he'd left. He partly opened the cupboard door to a specific mark on the carpet; likely, if someone opened it to search his belongings, they wouldn't know to close it exactly on the mark. He deliberately lay a wet towel on the cupboard top—draped over the edge in a way he would know if someone moved it to search the drawers. Plucking a number of wet hairs from his head, he went around the room placing one over each of the electrical socket points. Each hair was stuck half over the wall socket cover and half on the wall. If anyone removed the covering to install a spying device, the hair would be displaced.

He left the hotel room, locking the door after him and hung a "Do Not Disturb" sign on the door handle—to keep hotel staff out. He looked up and down the corridor, making sure no one was around, plucked a hair from his head and licked it. Then, by using the same trick as inside the room, he kneeled down low and stuck it across the door and doorframe, so no one except possibly a professional intrusion team would find it. Satisfied his intrusion detection method was in place, he headed downstairs to get breakfast.

Downstairs, the dining room was quiet. Two men dressed in business suits were sitting at different tables, both eating. They never even looked up as Josh entered. He took a seat at a table in the corner; sitting against the wall, able to watch the two men and the door. The waitress came over and offered the menu, but Josh asked for a cooked breakfast and coffee without looking. He knew what he wanted and he wanted it fast. In a short while, the waitress brought the meal over; she was used to the impatient business types trying to get a head start in the day. Josh looked at her. She already looked worn out and the day was just beginning.

"Thanks Christina," said Josh gratefully, after reading her name badge.

She looked at him differently. All she usually got was an insincere "thank you" from the passing patrons, once she'd placed their meals on the table.

"You're welcome," she replied in English, with a German accent. She then walked back to the kitchen, but looking a little less tired as a result of just that one moment of genuine human interaction.

Recognising and appreciating people for whoever they are, and for whatever job they do, was something Josh was getting better at. He practiced it daily, not just to build useful contacts in the field that could potentially help him, but to raise people's spirits. It was something he picked up from Sofia the first time they met. She had a natural inclination and ability to raise people up, and to Josh, that was something rare in a person and worth fighting for.

Josh threw his meal down his throat. He sipped the last of his coffee and stood up from the table. Seeing him, the waitress came over immediately.

"Can I get you anything else?" she asked cheerfully.

"No thanks Christina; that was great. Thank you. I've left the money on the table."

Christina smiled, took the money, and walked to the till to ring in the payment. Josh was using cash as much as he could, rather than card, to avoid an electronic bank trail. He knew intelligence agencies had access to banking systems, either by way of a bank's authorisation or, if not authorised, through hacking their computer systems. Some agencies would even go as far as having their spies recruited to work in banks on a full-time basis, solely for easy access to banking records. Either way, Josh needed to stay off-grid as much as possible.

BEEP BEEP, BEEP BEEP! BEEP BEEP, BEEP BEEP!

His phone began ringing in his pocket. He took it out and looked at the display. It was the "office" back in London.

"Took your time," he thought.

His passport had finally been flagged up on their system. They were trying to contact him to censure him for travelling abroad without permission. Josh ignored the ringing, pushing the button on the side to silence it. The call stopped but immediately began again. He thought it better to answer, or they would send out a team to investigate. Until they knew he was safe, they wouldn't back off for threat of losing one of their own.

"Yeah?" he answered.

"This is Control, please verify," requested the robotically sounding voice of the operator.

"Brannon, 1,5,3,1."

A pause followed as the security system checked his voice pattern and ID. "Confirmed," replied the operator. He was checking two things; one: Josh's identity through voice analysis and two: that he wasn't under any duress. Had he been, Josh would have given the "Under Duress Code" instead of his ID.

"Brannon, you are ordered to return to London immediately and report to your senior case officer. A flight back has been booked for you at Munich airport which leaves at midday. Collect your ticket from the Lufthansa check-in. Please confirm your orders."

"I'm taking some holiday. I'll be back in a couple of days or so," replied Josh.

"Acknowledge your orders Brannon," insisted the operator.

The operator's sole task now was to get compliance of orders, or he would have to report non-compliance and the matter would escalate to a more senior level. They could then send a local liaison to encourage Josh to return, but that would end up being a little too embarrassing for the company; not being able to control their own operatives. Now they knew he was safe, they would likely just send someone out from London to bring him back, or leave the matter until his return. Then he would face another disciplinary.

"Sorry, gotta go, going to take a trip to the zoo. Tell Harris I'll bring him back a souvenir," replied Josh sarcastically, then pushed the button to hang up. The operator never phoned back, so was likely satisfied Josh wasn't under any form of duress, but would now go on to report non-compliance of orders.

"Now that's out of the way, time to get going," he thought.

He removed Sniffer from his pocket and rechecked the signal location of Dr Faust's phone. It was still emanating from the institute. Josh was beginning to get suspicious; the phone's location not having moved at all. He wondered if he was heading into a trap; if they knew he was coming. It didn't matter though; he was going anyway.

Josh put Sniffer away in his pocket and walked out of the dining room, through to hotel reception. The front desk clerk was finishing up with booking out a visitor as Josh walked up to the desk. The desk clerk didn't speak English, so with some difficulty and unusual sign language, Josh mimed to him to not let anyone in his room, including housekeeping, until he booked out. He appeared to understand, so Josh left it there and walked out of the hotel.

It took a fifteen-minute walk along the well-kept paths to get to his target location—the Kraepelin Institute of Psychiatry. He approached a side-road, leading from the main road into the institute grounds. There were two four-storey buildings, one on either side of the road, a small security outbuilding positioned in front, with automated security barriers across the roadway.

Security looked lapse; no fencing, just a one-man post that seemed to be there just for appearance's sake. Josh waited. Two men were walking from the opposite direction and turned into the side-road towards the institute. Josh tagged on behind. The two men were talking and paid no attention to security as they walked on by. Josh continued on their tail, looking from his peripheral vision to the left, at security. Without directly looking, he could see the security guard sitting behind a glass window looking down; probably reading. Just as he suspected, security was lapse.

Once passed the security barrier, Josh quickened his pace to catch up with the two men. "Excuse me!" he called out from behind.

Both men turned, looking bothered at having their conversation interrupted. Josh was unsure if they spoke English.

"Do you know Doctor Faust? Doctor Anthony Faust?"

One man spoke in English with a German accent. The other looked blank, obviously not understanding what Josh had just said.

"You're here to see Doctor Faust? What is your business with him?" rudely asserted the older of the pair.

Josh picked up on the man's self-importance right away. He didn't even answer the question but counter-questioned, seemingly trying to control the conversation. Josh matched the man's arrogance to create some kind of rapport, that hopefully the man would relate to and thus become somewhat more useful—providing Josh the answer he needed.

"He's a busy man, so where can I find him?" asserted Josh, in a likewise rude manner.

"He's in Neurogenetics Research!" snarled the man, pointing the way.

Both men turned their backs on Josh, ignoring him further, and continued on, picking up their conversation where they seemed to have left off. Josh was beginning to get a real feel for the place. If everyone were like these two, well, Josh was going to have an easy time of extracting information. Getting information from dislikeable people was always easier on his conscience.

Walking in the given direction, Josh was keeping a sharp eye out, in case he was indeed walking into a trap. He reached an expensive looking double-winged concrete building; the wings joined in the middle by a fancy glass building. The whole structure was an architect's wet dream. Obviously, someone was throwing a lot of money into neurogenetics research and development. The building was marked with a shiny brass plated sign: Neurogenetics Research Department.

Standing on the opposite pathway, across the road from the building, Josh watched the entrance—a door in the glass section of the middle structure. There were very few personnel entering; access only being granted using security key-card. He needed to "borrow" one for himself, so watched and waited for the next person to come along.

WHOOSH!

Suddenly Josh froze; déjà vu struck. Something or someone was creating a Time-fold phenomenon. He pulled himself out of the inward fixation and looked, looked hard. A figure grabbed his attention, staring directly at him through the glass of the middle structure and standing motionless. The figure was unclear in features and detail but characteristically familiar. An idea of identity flashed in Josh's mind but was immediately discounted, so passed into a forgotten memory.

WHOOSH!

Josh was struck again; his mind pushed elsewhere. It was unusually odd to be hit twice so soon. He quickly pulled himself back to the present. The figure behind the glass hadn't moved one inch—as though a mannequin in a shop window. Josh continued watching, waiting for the figure to make the first move. But it seemed that it was also waiting, waiting for Josh.

Josh's instinct was telling him to get out of there, that he was entering a trap, something he had considered earlier. However, Josh was experiencing an incredible pull towards the unknown figure; the powerful traction caused by a strong desire to know. He wanted to know something he already suspected and had partially witnessed, but had buried the idea and labelled it as lunacy. The first moment of suspicion popped into his mind during Operation Sting Bolt; during the crazy encounter with his old friend Liam. Seeing the CCTV footage at the hospital, of Sofia being taken, gave him added confirmation; but still it was unbelievable. Now he had to confirm his doubts.

Against his better judgement, Josh slowly walked towards the building, his eyes glued to the figure. His peripheral senses were acutely high, scanning for threats. He continued walking tentative steps; all the while the figure remained motionless. Josh approached the glass. It was like looking into a mirror. He could see his own vague reflection as you would naturally expect, but a third, more real identity, was standing on the opposite side of the glass: the facsimile! Josh was looking at the facsimile of himself, not as the boy, but as his current self.

Once he had gotten over the initial stage of disbelief, Josh began noticing the facsimile's blank expression. Unlike the boy fac—who was self-aware and self-animated, this one looked defective. Its blank wooden-like stare, made it look like the mannequin Josh first thought. It was as though the actual person had been trapped inside the shell of the body. Josh then realised where he had seen this expressionless look before. It was the same look Jennifer Baxter had had when she attempted to stab him in the park: her uncontrolled action caused by the GeneRobotix GRX-5 chip that was implanted in her.

Suddenly, the facsimile moved. It turned and walked further into the building. A "clunk" sounded from the security door indicating the lock had been released. Josh took it as a sign he was being invited in, and he suspected by whom. Regardless, he entered the glass building. The door closed behind him, with the clunk sound of the lock being re-engaged, as he knowingly walked into the trap.

The facsimile walked through another door into one of the building wings. Josh followed, curiosity drawing him in further. He knew Dr Faust would be watching from somewhere remotely, probably via camera, but if this was a means to finding him and Sofia, Josh didn't mind playing the caged rat in Faust's experimental game.

Josh walked through the same door into a corridor. Branching off the corridor were several rooms, much like laboratories with sophisticated equipment. The rooms were separated off by large glass windows. Josh watched the facsimile pass through another doorway off the corridor. He followed along but stopped short of entering, as he knew that was what was required of him. Unlike a trained rat, instead of entering through the same doorway, he paused. The room was empty, with padded walls. The fac was standing near the back wall facing the doorway. As Josh had anticipated, it was a dead end, a trick to get him into the room. This was supposed to be the end of the line for him. But now, he was done playing their game. It was time to start playing his own and stir up the snake pit he had entered.

Instead, Josh pulled out his weapon from inside his jacket and pulled back on the slide—letting it spring forwards, loading a round into the chamber. He entered the laboratory next door and began systematically searching the rooms. One by one he entered a room, and if locked he kicked it in. Each room was empty. He headed back to the main glass building he first came through and proceeded through to the opposite wing.

The wing had a similar set-up—rooms coming off the corridor. Likewise, he swept the rooms, searching for Sofia or Faust, even kicking in doors if they presented a problem. Again, empty. Josh made his way upstairs. He tried the handle of the first door he came to but the door was locked. With a forceful thrust of his shoulder against it, he broke the lock, swinging the door open in the process. Inside was a man wearing a white laboratory coat with a shocked look across his face.

"Where's Faust?" demanded Josh loudly.

The man said nothing so Josh rushed over to help him speak. He took hold of the man's white coat, grabbing the material in his left fist and pushed him hard up against the wall. Staring at Josh's gun, the skinny spectacled man started jabbering in German. Josh pushed him into his seat.

"Faust...Doctor Faust!" shouted Josh.

The intenseness in his eyes caused the man to shake with fear, to put his hands up in defence. Josh slapped them down.

"Faust, where is Doctor Faust!"

The man was a complete wreck, fear had consumed him. Josh had come at him too hard and as a result the man's adrenal "fight or flight" biochemical process had kicked in; except he wasn't able to fight or permitted to flee—causing him to experience a temporary mental breakdown. Josh left the man talking incoherently to himself. He was damaged as a useful source.

Josh left the office and continued opening and kicking in doors, looking for Faust or Sofia. About to break open another door, he turned. Standing at the end of the corridor was the facsimile. Josh knew what was coming. He knew from the very moment, when he was supposed to enter the room downstairs with the fac, what the purpose of trapping him was. This was a further test of the "usefulness" of the GRX-5 chip on a human being. It wasn't just about the ability of controlling a nation, but turning a human being into a killing machine. This was a psychotic's absolute test.

CHAPTER 19

JOSH AND THE FACSIMILE were standing, facing each other in the corridor, ready to do battle. Everything about them was identical to the last gene; the only exception to their complete carbon copied bodies were the clothes they wore. This was the most absolute form of identical twinship a geneticist could ever hope for. Their physical appearance, DNA, each chromosome, and every cell in their bodies matched down to the last. Even the arches, loops and whorls of their fingers and thumbs, exactly the same: an anomaly which would baffle any fingerprint expert. To have two "originals" existing in the same time and location defied modern science.

Time was stretching during the motionless stand-off. Facing this fac was the most bizarre experience Josh had ever had in his lifetime's existence. Being in the same time and space as the boy facsimile—experiencing his younger self—was most unusual, but to be standing in front of a body, that should only be a reflexion in a mirror, was daunting.

Josh was waiting, watching what his familiar opponent would do. He couldn't deny it, but the best match one could go up against was themselves. Josh was assessing his opponent's fighting abilities and skill-sets, and then having to re-evaluate his own plan to make changes. In effect, he had to look inwardly at himself as to what he would do and then change that plan to another, due to the fact the other would likely be thinking the same plan.

The retrospection and planning and rethinking the plan were causing too much thinking, and subsequently too much hesitation. He wondered if his opposite was having the same problem. He then realised his plan should be to have no plan at all, but to just take action. Spontaneity was the key factor to defeating himself—the facsimile, and no pre-thought, pre-planned action, was going to win him through. He knew he had to be in the moment and act accordingly; not planning from past experience or planning from suppositions of the future.

Josh emptied his head of all thought, getting rid of all the considerations and tactical calculations he had been making, which were in fact causing his abilities to jam up. The calmness of mind allowed him to acutely tune his senses to what was coming. He was ready!

The facsimile began with a fast pace towards Josh. He waited as the fac closed in. His opponent clenched his fist, something Josh would never do until the final moment, so as to not give away his move. Something was wrong. Something was missing. He then realised he was facing how someone else would probably fight. He wasn't about to fight himself or someone with identical skills as himself, but an inexperienced controller or scientist manipulating the body.

The blank emotionless stare of the facsimile was a clear sign of how Josh knew he could defeat him. Dr Faust, or one of his minions, was in command of the body through the implanted chip: but only the body. Josh knew Faust had control of the strength of the fac's body but not the strength and skill of its mind. The facsimile would just be an extension of Faust's arm without the ability; an inadequate, unthinking robot. Without access to the fac's innate skills and knowledge, Faust would be defeated. Josh realised the fac wasn't the enemy but reaffirmed that Faust was.

The fac raised its arm and swung a fist at Josh, who—easily seeing it, moved out of the way. Although the fighting skills of the controller—who was moving the facsimile around—were weak and clumsy, Josh knew the fac's body could still land a powerful punch. Under pathetic guidance, the facsimile continued waving its arms around and striking out as though in an amateur schoolyard fight.

Holding back on his own punches and not taking opportunity to retaliate, Josh was assessing the extent of Faust's control over the fac's body. Dodging the punches, he was trying to ascertain to what degree Faust could use people against their will. Verbal communication seemed to be a problem, although there were split moments Josh sensed something tacitly; something coming from the person trapped inside. It was recognition of something other than the body itself, something that was a resident of the shell. What he couldn't figure out though, was how they were able to "see" through the body without the use of any noticeable visual equipment.

While continuing his volatile study, Josh caught a powerful left hook from the fac to the right side of his face, sending a shock of pain throughout his jawbone. That was it, "enough is enough now," he thought. He needed to subdue his opponent and in a way that wasn't damaging to either of them. The only way he knew how, which had worked previously, was through a momentary blast of electricity to the back of the neck area, and the implanted chip.

Minding the swings and punches, he gradually led the fac into a nearby room. Maybe it was a mistake as it picked up a chair and hurled it at him. Josh ducked down to the floor to avoid it. He spotted a wire lying under a table and grabbed it. Yanking it with force, a computer from the table jolted across the table, causing it to crash to the floor. He pulled harder on the cord, breaking the wire from the computer tower, exposing the bare copper strands inside. Standing over him, the facsimile reached down and grabbed

Josh's jacket. It was another clumsy mistake. Using his legs, Josh kicked out with force against the legs of his opponent, and whilst off-balance, twisted the fac's body around to expose the back of its neck. Josh hadn't checked if the wires were live but time was against him. Still holding the cord firmly, Josh pushed the bare wires into the back of the fac's neck. ZAP!

Not only did Josh zap the facsimile with electricity, but also himself, by way of connection to its body. The sudden jolts passed through them both like a heavy pulsating drill. It lasted a couple of seconds longer than necessary, as Josh had trouble letting go. He eventually pulled the electrical cord away, disconnecting it from the fac's neck and threw it aside. The facsimile flopped on top of Josh, stunned like a pig in slaughter. He pushed it off, allowing the fac to roll limply to the carpeted floor. Josh then quickly jumped to his feet. He watched closely, anticipating his trick may not have worked for a second time, so readied his weapon in case he needed to use deadlier force.

A groan of pain came from the body. It was the first spoken communication from the facsimile. Although not really words to understand, the communication of pain was actually a good sign. Josh was hopeful. The facsimile was beginning to slowly push itself up off the floor. Josh stood back, creating a safe distance between them. The fac stood upright, turned to Josh and once again they faced each other.

"You took your fucking time," moaned the fac.

Josh smiled at the facsimile's choice of greeting. "Well, you looked as though you were enjoying yourself," he replied dryly.

The facsimile stared hard at Josh, then slowly broke into a smile at the wry humour. But the smile was short-lived and quickly faded. He became serious and focussed. "We need to get out of here fast," ordered the fac. "They'll be coming!"

Their new union was cut short by factors unknown to Josh. It seemed his counterpart was more in the know than him. The seriousness cut in once again and without hesitation they headed for the door, bumping into each other as they both tried to take the lead. Josh looked at his new partner and gestured with his hand.

"Ladies first," mocked Josh, and he moved aside for his partner to leave first.

The fac smirked, shook his head at the joke and led the way through. Josh followed. He put his weapon away as they headed out of the building wing into the glass mid-structure—where they first came face-to-face. The fac stopped still on the spot looking lost. He turned to Josh.

"My orientation is vague. You'll have to lead."

Josh nodded. They raced to the glass door and tried to open it. It was locked. With a heavy shove of his shoulder against the metal frame, the fac broke it open and walked through. Josh followed. They marched quickly along the road towards the security barrier of the institute. Passing by, Josh could see the security guard looking down; oblivious to what had just gone on under his watch. Continuing on to the junction, they then turned the corner onto the main road. It wasn't long before two black cars suddenly appeared from around the bend in the road, stopping fifty metres or so short of them.

"You ready?" asked the fac.

"Ready," replied Josh, reaching under his jacket to grip the handle of his gun.

Both cars screeched into sudden high-speed motion towards them. The first car bearing down on them mounted the curb, knocking a bin from the pavement. Josh pulled his gun fast, aimed and fired two shots, one straight after the other at the driver's side windscreen. The car swerved and crashed head-on into the corner of a building; steam and hot water spraying from the radiator.

The fac sprinted towards the wreck as Josh covered him with his pistol. The second car was on them in seconds. A weapon pointing through the open passenger-side window began spraying bullets in their direction. Josh dived, hitting the pavement hard and crawled furiously to the crashed car for cover.

Suddenly, a rip of automatic gunfire projected a hail of bullets at the second vehicle. The facsimile began returning fire using a Chinese QCW-05 submachine gun he removed from the crashed vehicle. He sprayed the car's passenger side as it drove by, punching holes through the door. The gunfire from the second car was stopped dead; the fac taking out the shooter. The driver of the car, defeated, sped off along the road out of sight.

Josh focussed on the crashed car, pointing his gun, but the fac had already taken out the passenger. Initially, Josh had put two bullets in the driver, causing the crash, but the passenger, although stunned, was still alive. The fac snapped the passenger's neck before taking his weapon. Josh and the facsimile were the perfect team.

Amidst the intense noise of the fire-fight, the security guard back at the institute had called the polizei—German police. The sound of sirens could be heard in the far distance. Josh and the fac began hastily frisking the two Chinese occupants. Both had official diplomatic identification cards and both, as Josh knew, were agents of the Chinese Ministry State Security. This was the second run-in he had had with the MSS lately. And both times it didn't turn out well for them.

"We need to go!" insisted Josh.

"Yeah, roger that. But we need to gear up first," replied the fac; grabbing two full magazines from the dead MSS agent's ammo pouches strapped to his body.

Josh followed suit; taking the dead driver's submachine gun and ammo from under his suit jacket, as well as his Chinese

QSV-92 semi-automatic pistol. As a quick trade, Josh took his newly acquired black market pistol, rubbed it over with his jacket—removing his fingerprints—and placed it in the driver's hand. If the gun had a history of crime attached to it, then the Chinese would have some explaining to do with German authorities.

"You know that won't fool em for long?" the fac pointed out, referring to Josh's gun swap. "They ain't gonna believe the driver shot himself with his own gun through the windscreen."

"But hopefully it'll send them on a bit of a goose-chase. It'll give us a little breathing time," added Josh. The fac agreed.

The early morning incident was over just as fast as it had started. They finished concealing the Chinese weapons on their persons and hurried off. Instead of moving along the main road and bumping into the polizei, they cut through between two buildings, heading along a narrow pathway directly away from the scene. Pacing with speed along the pathway, Josh taking the lead, they continually scanned for further surprises: although Josh was well aware, that to his new partner, the last "surprise" wasn't in fact a surprise at all. Josh was eager to reach a safe place so he could find out what the fac knew.

Sirens were wailing in the near distance; the polizei likely just about arriving to witness for themselves the scene of destruction near the institute. The pair had made some ground between them and the scene, but they weren't out of danger yet.

"We need to get back to the hotel. It's close by," said Josh.

"No. We need to keep moving," insisted the fac. "I have a tracker in me; they'll know where we are."

"Who?" asked Josh.

"Faust, the Chinese. They'll want us both dead. We need to keep moving."

"Where's the tracker?"

"I'm not sure. We need to find somewhere we can set up an ambush."

"I know of a place and someone who can help," replied Josh. He took out his phone and speed-dialled his new contact in the city.

"Hallo, Englisch sprechen bitte," a familiar voice answered the call; speaking poor German with an Arabic accent.

"Farhad, its Josh, Josh Brannon. I need your help urgently!"

"Josh, where are you? I will come now!"

"Meet me at Scheidplatz U-Bahn station. I'm nearly there. And set up a meeting with your friends at the same location in one hour. Tell them I have a business deal for them."

"Okay! I'm going now Josh. I make it fast. Ten minutes!"

Josh hung up and looked at the fac. "ETA on car pick-up, ten minutes."

"We might not even have two," said the fac, looking in the direction of the station.

Two speeding black 4-door Audi saloons had just driven up from the opposite direction, making a sharp U-turn in the road and parked outside the station. The car doors swung open and two men from each car stepped out—one from the front passenger's side and one from the back. It was the Chinese MSS.

Quickly responding to the threat, Josh and the fac darted behind a small bushy area near the entrance to the Luitpold Park. They pushed through the bushes to the forward edge to observe the station, in particular the Chinese, some two to three hundred metres away. Both were making a threat assessment in their heads; figuring out the number of hostiles, weapons, likely skill-sets, back-up support and communications.

"I estimate three-up in each vehicle—driver still mobile with two foxtrots, six hostiles total. Looking at their dress code, probably kitted up the same as the others," stated the fac.

"Agreed," replied Josh. "I see one foxtrot with a handheld device; any thoughts?"

"Comms; mobile or sat phone maybe?"

"No. Look what he's doing with it. It's some kinda scanner or tracker. It's a tracker! They've got access to your output signal. That's how they were able to cut us off so fast," revealed Josh. "They'll get direction on our location soon enough."

The fac looked at Josh. "Okay, plan. We draw them into the park. You move off first and set up on that high ground." The facsimile pointed through a gap in the bushes to a high point in the park. "You'll be able to dominate the area and give me fire support. I'll wait here until they've got my location, then I'll move in and come out through the trees into the open ground below you. They should follow."

Josh agreed with the plan. "They'll probably leave one man with transport, so you'll have at most five on your tail. So don't fuck around and stop to get a look at the scenery, okay?"

"I hear ya. Now get going!" ordered the fac.

"Good luck," said Josh, and with those last two words he sprinted off into the park. He needed to get into position and settled fast. He ran in a direct line through the trees and bushes, avoiding the winding pathway which would take too long. He continued sprinting as best he could, once he hit the incline up the hill to the high ground. His breathing was heavy but his focus and determination was strong. He reached the top and quickly assessed the location for the best firing position. He could see the open ground below—he had a firing arc of about ninety degrees. He looked around for park visitors of which there were a few but of no big concern. It was a good spot.

Josh pushed his body backwards into a bush and lay flat on his belly. He removed the Chinese submachine gun from under his jacket, checked it over and made it ready for firing. He placed two spare magazines next to him for faster reloading. His breathing was still heavy from the sprint, so by taking slow deep breaths he was able to control and steady it. He rechecked his position and firing arcs and began ranging—picking out objects and mentally estimating their firing distances.

He set the weapon to "single shot" mode; knowing the distance he had to fire was long, and that automatic fire at that range would lose him accuracy. The distance he had to fire was overstretching and reaching the maximum firing range capability of the weapon. He needed well-aimed single shots and a bit of luck to hit his targets. He lifted the weapon into his shoulder and looked down through the sight. He shifted his body around to get natural firing alignment to the ambush area. He rested the weapon, still with the butt in his shoulder and waited. His ambush was set.

CHAPTER 20

HIS BREATHING WAS STEADY and mind focused on what was about to come. Josh had mapped out in his head the various tactical solutions to the many variables that the situation could unfold. He watched the open ground below his position—a beautiful, slightly undulating grassy green park with a snaking path. At most, at any one time, only about two or three unsuspecting park walkers crossed the kill zone. He knew the Chinese wouldn't want open warfare and would try to keep things quiet; unlike earlier. More than likely, they would try and capture the facsimile; perhaps wound him to make it easier. But they had no idea what was waiting for them.

From the right edge, out of the line of trees, fast movement caught Josh's eye. He focussed in like a laser; it was the fac. He was running into the open ground below. The bait was successfully leading the prey into the ambush. Josh raised his weapon; barrel pointing down into the open area. As anticipated, five of the six Chinese MSS agents were following the fac out through the trees. They were stretched out in extended line across the kill zone—perpendicular to Josh's position—apart from one who was ten metres back. None of the MSS agents had weapons drawn; a mistake they would not live to remake.

Josh began making a critical assessment in his head before taking his first shot. "No wind, range to target three hundred, moving right to left."

He quickly calculated distances based on his earlier ranging of known objects in the kill zone—a park bin three hundred and fifty metres away, a small mound two hundred and fifty metres. Knowing these objects' ranges he could easily gauge the MSS agents' distances nearby. He also worked out the order of priority in which to take out his targets. He judged the agent following ten metres behind, who appeared to be calling out orders to the others, to be the officer in charge. He was to be the first target and who Josh had just ranged. Second target would be the first man closest to Josh in the extended line—a sure kill. Then it would be a free-for-all between him and his partner: the fac.

The facsimile purposely slowed down his pace and looked left up the incline in Josh's direction—a sign to unleash hell. Josh knew the first shot would give the game away, so had to make it count. Aiming, looking at his first target through the sight, Josh stopped his breathing to steady the weapon. He was aiming just in front of the moving target's body, allowing for time and travelling distance of the bullet to target. He squeezed the trigger. BANG! The butt of the weapon kicked back into his shoulder with the first shot fired.

Following through, Josh watched to make sure his intended target went down. A fraction of a second later the suspected leader was pushed over onto the ground—a sure sign he had been hit. Without further thought Josh aimed at his second target the same way. BANG! Another agent dropped to the ground. This time, because the target was closer, Josh could see the bullet strike. From the blood signature midway up the side of the man's torso, the bullet landed precisely where intended—centre mass of the body.

After the two quick deadly shots, the remaining agents instantly dropped to ground for cover; pulling their weapons out from concealment. The shots gave the signal to the fac that the ambush had been sprung. He immediately stopped running, turned, and engaged the remaining three MSS agents—taking out the middle man who knelt up to take a shot. The only two civilians in the park, who were caught in the cross-fire, quickly ran off screaming.

The two remaining agents began shouting and returning automatic fire at the fac. They seemed to be in confusion; the expected result of the ambush. Josh watched the fac throw his body down to avoid the bullets and crawl to cover—a slight depression in the ground. He then began returning fire to keep the MSS agents occupied whilst Josh zeroed in on his next target.

An MSS agent was positioned not far from the park bin Josh had pre-sighted at three-fifty metres away. The agent's body was covered by bushes but his head, bobbing up and down whilst firing, was a clear target. Josh aimed, stopped his breathing, then took the shot. Just as the agent raised his head to fire his own shot, Josh's bullet struck. Red matter flew into the air from the opposite side of the agent's head. He was silenced.

The final agent, now realising he was on his own, began making a tactical withdrawal back towards the trees. He was trying to break his way out of the ambush area. Josh watched his pattern of withdrawal: ten metre dash, turn and fire two shots; ten metre dash, turn and fire two shots. Josh estimated the agent's next firing position and prepared for a final shot. BANG! The agent ran into Josh's marksmanship shot and joined his comrades in the hereafter. The whole fire-fight was over in a few minutes, from first shot fired to the last man down.

Josh grabbed his spare magazines from the ground and broke cover from the bushes. He raced from his hide, down into the kill zone. The fac was also moving in.

"SIT REP!" shouted Josh to his partner as he took a protective stance over the area.

The fac responded with a quick situation report. "No injuries, one full mag left, one enemy killed!"

"Roger that!" acknowledged Josh and shouted out his own report. "No injuries, two and a half plus mags left, four enemy shot!"

"Roger!" shouted the fac. "Sweep and clear!"

Covering each other, Josh and the facsimile systematically checked all of the MSS agents to ensure they were indeed dead. They jammed the muzzles of their weapons hard into the bodies to make sure they weren't playing possum—there were no moans or groans from the forceful jabs. Swiftly checking the bodies for intelligence, all of them were clean except for their diplomatic cover IDs. Satisfied with their expected result, Josh and the fac quickly replenished their ammo—stripping the bodies of their full magazines and discarding their own empty or partly filled ones.

"Your shooting is shit, you need more practice," teased the fac. He was looking at the entry wound of Josh's last target—a difficult shot for anyone to make in normal conditions, let alone during an enemy engagement.

Josh just smiled and shook his head at the brotherly wind-up. "We've still got one left, the one securing their transport; that's if he hasn't already bolted."

"I'll act as decoy again; attract his attention. You come at him from behind," said the fac.

"Agreed."

They started running back to the road; concealing their weapons to avoid further public interest. Before reaching the main road near the station they split up—Josh heading right and the fac left. Josh came out through the edge of the park into the open. He looked towards the station and the location where the last MSS agent was expected to be. "Shit, one car left. He's gone," thought Josh.

He continued cautiously walking along the pathway towards the station and the abandoned MSS vehicle. A small crowd had gathered near the edge of the park who were chattering like monkeys in trouble. They had heard the gunfire and screaming of the two civilians who were caught up in the initial firing. As Josh got closer to the car, he saw the fac was moving in. He also noticed the last agent had made a fast departure. Both met up by the abandoned vehicle.

"We need to go. There's too much heat here," said the fac. "Police will be on their way. And the Chinese will send more agents."

Josh was frustrated and reached for the car's door handle but the fac grabbed his wrist and stopped him. "You don't want to touch that car."

"I need to get inside. I need intel on Faust or Sofia!"

"We'll get it. You know the car will be clean; the agent will have seen to it. And he's left a loud nasty surprise we don't want."

Josh was getting desperate. There was too much public attention and little progress in the case. He had always been taught to keep a low profile but things were dramatically getting out of hand. He took his attention off the car knowing his partner was right. Knowing he was also right—after all, they are the same person. It was odd though that his decisions seemed different than the fac's. How was the fac so certain that the agent had left a "loud surprise"?

"Where's your friend?" asked the fac.

Josh looked around the area. "He's not here. Wait! Over there; that taxi pulling in."

Farhad had literally just arrived and parked his taxi by the station. Josh and the fac walked over. Through the taxi windscreen, Josh could see the confusion slowly dawning on Farhad's face. He knew he was going to have to explain things to him but right now he had no time. He needed to focus on the next step of his plan.

"Joshua...," Farhad hesitated as both Joshes entered the taxi at the same time. "How are you?" He was gazing at them the same way someone would stare at monkeys in a zoo—with great fascination.

"Farhad, we need to leave, NOW!" ordered Josh.

Farhad snapped out of his rude inspection of the pair. "Sure, certainly...I will take you," he said, turning his attention to the road. He pulled away, driving out from the station slipway onto the main one-way road. He drove up to the next set of traffic lights and made a U-turn, back in the direction of the station, on the opposite side.

As they drove by, a fleet of five cars pulled into the station at speed. A second but larger force of Chinese government agents had arrived. At least fifteen MSS agents exploded out from their vehicles, racing in the direction of the park. This time they weren't bothered about staying out of the limelight, giving the small crowd of spectators some added excitement to chatter about. Both Joshes knew what they would find, and that they would want some serious payback.

"Farhad, is the meet with our local friend set up?" enquired Josh.

"Yes, we go there now. He will be waiting for us."

"The arms dealer?" interjected the fac.

Josh turned to the facsimile looking surprised; although he shouldn't have been. "Yes. The 'arms dealer'," he repeated. "And you know of him, how?"

The fac looked at Josh but said nothing of what he knew.

"You've met him before," stated Josh.

The fac remained silent; not denying nor confirming what Josh was suggesting. But the facsimile's surprising question, coupled with his suspicious silence, triggered Josh's open speculation. Using the premise that the fac had met the arms dealer, Josh began pulling the idea apart: logically testing it for accuracy and truthfulness.

"If you met the arms dealer, why didn't he recognise me as being you? Why didn't Farhad recognise me in you?" questioned Josh. "Farhad! Have you seen me before?"

Farhad looked in the rear-view mirror; he was silently confused. "Well, yes Josh. You came to my home."

"What about before that; before meeting at the airport last night?"

"Um...no. I don't believe we have met. But I don't remember every pick-up I make."

"I mean, have you met me before, and taken me to the arms dealer?" Josh was more accurate in his questioning.

"Why no! I have never taken anyone to the arms dealer before," answered Farhad. "Now that, I am sure."

Josh turned to the fac for an answer; not saying anything further but staring directly at him with an intensity the fac couldn't ignore.

"We don't have time for explanations," said the fac. "I will tell you what I know later. Right now, we need to prepare for what's coming. They will be following."

Josh eased off, knowing he would hold him to that promise.

"How long Farhad?" Josh changed the subject.

"Shortly Mister Joshua, shortly." Farhad was driving as fast as he dared; to avoid getting stopped. "May I ask you the most obvious question on my mind right now?"

"No Farhad, not now." Josh knew he was burning to know why there were two identical "Joshes" sitting in his taxi, but as the fac said, they didn't have time for explanations. Farhad said nothing; he was unusually dumbfounded. He focused on the road and continued driving.

They drove southwest, returning to the old industrial complex in Obersendling, where Josh had met with the local arms dealer. The taxi slowly creeped in. The complex looked less haunting in the day than it did the previous night. It was still quiet from its abandonment and dirty from neglect, but the daylight made it much less sinister looking. Farhad parked in the same place as the night before—by the wall, and all three stepped out of the taxi.

Josh turned towards the main building. The same two heavies were standing guard by the doorway, suspiciously looking the trio over as they approached. Leading the group, Josh stopped in front of the guards. They looked curiously past Josh, getting an eyeful of the fac, then looked at each other. Raising their eyebrows in surprise, they waited for the other to say something. Josh could see their confused hesitation.

"My brother," said Josh, drawing the guard's attention and resolving their confusion.

The guards looked at each other again, shrugged their shoulders and one stepped aside, allowing entry. The routine was the same; one of the heavies leading the way and the second escorting them in from the rear. They walked into the familiar space of the empty warehouse. The arms dealer, waiting by the table with another heavy, called them straight over. Josh had already proved his credentials from his earlier purchase and was now treated as a trusted business client.

"Welcome my friends!" the arms dealer called out, raising his arms in a friendly manner.

As the party approached, Josh could see the arms dealer squinting and focussing on both him and the fac. As with everyone else, he too was surprised. Still, he wasn't one to let strangeness get in the way of a good deal.

"You bring your twin with you," he said openly. It was the first time someone had identified the Joshes in that way.

"Yes," replied Josh.

"Well good. We can make more deals and..."

"I have a better deal for you," interrupted Josh. Farhad looked concerned and the fac remained quiet but ready, allowing Josh to have control.

The arms dealer paused for a moment. "What 'better deal'?"

"I need your help and the help of your men."

The arms dealer frowned, "You don't need weapons? What do you mean?"

"At any time now, a small army will be coming to take us all out."

With that surprising statement all three heavies drew their weapons and stood firm, pointing at both Joshes and Farhad.

"You betray me!" shouted the dealer and likewise pulled a pistol out from under his jacket.

"No!" Josh raised his voice to get through to the arms dealer, to get through his state of panic. "You help us deal with this small army and you get much reward."

Josh was talking his language by mentioning "reward". It worked. The arms dealer calmed a little, putting his weapon away. The three heavies though, kept their weapons trained on them just in case.

"Reward, what reward?" The arms dealer's greedy eyes grew larger.

This was the deal Josh hoped would be accepted—if not, they were on their own. "A big selection of the best Chinese weapons on the market; plus, their vehicles."

Watching the dealer's response to the offer, Josh waited and prepared himself in case they would have to fight their way out. The fac, still quiet, was aware of dire potentialities—the many ways in how the deal could go sour—and was himself working out multiple contingency plans of escape. The dealer was frowning, moving his eyes and lips around as though the decision-making cogs in his head were taking up all his memory. He suddenly straightened out and looked firmly at Josh.

"What weapons and who is this small army? I cannot fight polizei."

"It's the Chinese—a gang, around twenty well-armed men carrying these," and Josh opened his jacket to display the submachine gun and semi-automatic pistol taken from the MSS. "You get to keep everything, including their top-of-the-range Audi saloons. You'll just need to disable their trackers."

The fac knew Josh had left out some of the finer details for a good reason. Letting them in on the fact these were Chinese MSS would make the deal less sweet. Josh was working them round with the best deal he could give. The arms dealer reached for the weapon strapped to Josh's body and touched it. He was already calculating the costs and expenses in his head. He could gain a lot at the expense of maybe one or two of his men, but business was business and he recognised a lucrative deal.

"Done!" he said smiling.

"Good!" smiled Josh. "We will need to prepare."

The arms dealer began speaking to his men in Arabic, giving them orders to get armed to the teeth. They began picking up the armament stock meant for sale from the table—opening boxes of ammo and loading magazines. Gun battles were nothing new to these guys, they were from Palestine.

Whilst the arms dealer was dictating to his men, Josh turned to Farhad. "This is not your fight. I want you to leave quickly."

"Mister Joshua, I do not abandon a friend in need. I will stay!"

"Farhad, you must also not abandon your family. You are a brave man and I welcome your favour as a true friend, but you must go and take care of your family now. I would not want to see them suffer from your death because of me."

Farhad listened to Josh's reasoning and nodded disappointedly. "As you command. I will listen to you and leave. You will be in my prayers and you will always be my friend." Farhad reached out and put his arms around Josh, giving him a customary Arabic farewell. "Thank you, Joshua...Josh, for the money you gave us. You are a good man." Farhad released his embrace, turned, and walked off.

"Where is Farhad going?" questioned the arms dealer.

"This is not his fight. I told him to leave; to be with his family."

"Ha, no problem! More for us!" laughed the dealer loudly.

"What's your name?" asked Josh.

"Aah! I usually like to keep that a secret, you know, too many competition and bad police trying to get me. But...well..., now we are friends and do battle together, you can call me Azzam."

"Azzam, thank you," said Josh gratefully. He had made a good contact and for the time being they were friends. But he was under no illusion that their friendship today could turn to enemies tomorrow. That was the game they were in.

The edge of battle was upon them. Everyone was kitted up and the fac had strategically placed Azzam's men. It was now a case of wait. They knew the Chinese wouldn't be far behind, following along by means of the fac's tracker.

"Fweet!" a short single whistle sound came from one of Azzam's men—a lookout on an upper balcony. He signalled to his boss they had visitors.

The fac, once again, was the bait. It was him they were tracking so made sense to use him to draw the MSS agents in. Josh had positioned himself up high again, so he could maximise his firepower and dominate the area. The plan was to let as many agents enter the building as possible before opening fire. He just hoped one of Azzam's men wouldn't get an itchy trigger finger beforehand and blow the surprise.

Everyone was quiet. Everyone was still. Josh could hear the slow creaking of doors echo through the empty building. He knew the MSS were sneaking around, but failing to be completely quiet while searching the building. The door to the warehouse slowly began to open. Whoever was behind it was being super cautious. It opened further. A figure slowly slipped through—a scout. His weapon pointed the way; moving around in sync with his body and direction of eyesight, ready to fire. He moved around the inner edge of the building, his back against the wall. He was probably feeling how Josh first felt when he entered the warehouse the first time: exposed.

Another MSS agent slipped through the gap of the doorway, again on high alert. He began moving along the edge of the opposite wall. More came through, one by one, peeling off left and right along both sides of the building. Josh counted ten so far and estimated half of their force. No more were coming through, indicating they were split into two search groups—one in and one outside. It was time to cut their force in half.

BANG-BANG! Josh's first two shots landed in the chest, taking out the tail end man and signalled for everyone to engage their targets. Suddenly, hell's gates were flung open and the devil's wrath was unleashed on the Chinese. The sound of multiple automatic gunfire reverberated like thunderous beating drums throughout the empty warehouse. The pounding of bullets tore into the Chinese, punching holes and ripping their bodies apart. It was a massacre with hardly a shot returned in retaliation. The firing stopped. Bodies of the MSS lay deathly still on both sides of the warehouse, their blood redecorating the dirty walls with bright red splatter patterns.

Despite their initial success, Josh and the fac's position—as well as Azzam and his men—were now revealed. The second MSS team would be planning their attack. Josh knew he had to take the fight elsewhere. He slid down a metal ladder from the upper to lower floor, to converge with the fac and Azzam.

"What now?" asked Azzam. He was buzzing from the fight and wanted more.

"They'll come round the back to try and surprise us," said the fac.

"The odds are a little more even for us now I think!" said Azzam boisterously and laughed. He called and waved for his men to come down to join him. "Reminds me of the battles at home in Palestine."

"Azzam, I want you and your men to stay here and hold them off. Keep them occupied while we go round the back to surprise them. Can you do that?" asked Josh.

"No problem," agreed Azzam and turned to his men, "Check your ammunition!"

Josh and the fac strode off. They slipped through the door of the warehouse; heading outside. On full alert, weapons at the ready, their senses were highly tuned, not only within themselves but in tune with each other. They could think and feel what the other was planning without having to say. Well synchronised, they were operating as though part of the same body: one organism. Their bond was truly brotherly.

Out in the open, all five cars belonging to the MSS agents were empty; doors left wide open. They had committed all personnel to their mission. Josh and the fac moved tactically around the building, when suddenly they heard multiple gunfire from within the warehouse. The Chinese, as suspected, started their counter-assault at the rear.

Josh and the fac quickly moved to execute their plan before the Chinese could overpower Azzam and his men. They followed the sound of gunfire and slipped through a rear door into an open office area. The automatic weapon-fire became louder. Across the room was another door. Both sprinted to it across the open space. The fac looked at Josh, threw open the door and ran through. Josh followed straight after. They began letting rip with automatic gunfire at the backs of the Chinese agents. The agents were caught in a deadly cross-fire and were losing men fast. Two agents spun round to engage Josh and the fac but were instantly turned into two piles of jellied flesh, after being ripped apart by several bursts of bullets: the Joshes getting to them first. Suddenly, everything became silent. The fight was over.

"AZZAM, ALL CLEAR! WE'RE COMING THROUGH!" shouted the fac, making sure they wouldn't be mistaken for the enemy.

"COME! COME!" shouted Azzam.

Josh and the fac walked through the line of dead bodies on the ground back to Azzam's position. Two of his men had been killed and the third slightly wounded—a bullet graze to his neck.

"This was a very expensive deal for me," warned Azzam selfishly. He wasn't so boisterous now, after counting his own losses. He didn't care about his two dead men, just that he now had to go to the expense of replacing them.

"I counted five new cars outside. And you've just got yourself at least twenty new assault weapons, plus ammo and whatever else they were carrying. You've got yourself a bargain Azzam," replied the fac.

Azzam quickly changed his tune and laughed out loudly. "You are right! Better start collecting my property. Maybe we can do business again. I think we make a good business partnership; you think?"

"Maybe Azzam. Maybe," replied Josh, not wanting to spoil the relationship by telling him to go to hell. "We need to leave now."

"Very well. You know how to get me if you need me again. Farewell." Azzam put his hand up and both Joshes promptly walked away.

CHAPTER 21

Taking the back roads so as not to be noticed, the Joshes made their way to Aidenbachstrasse U-Bahn. As they were about to descend the stairway to the underground station, sirens wailed nearby. Traffic instantly moved aside to allow a convoy of three police vehicles to push through. Without drawing attention to themselves the Joshes quickly made their way downwards. Both had the same suspicion as to where the convoy was heading and knew things were seriously heating up for them. They needed to get out of the area fast and lie low.

Standing on the platform, they waited for the next train to arrive. They stood well apart from each other to avoid the attention that their identical appearances would attract. The next train sped quietly into the station and slowed to a halt. The doors opened automatically and the fast exchange of passengers on and off began. Both Joshes boarded the train, getting into separate carriages from each other.

Taking the train through the city's underground, they made their way up the line to Bonner Platz—one station down from Scheidplatz, near the hotel where Josh had booked into. They couldn't chance getting off at that station, it was likely buzzing with polizei, cleaning up the mess the pair had made with the MSS agents near the Kraepelin institute.

The doors opened and Josh mixed with the other passengers stepping from the train onto the station platform. He looked over to see the fac, also standing on the platform, looking over at him. Josh turned to lead the way out and the fac followed a short distance behind. After ascending the stairway to street level—leaving the station, Josh made a three-sixty-degree scan of the area. He was looking for two things, one: any potential threat—whether the Chinese or police, and two: a medical facility or electrical shop. Knowing the fac still had a tracker embedded in his body they needed to remove it fast, before being hunted down again.

Marching along the pavement with the fac still following, Josh approached a local German woman. With some language difficulty he was given directions to a medical supply store across the way. Dodging traffic, the Joshes hurriedly crossed the four-way intersection to the store. As they entered, the proprietor standing by the doorway stared at length. Just like everyone else, he too was mesmerised by the identicalness of the pair. "Guten tag," he greeted in German.

They passed him by; not saying a word to the owner and headed down an aisle of medical equipment. Josh zeroed in and picked out a handheld X-ray scanner off the shelf. He opened the box and removed it. The fac located a power supply—a wall socket for Josh to plug it in to.

"Nein nein!" called the store owner, his voice raised. He raced over to stop them from using his merchandise. He began a stream of nonsensical words that the pair could only discern—from the man's irritated look—were harsh words.

The fac grabbed the man's shirt in his fist and pushed him against the shelving. Immediately, as fear came over him, the store owner stopped his censure.

"English!" demanded the fac.

"Englicsh…I speak little," replied the worried owner. "You use X-ray scanner for exactly?" he asked in broken English.

"How does it work?" asked the fac. Both Joshes ignored the man's question as they passed the scanner between them.

"Give me," said the owner cautiously and took it from them. "Who should I...?" he asked—his fear causing him to suddenly change his tune to become more co-operative.

The fac removed his jacket. "Me."

The owner set up the scanner and turned it on. "You move it over body like this and see," he said, demonstrating its use on the fac's body.

Josh snatched the device from the man and slowly continued scanning the fac. Following a systematic sweeping pattern left and right and up and down the fac's body, Josh suddenly paused. Just above the right hip, a small cylindrical object appeared on the scanner's display. The fac pulled at his clothing to expose his bare hip, so Josh could inspect the area.

"No scars. Must have been injected," said Josh. He turned to the store owner who was looking bewildered at what was happening. "I need a scalpel."

"You can't do here. You must go doctor." The owner was worried and his weak protest was ignored.

"The shelf, over there." The fac pointed to a display of surgical implements.

Josh fetched a scalpel and small pair of forceps from the display; ripping open and removing them from their packets. Standing next to the fac, Josh rechecked the location of the embedded cylindrical object using the scanner. With the scalpel, he made a small incision in the fac's skin, causing him to wince, and creating a little blood flow. Josh took the forceps and eased the ends inside. Prodding gently, he felt the instrument contact a solid object. He pinched with the forceps, gripping the object, and pulled out. All three looked at the bloodied implant: a micro-GPS tracker.

"We won't need this," said Josh, snapping the fragile capsule in two and pushing it into his pocket, so as not to leave any evidence behind. He replaced the bloodied scalpel and forceps inside their packets, also putting them in his pocket.

The fac tucked his clothes in and pushed a finger down on the material, over the small incision—applying pressure to help the blood in the wound clot. "Let's go!"

"Danke," said Josh, thanking the owner for his help—albeit enforced. He pulled out some money from his pocket and pushed it into the owner's hand—for payment of the medical equipment.

The pair quickly left the store, knowing the owner would immediately phone for the police once they were out through the door. They had to move fast. Josh changed course, heading back in the direction of the hotel. It was a risk going back but he had no choice, his effects were there which could identify him. With an aggressively fast walking-pace, the amount of time it took them to cover the distance to the hotel was short.

Standing across the road from the hotel, both Joshes waited and watched. "I'll go in first. Wait five minutes then follow me up. It's room five-five-four on the second floor. Knock three times, pause, and knock twice more. I'll open the door," said Josh.

The fac agreed with the plan. It would get them both inside without raising questions. At this stage, they had to be the same person from the same time and not the same person from different times. Walking in together would most definitely cause them to stand out and turn the heads of hotel staff and guests; something they wanted to avoid.

Josh marched across the road into the hotel lobby. He walked past the unmanned reception and up the stairs to the second floor. He stopped outside his door and looked down. He was looking for the hair he had surreptitiously stuck across the door and doorframe. It was still in place; an indication no one had been in his room since he had left that morning.

He opened the door and walked in. The wet towel he had draped over the cupboard drawers was still in place, along with the cupboard door—still open to the mark on the floor. He checked the sockets and electrical points. Everything was as he had left it. He walked over to the window that looked out from the front of the hotel. He looked across the road for his partner but he had already entered the hotel. Josh walked to the door and waited for the signal.

Knock, knock, knock—knock, knock.

He opened the door and the fac entered the room. Josh poked his head out into the hallway, checking it was clear before closing the door. He turned and immediately noticed the fac secretly checking the room. But something was off. Josh knew it was a standard operating procedure to check, as he was trained to do, but the fac was looking at the wet towel, and the bottom of the cupboard door and floor. He was checking the things Josh had arranged prior to leaving that morning, things the fac shouldn't know about. Josh became suspicious.

The fac turned to look at Josh. They were standing, facing each other again. This was the first safe moment they could both begin to take in the reality of the other. Josh approached the fac, looking at his eyes, or rather through his eyes. He could partially understand a physical form being replicated, being made into an exact copy of another—fingerprints and all; but to reproduce that which was driving the body? How could two life-forces that were potentially identical exist? Scientifically and spiritually, it would be impossible. Scientists and religious philosophers would be at loggerheads with the phenomenon. Josh was trying hard to discern something different in the fac from himself.

Interestingly, Josh noted the fac was far less interested in him as he was in it; as though it wasn't so unusual for him. That led Josh to the ultimate question he was avoiding to ask. Strangely, he knew what was happening before getting the answer from the fac.

"You've been here before." Josh changed his question to a statement. He already knew the answer.

"Yes," replied the fac.

Josh hesitated; truth revealing more of itself. "You're here...ahead of me...in my time."

"Yes."

"Right now...you are where I will be."

"Yes."

The fac didn't do or say anything, except stand and let Josh figure out what was happening and then, and only then, speak to acknowledge the truth Josh had self-discovered. The path to truth Josh was on was something the fac knew he had to find out for himself. No one could tell it to him, or he would likely reject and disbelieve it. He had to be shown and willingly accept that it was so. Too much truth had the potential to be overwhelming, particularly in those afraid of it—which Josh was not.

"I need to know everything. I need to know everything you know!" insisted Josh.

The fac smiled. "First, I need to grab a shower. I feel like shit," he replied, making the mood a little lighter than it currently was.

Josh smiled back. Their overall alikeness, including humour, made things easy between them.

"I'll use a dry towel as that one's still damp," said the fac, indicating the trick towel Josh had draped over the cupboard drawers earlier that morning. "You can hang it up now."

Josh puzzled at the strangeness of it all: the potentiality of the fac knowing what Josh had done and will do in the future. He couldn't hide anything as the fac had perhaps already done it—maybe even thought it. And the even strangest part of it all, was to know that he could possibly do the same things; follow the same path as the fac. Josh wondered, just how much of their lives were identical, how much was similar, and how much was different. He didn't know.

The fac went into the bathroom to shower whilst Josh phoned reception to order food; they had both expended considerable amounts of energy—hitting into their reserves and needed to replenish. He ordered two meals the same; he knew what he liked and therefore what the fac would like.

After putting the phone down, Josh moved over to the window. He stood looking down at the road, keeping an eye out for danger. It looked like a normal day in the lives of the passers-by; nothing out of the ordinary in their humdrum lives on the tread-mill of life. In some ways Josh envied them, envied the simplicity, and sometimes considered a trade—his life for the simple. But to forgo the hidden knowledge and truth of what was really happening in the world was not a wise compromise. Truth, no matter how difficult to swallow, is all that really matters. And now he needed to learn more of it. He needed to know the truth from the fac; his partner and newly found "brother": his twin.

Knock, knock, knock!

Josh walked cautiously to the doorway. Holding the loaded pistol he took from the Chinese, he stood to the left, stretched his arm out and pointed the barrel at the door—right angled to his body. He pictured in his mind where the visitor would be standing on the opposite side, and lined up the barrel to match where they would be. Any surprise attack, he would fire off a bullet through the cheap wood—hitting and taking out the visitor.

Knock, knock, knock!

"Room service!" A voice called through the door in English, with German accent, one that Josh recognised.

He unlocked and pulled the door open slightly. Looking through the gap, Josh double-checked it was only the person whom he was expecting. It was. He eased his pistol's hammer forward with his thumb, making his weapon safe, and promptly tucked it inside the back of his jeans. He then opened the door further.

"Hello Christina."

"Hello Mister Brannon, I have your order. I will take it to the table."

"Thanks. You can call me Josh."

He moved out of the way to allow Christina into the room. She carried the tray to the table and placed it down; moving the two plates of food from the tray to the table.

"Smells good. What have we got?"

The fac had stepped through from the bathroom, his hair still wet, freshly shaved and well groomed. Christina looked up; her mouth gaped at the sight of the fac. She couldn't help but stare at both Josh and his "twin", flicking her head side-to-side comparing the two. Her continuing head motion looked like it was stuck in replay.

"My twin brother," said Josh quickly. His answer settled her.

"You look so alike, it so amazing!" Christina began smiling like she had just discovered a miracle, or a bag of money, or something. "I'm sorry, I should not stare, but you look exactly the same!" she continued excitedly.

"I know, we get it all the time," replied the fac charmingly.

She chuckled, picked up the empty tray and began walking back to the door to leave. She turned to take another look at the pair; as though to turn any remnants of doubt she had about them into certainty. She smiled again at the unusual spectacle. Josh followed and let her out—closing and locking the door after she had left. He returned to face his "brother".

"Okay, I don't understand!" Josh was getting annoyed. "You say this—all this has happened before! Well, why didn't Christina recognise me then; when I first arrived? She should have recognised me—you, from being here before!"

"Sit down and eat. We're both running on empty." The fac took a seat at the table and reached for some cutlery.

He made sense; Josh was crazily hungry. He joined the fac at the tiny table and looked down at the meal he had ordered.

"Good choice," praised the fac and tucked straight into his food.

"I knew you'd like it," replied Josh.

They both shovelled the food into their mouths. Their table etiquette went overlooked as they chomped away at the meal and slurped heavily on their juice. Anywhere else, or with anyone else, they would have consciously minded their manners, but together, they allowed each other to be.

They finished their feast, refuelling their bodies, and leaned back with almost synchronised action. Josh gave himself a little thinking time before asking questions again. He was feeling a little like he was living in the past—with the first older facsimile he had encountered. Although Josh had come much further in his understanding, he was beginning to feel like he was going backwards.

"Josh, I need to get answers from you," said Josh, a little despairingly. He hadn't realised it, but it was the first time he had called the fac by their shared name, something the fac picked up on.

"Recognising me as you now," replied the fac.

Josh brightened up a little. "I want to know what you know—Josh." He repeated their name, but this time so he was fully aware he was saying it.

The fac began to give Josh more answers—or not so much as answers but a little more data to work with. "You remember what

Stephen Montague told you back inside the bunker about the Time-folds? You remember what he said? When time-dimensions overlap with each other they create false identities made of energy—facsimiles. That time can be intentionally shifted, changed around. Its direction can be reversed, forwarded, or even paused, like a recording machine?"

"Yeah, he also said I had broken away and was released from it...my own Time-fold trap. He lied! I'm back in the fucking trap again!" replied Josh angrily.

The fac quickly stepped in to quell Josh's temper. "Hold on, not so fast. He only told you what he knew at the time. Things have changed...are changing. View Corp is still learning from the data we helped to give them in the bunker, once we broke ourselves free. You have to now realise it's not just about ourselves anymore. The game is rigged, rigged against you, you always keep that in mind and you'll grasp the seriousness of it."

"I want to know from the beginning. What happened to you?" Josh had his full attention on his "brother" and was waiting for a lengthy answer. But instead of an answer he got a question.

"Tell me about your recent activities at the office; your involvement in an operation?"

"Operation Sting Bolt?" asked Josh curiously. His thoughts went straight back to the day he experienced the déjà vu in the house, where his colleague Malik was suspiciously shot and killed. "I experienced something very unusual. I recognised someone from my...our teenage years, who should've been dead but wasn't. And not only that, he was older."

"Liam," interrupted the fac.

Although he shouldn't have been, Josh was surprised the fac knew of it—knew of Liam. "That's right, how did you...ah...I'm asking the wrong question," realised Josh.

Things were starting to align; Josh's thoughts were beginning to align. The fac was watching him just as intently as he was watching the fac.

Josh continued his recollection. "It was a kill or capture Op, meant to take out an Islamic terrorist cell. But it was bullshit, a lie. There was one man—Liam—shot and killed, no one else. There was a second target, someone who apparently shot my colleague Malik and escaped." Josh was recalling the events and piecing things together. "Something about the whole thing stank...and I mean a cover-up. I think...," Josh paused from saying what was on his mind.

"What?" asked the fac, stepping in to help move Josh's train of thought along.

"...I think that whoever else was in the house that day, was taken by an armed police unit headed up by an officer, an officer I later killed that tried to take me out. I think that my colleague was killed by that same unit in order to cover-up who they had taken, because he was a witness to the snatch. I think...." Josh stopped his roll of thoughts on the craziest but most obvious idea yet.

The fac looked at Josh knowing his conclusion to be correct, but had yet to voice what he knew to be true. The fac needed to help him along. "Yes Josh, what's your idea?"

Josh looked directly at his twin, "...I think...I think that the second person in that house and who was captured was...was you!"

Both sat back at the revelation Josh had just come to. They didn't need to say anymore on that point once the truth had been recognised. It was time to move forward and Josh was willing and able to piece more together.

"So you were taken and implanted with a chip made by GeneRobotix," added Josh.

The fac nodded. "It's not a pleasant thing to know you're still aware, but not able to control your own body and thoughts," he troublingly revealed. "They say these implants, these chips, are for our own protection; to keep us safe from harm they say. Safe for who? The words 'protection' and 'safe' are used cunningly by governments that have insidious plans to control us. They have a hidden agenda Josh; one we are not meant to know."

Josh already had some insight of the political games being carried out by government officials: for power and fortune. He had himself looked at "TOP SECRET" files not meant for his eyes—files laying out widespread corruption and sly measures to undemocratically grab control.

"So why didn't Christina, the waitress, recognise me? Why didn't she recognise this whole situation again?" asked Josh.

"Because it's not her Time-fold," replied the fac candidly. "Our time-dimensions are not, or never have been linked. We have never seen each other before. She has never seen you before."

Josh frowned with confusion. "I still don't understand?" he questioned.

"Josh...Brother, this goes way beyond my understanding. I was told to think of it as every person has their own circle-like prison. They are living in their own circular time-dimension prison without knowing it. And those prisons can be manoeuvred, not only back and forth in time, but can be linked with others, one with another, to create dual or multiple Time-folds and facsimiles.

Yeah, it baffled the hell out of me until I got the concept of "rings"; rings that can link to any other ring. And where they join, creates a Time-fold. It's a simpler concept once you understand that. But always remember one thing. Although they can still manipulate events, we now have the ability to change the outcome. That's what happened to us in the bunker that day: regaining of free will."

Josh was beginning to grasp the idea. "Who told you all this? You said, 'I was told to think', who told you?" He had spotted the fac was telling it from another's viewpoint and not his own. Someone had been trying to get the fac to understand what he was now trying to get Josh to understand.

The fac looked deeply at Josh; about to give him an answer that he knew would be far from satisfactory to the question. It was to be an answer that would only create more confusion and questions. "Sorry Josh...but you did. We did. We pass it on to ourselves; through the Time-folds and facsimiles of ourselves."

Something suddenly dropped in Josh's universe. A heavy feeling inside of him dropped down like a dense weight to the floor at his twin's answer. It was truly unexpected and not the answer he desired.

KNOCK, KNOCK, KNOCK. The knocking on the hotel door interrupted the fac's revelations.

"My turn," said the fac, standing up from his seat. He walked over to the door and opened it slightly. He verified the visitor just as Josh did earlier. "It's Christina for the dishes," and he opened the door fully.

Seeing Christina at the door, Josh immediately sensed something was wrong. "WAIT!" he yelled out.

The cry caused the fac to turn his head away from the door and Christina, to look at Josh. A split second after the distraction the fac turned back, but it was a split second too late. A knife-blade was thrust in deep, up and into his heart, by Christina. Josh immediately sprang from his seat and in three long strides reached the door. With the palm of his hand and continued motion of force, he pushed Christina hard in the chest, catapulting her from the doorway. She flew backwards into the hotel corridor, slamming hard into the wall and fell to the floor. Josh caught his "brother" on the way down, sinking to the floor. It all happened in an instant.

Pulling the fac back further inside the room, Josh pushed the door closed; putting a barrier between them and Christina while he tended to his twin. He laid his "brother" on the floor and ripped away at his upper garments to expose the wound. A large chef's knife was deeply embedded in his lower chest at an upward angle; blood pumping its way out. Josh quickly grabbed a cotton pillow case from the bed and rolled it up tightly. He wrapped it around the knife blade just below the hilt—the piece of steel that hadn't penetrated the body—to pad the entry wound, hoping to reduce the blood flow. He knew it was serious as the blood's bright-red colour indicated an arterial wound. If he removed the knife, blood would most certainly pump out from his twin's body, causing almost instantaneous death. Josh grabbed a chair close by and pushed it over. He elevated his "brother's" legs, resting them on the overturned chair to force what blood was left in his body to rush to his heart—to keep the vital organ going. Josh picked up the hotel phone and dialled reception for immediate medical aid.

"J-o-s-h." Still conscious, the fac spoke weakly. "No."

Josh looked at him, knowing instinctively what he wanted.

"Rezeption, wie kann ich helfen?" The receptionist answered, offering help, but Josh put the phone down.

He leaned over the fac and looked at his eyes; they looked weak and grew weaker by the second as blood drained from his overworking heart. It didn't matter if Josh had called for medical aid; he knew his twin wouldn't survive the time it would take for a paramedic to arrive. His twin knew it also.

"J-o-s-h. F-o-r-g-e-t…S-o-f-i-a." The fac was slowly slurring his speech.

"What do you mean?" Josh was shocked by the unclear statement and wondered if the fac really knew what he was saying.

"F-o-r-g-e-t…S-o-f-i-a," he slowly repeated.

By repeating himself, Josh realised his twin knew what he was saying. "Why forget about Sofia, why?" demanded Josh.

"K-n-o-w…y-o-u-r…e-n-e-m-i-e-s," mumbled the fac, the last words to pass his lips as his eyes glazed over. He was dead.

CHAPTER 22

THE FAC WAS JUST a shell of a body lying on the floor; a lifeless body. Leaving his dead "brother", Josh turned to handle the immediate threat: Christina. The door was still closed and she had made no attempt to re-enter the room, as though her task was done. Josh knew why she had executed his twin. It wasn't of her own choosing but those who had manipulated her mind into doing so. He knew she was chipped, just like his twin had been.

He opened the door, half expecting to see her on the floor against the wall where she had fallen—after the forceful shove he had given her. She wasn't there. He looked up and down the corridor but she was gone, nowhere to be seen. It was one less problem for him to handle. Now he had to deal with his twin. He closed and locked the door then turned back around to deal with the body. Josh was completely stunned. His twin was also gone. He had literally vanished!

This was the first time Josh had experienced a Time-fold shift so clearly. Other times it had been experienced under a cloud of mental haze. The overlap of time had been closed. The "linked rings" as his twin suggested had been pulled apart. Whoever was controlling it, were now cleaning up. Had Josh stayed to watch a little longer, he probably would have witnessed first-hand his twin's vanishment. Still, like a magician's trick, it was the strangest of things.

KNOCK! KNOCK! KNOCK!

There was a heavy knocking on the door. Immediately Josh reached for his weapon and pulled back the hammer with his thumb; it was still cocked with a round in the chamber. He pointed it in the direction of the door, ready to fire in case Christina had returned for a second kill. He cautiously walked over, still pointing the barrel of the gun, and tentatively unlocked the door; pulling it open slightly. He looked through the narrow gap of the doorway and, upon seeing the visitor, stepped back inside the room.

The door was pushed wide open by the visitor. "Expecting trouble Brannon?"

"Always expecting trouble these days Franks," replied Josh, as he eased the firing hammer forward and pushed the gun into his waistband.

Franks was standing in the doorway with another man from the office. "You know why we're here Brannon. Harris has ordered us to bring you back. You're in a world of shit." Franks didn't mince his words.

"Well, that's nothing new," replied Josh. "I'm done here anyway." Josh looked around to make sure the fac had indeed vanished; gone back to his own time. He had. Even the fac's blood and the knife Christina had stabbed him with had vanished. The carpet was just as clean as when he had arrived—no blood.

"Nice holiday?" asked Franks insincerely.

"Eventful," said Josh with a single smirk. He needed to regroup and re-plan his next steps. He still hadn't located Faust who had been three steps ahead of him the whole time. More than likely, he had left the country, probably even before Josh had set foot on German soil. The whole thing was a trap, one instigated by Radnus at GeneRobotix.

"Just gonna grab my things." Josh picked up his bag and walked around the room collecting up what little he had brought with him. He closed the bag and gave the room one last look.

"Yours?" asked Franks, looking down at the Chinese pistol Josh had tucked away.

"Belongs to a friend." But Josh knew Franks didn't buy his lie. It didn't matter though; Franks was only there to bring him back, nothing more.

"Well, we better offload it before we get to the airport," suggested Franks, and Josh agreed with the recommendation.

All three left the room and headed downstairs into the hotel lobby. Josh approached the receptionist standing behind the desk, to book out. He dropped his room key on the counter and paid up in cash with what little he had left.

"Can I speak to Christina before I leave?"

"Sorry, she's gone home. She's not feeling well," answered the receptionist in English.

"Well, tell her from me everything is okay. And not to worry about the mess she made in the room earlier; I think she was upset by it. I'd appreciate you calling her right away to let her know."

"I will. And thank you for your stay, Mister Brannon."

Josh walked away to join his comrades and all three headed out of the hotel. A taxi was still waiting outside with the meter running. Franks had ordered the driver to wait whilst he fetched his assigned subject: Josh. They got into the taxi together; Franks sitting in the back with Josh. Obvious to Josh, Franks had been told to keep a tight rein on him. It was fine, he wasn't going anywhere; his personal investigation there was over.

Franks looked over after slamming the taxi door shut. "You got some nice damage." He was referring to the visible bruising and scrape marks on Josh's hands, face, and neck; damage caused by the fight with the fac and Chinese agents. Franks was silently making an assessment and inspection of Josh.

"Been hell of a holiday Franks; hell of a holiday," replied Josh evasively, knowing everything said and observed of his state would go in Franks's asset recovery report.

The taxi pulled off, heading for Munich airport. Whilst travelling in silence, Josh looked out of the window, contemplating his trip. It had not only gained him new enemies but also new friends. Josh sincerely hoped Farhad and his family were well. As for Assad the arms dealer, well, Josh knew his "friendship" would always come at a price, and friends like that were not worth having. Throughout the ride, Josh continued flicking the many various thoughts of the trip around in his mind; one thought in particular: Sofia.

They arrived at the airport; the taxi driver parked near the entrance. Franks's colleague dipped his hand in his pocket to pay the fare as Josh and Franks stepped out. The pair began walking into the terminal building to departures.

"We're flying business class. Company's footing the bill," said Franks, raising his eyebrows in appreciation.

"Your colleague, he's quiet. Not seen him before," said Josh.

"Mason? Yeah, he's new. I'm showing him the ropes before they cut him loose. He was interested in meeting you though."

"Why's that?" asked Josh.

"Guess he likes your rep."

"My rep? I have a reputation?" Josh was curious to know what that was.

Franks looked surprised at Josh not knowing. "Yeah. You're a wild card, not a team player, which is why we're here. You need to learn to toe the line Brannon. We do what we're told to do and nothing more. We stick to orders, that's what we do. But you...you're unpredictably dangerous."

In spite of it meaning to sound like a bad evaluation of his character, Josh liked it. It wasn't meant to be, but to him it was a compliment. To him, the ability of being able to think for oneself and go beyond just taking orders was an honourable quality in a person. Josh was fully aware, that those who don't stand up to irrational orders, are themselves dangerous people to have around. These are the type of robotic tools that psychotic politicians love to have in their pockets, so as not to challenge their insanity and crazy policies.

"Well, here we are." Franks had escorted Josh to a special lounge, away from prying eyes and potentially upset Chinese MSS agents out scouring the city for him—if they had any left alive that is.

"Our flight leaves in two hours. Put ya feet up and have a drink Brannon." Franks plonked himself in a comfy lounge chair and began perusing a drinks menu that was left on the arm. Josh followed suit; resting his tired and battered body in a seat opposite Franks.

Mason—Franks's colleague—caught up; taking a seat next to Josh. "So how was your holiday?" he asked.

"Riveting," replied Josh sarcastically; thoroughly uninterested in Mason's banal question.

Franks laughed loudly at the snub and began shaking his head. "How to win friends hey Brannon?" he mocked, and continued checking the drinks menu.

All conversation between the three dried up quickly; Josh uninterested in what either company man had to say, Franks not caring at all, and Mason—the new guy—not sure if he would get shot down again if he opened his mouth, so didn't. It was perfect. Quiet was what Josh wanted. Internally, he was planning ahead as to what his next move would be, so didn't want to engage in pointless chit-chat.

An hour and a half had passed by when they were called by the airport hostess to begin boarding. Josh grabbed his bag and with his two chaperones followed the lady. At the security gate, Franks handed over a diplomatic authorisation document giving them all dispensation to walk through unchecked. He had ensured Josh dispose of his "friend's" weapon prior to entering the airport, as they still had to pass through the metal detector. Only Franks and Mason had authority to carry concealed handguns.

Moving through onto the Lufthansa flight, they settled into their seats. Franks was making a big deal about escorting Josh back, by making him sit by the window. Where he thought Josh would abscond to, during the mid-air flight, was mindboggling to think. But Josh willingly went along with his stupidity, for now.

The plane was filled and all passengers secured: the doors closed. The flight taxied the runway and with a powerful thrust of the engines they took off—they were on their way back to London.

Two hours later, after a quiet trip, the wheels of the Lufthansa twin-jet Airbus touched down at London's Heathrow airport. After taxiing to the arrival's terminal, the trio vacated their seats and were given privilege over the other passengers upon leaving. As soon as they cleared through customs Franks called the office to let them know they had landed.

Franks and Mason escorted Josh to the airport's staff car park, where they had left their car that morning—before leaving for Munich. As with all operatives, they checked the car over for nasty surprises before unlocking it. They got in, and with Franks driving, drove to collect Josh's own car—still parked in the short-stay parking at Heathrow. Franks instructed Mason to drive it back; to follow on behind while he drove with Josh. He just didn't want to let Josh out of his sight. The three started off for central London and back to the office.

21:00hrs: Josh checked and adjusted his watch for local time. Darkness had set in and the street lights were shining brightly along the roadside. "Am I seeing Harris tonight?" he enquired.

"Yeah. He specifically wanted you in. Bit late for a bollocking in my opinion, but you know Harris; likes to dot the i's and cross the t's."

Josh said nothing.

The journey into central London seemed to take longer than the flight – perhaps it was the thought of what was coming that made it seem longer. Josh didn't care about another bollocking, but what he did care about was losing his job. The job was a means of getting to the truth. He had access. Without the job, his access to classified material was gone.

They arrived at the office, pulling into the secure parking. Franks was being a complete jobsworth by escorting Josh directly to Harris's office. Maybe he was looking for a promotion from the devil.

"Wait here," ordered Franks, as he knocked on Harris's door and walked in – closing it behind him. Josh let him have his moment of power. At any other time, things would have turned out differently; Josh would have laid him out.

Although he had managed to doze off for a while on the flight, Josh was feeling tired – mentally as well as physically. His mission had failed. He failed to find Sofia and it weighed heavily on his mind. He had no idea what he was going to report. He didn't know what Harris knew, and anything he would reveal, Harris was sure to corroborate it with what information he already had.

The office door opened. "You can go in now Brannon," said Franks, his tone manifesting a distinct level of superiority over Josh, as though superior in rank – which he wasn't.

Josh walked in and closed the door on Franks. Harris was sitting behind his desk with Marion – the HR lady – sitting nearby; ready to take notes. Without waiting for permission, Josh took a seat and folded his arms in defiance. He wasn't going to let Harris think he had gotten the better of him, which is what he always strived for.

Harris began his opening statement. "Well Brannon, he we are once again. You have a problem with authority and that's a problem for us." Marion began scribbling away in short-hand everything that was being said. "What do I do with you? What would you do with you Brannon?"

"Is that a rhetorical question sir, because I can easily answer that?" replied Josh cockily. He was intentionally pushing the boundary.

"Yes Brannon, it is rhetorical!" snapped Harris. "I want to know why you disobeyed company policy yet again, and why you took an unauthorised trip to Munich while on suspended leave?"

Josh snapped back, "Simple sir! Cleaning up a mess!"

"Oh, you mean the case with GeneRobotix. Well, how did that go then?"

"Not very well," said Josh honestly.

"You're right Brannon. It didn't go well!" Harris picked up a brown file from his desk and opened it. He removed some photographs and laid them out one by one on the table for Josh to witness. "This is Mark Radnus, CEO of GeneRobotix. He was found hanging in the stables at his home in Hertfordshire. Any thoughts on the matter Brannon? I mean, you did go and visit him at work, and by all accounts 'roughed him up.'"

Josh knew what Harris was implying, but to outright accuse him of killing Radnus would be illogical. Even Harris would know the evidence to be circumstantial at best.

"I would go on record to suggest it was a Chinese hit. They are trying to cover up their part in the purchase of the chips made by Radnus's company: GeneRobotix. You have my earlier report sir. I stand by my findings in that report."

"Ah yes...your report." Josh could sense Harris purposely stalling and fishing for a response. "...It seems your precipitous actions as of late Brannon, call into question the veracity of your report. I'm afraid it is no longer a valuable or viable source of intelligence, and will be officially regarded as such. Which means, we are now back at square one—your insubordination and lack of respect for your seniors, as well as company protocol."

Harris was whitewashing the whole case and it wasn't looking good for Josh. He was sitting quietly, trying to figure a way out of the trap that was being set up around him. Harris was constructing a fictitious wall that had an official stamp of approval. Josh knew his evidence was sound and could easily be verified, but that wasn't the purpose of the meeting. Harris wanted him out, regardless of any facts.

Harris looked like a judge; one about to pass a sentence of death. "My official findings are, that you wilfully disobeyed the orders of your suspension, as well as your senior. That your wilful disobedience caused for the use of company resources to bring you back, resources better allocated elsewhere. And that you potentially put your comrades in danger, in order to bring you back.

I conclude that, forthwith, you are to be summarily dismissed. You are no longer permitted to continue with any active, or inactive assignments. You will hand in all company equipment and documentation. You will turn over details of all human intelligence sources you have built up during your time here. If you fail to concede to my official orders, you will be prosecuted under the Official Secrets Act of which you are bound. Do you wish to say anything Brannon, for the record?" Harris had tightly tied the knot, leaving Josh no wiggle room to manoeuvre.

Josh let out a sigh of disappointment. "What can I say? What can I say against lies that are officially allowed to endure, except that they're lies. You accuse me of disobeying orders...I say those orders were wrong. The right and wrong of a person's action is not based on whether they blindly obey an order, but whether one's action does the most good, or the least harm. You sit in judgement of my actions, when your own are questionable. A seat of power doesn't give licence to wield an unjust sword. What you fail to recognise sir, is that your lies will be your undoing."

"Thank you Brannon. Your poetic speech has been noted. Franks is outside to finalise your dismissal process and escort you out. After which, if you need anything further, you will be required to enter through the front door as a visitor. That will be all."

With an air of satisfaction, Harris pushed back in his chair—with an arrogant victorious look on his face—and waited for Josh to leave. Josh rose from his seat and quietly walked out of the office. He knew it was over. He was met by Franks again, who was still outside the door; already privy to the outcome and his dismissal. As ordered, Franks began escorting Josh around the building—his final day at the office.

Later that evening, a secret meeting took place—held in a secret location between three people. The three, standing in a secluded wood just outside the M25 motorway, were discussing a recent sensitive topic. Under the illumination of car headlights, they discussed intelligence operative Josh Brannon's impromptu dismissal.

"Who gave you the authority to dismiss him?" questioned Chris Nugent—Brannon's recruiter.

"I thought it best under the circumstances," replied Harris cautiously. He was trying to seem assertive but his nervousness poked through his fake character.

"What circumstances?" replied the third person. It was Sir Godfrey—the politician Brannon had bumped into, during Operation Sting Bolt.

"He was becoming a liability," answered Harris. "I thought...."

"That's your problem!" Sir Godfrey harshly interrupted, "You thought! Thinking is NOT your responsibility, following orders IS!"

Harris began looking nervous, his cowardice noted by his superiors. Sir Godfrey continued in a milder tone. "You acted in good faith Michael, we know that. You're a good soldier and we need you."

Relieved by his superior's praise, Harris began backtracking on his rash firing of Brannon. "I can reverse the decision on his dismissal. I can bring him back in. Put him on a final warning to keep him in check." Harris was continuing to make himself look incompetent and weak.

SNAP! SNAP!

"That won't be necessary," answered Nugent, to the warm corpse now lying on mud and leaves.

While Sir Godfrey was talking, Nugent pulled a suppressor pistol out from his coat and put two bullets in Harris's chest—killing him instantly. With the bright headlights shining in Harris's eyes, he never saw it coming—it was the plan all along. Harris had become a weak link, a burden to their progress, and his termination became necessary.

Without conscience, Sir Godfrey turned to Nugent. "What about Radnus?"

Nugent slipped his pistol back inside his coat. "The coroner's initial report is suicide," he replied.

Sir Godfrey nodded, "Good, make sure it stays that way."

"And Brannon, what of him?" asked Nugent.

Sir Godfrey began wiping his shoe on Harris's coat, to remove some mud. "Brannon...we know what's next for him. Leave him to walk his path. Let him look for his Sofia. Let him find her secrets. Then bring him home again."

Sitting quietly in his car, Josh had returned to his apartment block after completing his dismissal process with Franks. It was dark; only the dim illumination of street lights shining through the window made it possible to see at all. He was feeling low, that he had failed Sofia. "What now?" he thought.

He began thinking about his twin's last words, what he had said about "forgetting Sofia." Josh's thoughts had gotten stuck on those dispiriting words—not knowing why he had said them. But then Josh began recalling what else he had said. It was unclear at first, due to the former idea about forgetting Sofia, which had consumed his thoughts. He tried to recall it precisely, tossing the words around in his head until finally it popped through: "Know your enemies!" he said out loud.

He then remembered the note, the note that was stuck on his car windscreen before leaving for Munich. He reached down into the door's side-compartment and retrieved the folded paper. He unfolded it and looked at the words: "KNOW YOUR ENEMIES". They were the same words his twin had uttered just prior to his death! But to Josh's complete surprise, written in what appeared to be the same handwriting—just below those words—was now a new phrase: "KNOW YOUR FRIENDS".

Book 3 Release

I sincerely hope you enjoyed *GEMINOS,* and the Josh Brannon series so far. I will be continuing Brannon's journey—in Book 3—which will become ever more perilous, coupled with action-packed suspense. So stay tuned!

Want To Be Notified of The New Release?

Join my Readers Club to be one of the first to get notified:
www.nigelbillington.com

About the Author

I'm a self-published British author who grew up in the county of Dorset, in the South of England. If you want to know more about me or my books, please visit my website **www.nigelbillington.com**

If you enjoyed this book, you can help me out by leaving an honest review...

As a self-published author, reviews are an essential way of getting more attention for my books. Honest reviews of my books help to support the continuation of my writing. So, if you enjoyed this book, I would be deeply grateful if you could take a few moments of your time to leave a review, wherever you obtained this book. It can be short and sweet, or as long as you want.

Thank you so much!

Join My Readers Club

Join The Others in My Readers Club

When you join my Readers Club you'll be first to get the LATEST on what I'm up to, my SPECIAL book promotions, and news of my future NEW book releases. PLUS, you will get my EXCLUSIVE novellas and short stories for FREE. I look forward to hearing from you!

Join my Readers Club here: www.nigelbillington.com

www.ingramcontent.com/pod-product-compliance
Lightning Source LLC
Chambersburg PA
CBHW031937240626
47153CB00003B/763